HEAD ABOVE WATER

Hailey Edwards

COPYRIGHT INFORMATION

Edited by Sasha Knight

Cover by Damonza

Interior format by The Killion Group

CHAPTER ONE

I disembarked my flight from Mobile, Alabama with a laptop tucked under my arm and the breathless expectation of a reunion with a certain hazel-eyed warg only to be met with a sea of eager faces, none of which brightened in recognition of me. I stood there, heart in my throat, but the man who shoved through the outer doors and strolled into the lobby wasn't Graeson.

"Hey coz." Isaac greeted me with a brief hug that brought his burnt-metal scent into my lungs. He dropped the keys to my pickup into one hand then pressed a paper cup of chai into the other. The latte was welcome, but even piping hot, it did little to ease the ache from what somehow stung like rejection. "Nice suit. Trying to impress the boyfriend?"

"No. I'm not," I huffed. "I had a meeting." Wearing jeans, a white tee with a black and red checked flannel shirt buttoned over it and ratty sneakers, Isaac had no room to judge my wardrobe choices. "Since when are you the fashion police?"

"I'm not." He shuddered. "One cop in the family is plenty." He picked at a dried mustard stain on his shirt pocket then started cleaning the yellow crust from under his nail. "So is Cord meeting us here or...?"

"No." I scanned the now-empty lobby one more time then checked my phone before turning to go. "He's not."

Cord Graeson and I weren't actually dating. That was just the lie he had told my family. Being a fake boyfriend, he wasn't obligated to do the couples thing and meet me at the gate. Though it might have been nice if he'd at least texted me an excuse instead of hanging me out to dry with Isaac.

"You want to take point?" Isaac jingled his own keys in hand. "You're the one familiar with the area."

"Not hardly." The state of Georgia and I were acquaintances, not friends. "I've been to Villanow once."

"That's once more than Mom or me." He tossed his keys in the air then caught them. "Keep it between the lines, Cammie. Mom will watch your six. I'll take the rear."

Outside the airport, the caravan waited. Four silver Airstream trailers, three trucks, two parking violations and Aunt Dot. Stepping into the parking lot felt like coming home.

I climbed behind the wheel of my truck and settled in for the forty-five minute drive ahead of us. All those empty miles allowed me to work up a good head of steam over Graeson's absence. We had a missing changeling to find and a serial killer to put down—for good this time—and he was burning precious hours by playing hide-and-seek.

Two quarters of the way into our trip, I stabbed the button on my infotainment screen and gave the voice command to call Aunt Dot, who was hauling Theo's trailer in addition to hers.

"ETA fifteen minutes." I drummed my fingers. "Don't run me over this time, okay?"

"That was one time, and I paid the insurance premium to have your trailer repaired." She puffed out an insulted breath. "The audiobook I was listening to was *intense*. I wasn't prepared when you made a sudden stop."

At a red light.

Hence the fifteen-minute warning.

"Maybe turn off the radio until we get where we're going?" I suggested.

"You dent one bumper, and people act like it's the end of the world," she muttered, ending the call.

The remaining miles slid past my windows, a montage of evergreens that blurred after a while.

Our caravan rolled to a stop on neutral ground, a stretch of country road shaded by forest that marked the eastern border of the Chandler pack lands, in time for a cricket serenade. I exited the vehicle and checked the coordinates Graeson had rattled off to Isaac after he'd finished buttering up Aunt Dot, but our welcome party consisted of a turkey vulture and the picked-over remains of what might once have been a beaver.

Great. I had been stood up. Twice in one day.

Isaac laid on the horn, and my middle finger itched to rise. The blame for this visit sat squarely at Aunt Dot's feet, not mine. She had accepted Graeson's invitation without consulting me, not the other way around. Choosing that moment to stick her head out her window, Aunt Dot winked at me like this was all part of some grand adventure, and I made a fist instead.

"Well?" she hollered as she craned to see around my trailer. "Where does Cord want us?"

"He's not here," I called back. "I guess we wait."

Arms crossed, I leaned against my truck's front bumper. A forest of pines, hickories, oaks and the occasional dogwood tree created a natural barrier to protect the wargs' privacy. I kicked at one of the clumps of grass responsible for the bumpy drive and watched the clod go sailing. It landed with a dull thud, and a heartbeat later twin specks of gold winked into existence deep in the velvet-dark heart of the forest.

"Maybe I spoke too soon," I murmured, straightening.

One blink. Two. The apparition vanished, and the woods went silent. Chills swept down my arms in a prickling cascade. Eerie quiet lured me nearer to the leaf-strewn line separating the single-lane road from the encroaching wilderness.

Wind swirled blond strands of hair into my eyes and kicked up dust at my feet. Leaves rustled over my head as if the hickories were shooing me away, warning me to climb back in the cab to safety. I rocked back on my heels, prepared to heed their warning, until a pitiful whine from the underbrush played on my heartstrings. "Graeson?"

A door opened behind me. "Pumpkin?"

"It's fine." I flung out my arm to keep her and Isaac corralled at their vehicles. "Get back in the truck."

A throaty rumble issued from the woods that grated like laughter in my ears. Fear dug talons into my spine a second before the wolf I had assumed was Graeson leapt for my throat. Black as the oncoming night, the sinuous beast widened its maw. All those months of marshal academy training snapped like a rubber band in my brain, and I swung my left forearm up high in a defensive pose that absorbed the impact of the wolf's body smacking into mine. Teeth grazed the tip of my nose as I shoved up with my right arm, turning as I used the wolf's momentum against it and flung it aside.

It landed nimbly on all fours and, as if its legs were spring-loaded, pivoted and launched itself right back at me.

The fingernail of my right hand's middle finger wobbled and fell off. A sickle claw extended from my nailbed. Clacking teeth grazed my chin before I cinched my hand around the wolf's throat. Spur fully extended, I punched its curved tip through the thick fur protecting the beast's throat, sucking in a gasp as its blood wet my fingertip, its magic flowing over my tongue.

The wolf hit the ground hard, flung its head side to side, then bunched for a third strike.

Ebony fur erupted down my right forearm, the bones lengthening as my fingernails arrowed into claws. Droning white noise buzzed in my head, persistent bees, as a cacophony of *presence* clashed against a chorus of indistinct words without substance or meaning.

The pack bond.

"Cam," Isaac roared.

"Stay back," I growled. "I can handle this."

The coiled wolf lunged, and I threw my weight behind swinging out with my clawed arm. Nails swiping across its neck, I ribboned the column of its throat. Crimson sprayed my face, my shirt, running hot and slick through my fingers. Gurgling wetly, the beast thumped on its side.

This time it stayed there.

Strong hands clamped over my upper arms, and I yelped at the pinch. Isaac spun me on my heels until the carnage I had wrought was hidden behind my back. Struck dumb by the sudden violence of the attack, the stickiness coating my palm, I let him fold me against his chest until the shock dulled enough for anger to flare in its place.

His chin bumped the top of my head. "What the hell?"

Breathless, I couldn't speak and didn't know how to answer. The fingers of my right hand—sleekly furred and razor-tipped—trembled where they scrunched his T-shirt into a fist.

Hard pops brought a lump to my throat, and I pivoted on my heel. The animal seized, back arched. Lips peeled away from its teeth, claws raked furrows in the dirt. Its gasping whimper as a human shape emerged caused me to dig my nails into my palms. That had to hurt.

A high-pitched whine accompanied the final, vicious crack of bone. The rich pelt shed and left a woman with dark-brown skin panting on the cushion of leaves. Her breasts were full and her hips lush, her body sheened with sweat. Short twists of burgundy hair covered her scalp, and even stained with the effort of her change, she was a beauty.

A beauty whose throat I had ripped out in self-defense moments earlier, whose flesh knitted together as I watched. Eyes the color of topaz soaked in Isaac like he was a tempting cut of prime beef that would tear softly under her teeth. It tempted me to test her regenerative capabilities by removing her windpipe for a second time. My cousin was not on the menu. Neither was I for that matter.

"Who are you lovely dishes?" she rasped, sitting upright and curving her legs under her. The pose was comfortable, not modest. Wargs weren't prudes in either form. "Wander where you don't belong out here, and you might get gobbled up."

A glance down confirmed I had, stupidly, allowed her to lure me onto Chandler land without a warg escort. "I'm Camille Ellis. Cord Graeson invited us. We're his guests."

Magic shivered over my skin, contracting, and I lost my grip on the borrowed energy. Fur fell out in clumps down my forearm, my fingers shrank and nails reformed into perfect ovals. I eased forward, angling so Isaac stood a step behind me. "Who are you?"

"Handsome here can call me Aisha." She licked her lips in Isaac's direction before snapping her gaze to me. "You, beta, may address me as *alpha*. I'm Bessemer's mate. These are our lands where you trespass."

Oh. She was one of *those* women. Each time I transferred to a new marshal's office, I got dropped into the frothing miasma of office politics. Thanks to those experiences, I recognized a power play when I saw one. If I bowed to her now, she would never let me off my knees.

"Aisha." I cleaned her blood out from under my nails. "Can you tell Graeson his girlfriend is here?"

An unladylike snort ripped through her. "Wargs don't have girlfriends, fae. We mate, and it's for life."

My every instinct is telling me you belong to me.

Graeson had said that to me right before giving me an impromptu haircut.

Too bad his every instinct hadn't informed him when my flight was arriving.

"A wise woman once cautioned me never to get into a pissing match with a warg." That wasn't strictly true. I'd read it in the stall of a ladies' restroom years ago. "Tell him or not." I spread my hands as I backed onto land owned by the state of Georgia. "I've got nothing but time."

A lie if ever I'd told one.

CHAPTER TWO

We elected to set up camp off the shoulder of the road, a stone's throw from Chandler lands. Close enough to accommodate Graeson and Dell visiting, but far enough to keep us on the right side of fae and human law.

We looped our caravan into a tight arc formation: truck, trailer, truck, trailer, trailer, truck, trailer. Magic flowed easier through circles, and the shape gave us a compact shared backyard within the boundaries of the protective magic Aunt Dot cast while Isaac and I made the trailers level on the uneven ground.

Sweaty from establishing our base, we each retreated to our homes for a much-deserved rest break. The satellite dish mounted to Isaac's roof twitched to wakefulness as I scanned the woods for signs of life and found none. The soft murmur of Aunt Dot's soaps drifted from her living room window and coaxed a sigh of contentment from me. Even with crusted blood on my hands, it was good to be home.

Home being relative considering Gemini were rooted in people and not places.

I climbed the two steps leading into my trailer and grabbed a hot shower. I remember sitting on my bed to dry my hair, but the heat must have flipped my switch, because I woke to a quiet camp and found a note taped to my door. Aunt Dot and Isaac had gone into town for supplies, taking the grocery list off my fridge with them.

After stretching out the kinks in my back, I hauled my laptop out of the bedroom and into the kitchen. One of my favorite nooks in the whole house was the booth with built-in dining table. Sliding across the vinyl seat, I set up my workstation—computer, sticky notes, pen, legal pad, pencil and freeze-dried banana chips—then opened my web browser.

A quick check of my empty inbox set off a pang in my chest. Thanks to my forced leave of absence from the Earthen Conclave due to my friendship with the now-missing Harlow Bevans, and the murky nature of my relationship with a certain absentee beta warg, I was cut off from my usual resources and most of my contacts. Most. Not all. I still had one willing to stick her neck out for me. And then I had Graeson. Maybe. I'd thought we shared the same goals, but now I wasn't as sure.

Fist pressed into my cheek, I rested my elbow on the table and started combing over my notes on the Charybdis case files, focusing on the kelpie we had taken down in Abbeville, Mississippi. When nothing new jumped off the page, I rubbed my eyes and began pondering dinner options.

A noise at the front of the trailer raised the fine hairs down my arms. The scritching of claws against metal dumped a load of adrenaline into my system. Was Aisha back for round two? Heart clogging my throat, I hauled myself out of the booth, crept to the door and peered out the window.

No one was there except for a mosquito hawk who thumped against the fist-sized exterior porch light mounted beside the steps.

Cocking my head, I filtered out the ambient noise until I heard the soft hum of the wards. They were intact, so if we had visitors, they were the friendly sort. Holding on to that comforting line of thought, I unhooked the inner screen door then shoved both it and the outer metal door open. I froze with my hand on the latch and swallowed convulsively.

White fur, matted with saliva. Slender ears perked for sounds they were past hearing. Head twisted perpendicular to its spine. Muscular hind legs still twitching.

A rabbit.

I really, really hoped this wasn't the warg version of a welcome present. Or an apology. Aisha didn't strike me as the kind to make amends, but I could picture her thinking nothing said *I'm sorry* quite like a fresh kill left to bleed out on your doorstep.

Chiding myself for getting choked up over a bunny, I took the first step down then leapt to the ground, knees protesting as they absorbed the impact. Nape crawling with the sensation of being watched, I forced myself to squat and trace the furrows etched into the metal siding with a fingertip. A sweeping glance under my lashes told me the gift-giver hadn't waited around to witness its reception. I picked the furry corpse up by the ankles and set it on a spare cinderblock while I decided what to do with it.

"Ellis."

Pivoting my weight to one side, I witnessed the moment Graeson exited from between two enormous oak trees. His rumpled shirt looked marginally fresher than his wrinkled jeans. His feet were bare and stained brown with grime. When he smiled at me, my pulse kicked up a notch. "Where have you been?" I stood and dug my bare toes into the soft dirt to anchor myself. "I met your alpha female earlier, and by *met* I mean she went for the jugular."

The woman who stepped into the clearing behind him was as tall and lanky as a teenager, with sun-kissed skin and a splash of freckles across the bridge of her nose. Her china-blue eyes shone, and her strawberry-blond hair spilled over her shoulders as she bounded toward me as naked as the day she was born. She smacked into my side and wrapped her arms around me, almost toppling us both.

"Sorry about the boobs. Pretend they aren't there." Impossible to do when her nipples were almost stabbing me in the throat. "I had to change to keep up with Cord." She squeezed me harder. "I'm so glad you're here."

"No thanks to some people," I grumbled at Graeson while awkwardly returning Dell's hug.

Molten-chocolate eyes striated with mossy green ensnared me. "I should have been here waiting for you. I'm sorry that didn't happen." He caressed my cheekbone with his thumb. "I planned on meeting you at the airport to avoid a scene like the one you described." He traced the rigid line of my jaw until his hand slid off my chin. "But you're still here and not a scratch on you. Looks like you handled yourself."

The urge to swell under his pride rankled. It must be the warg blood in my system. "Yes, well, I'm not a total damsel."

"Bessemer—" Dell began in a rush.

I cut her off with a gesture. "Let him speak for himself, Dell."

"You were worried about me." His lips hooked to one side in a crooked smile that threatened to disarm me. "Did you think I'd stand you up on purpose?"

"You bamboozled my family into coming to Georgia." I would not be taken in by an unspoken promise and a nice set of tattoos. The thick black bands wrapping his wrists, cypress forests sprouting up his forearms, was the only ink delineating a canvas I had seen nude almost as often as covered. I barely recognized him in honest-to-goodness clothing. "I ought to wring your neck for putting them in danger."

I would have too, but Aunt Dot and my cousins could take care of themselves. Unlike me, the weak link, they had honed all their skills to a killing edge. Gemini were peaceful, but we weren't pushovers. A wanderer's life meant traveling through hostile fae territory on occasion, and when you're on the highway alone, you learn to defend yourself, your family and your belongings, or you fast become roadkill.

"Bamboozled," he echoed.

"You've got thirty seconds." I started tapping my foot to give my nervous energy an outlet. "Give me a reason to stay, or I walk."

"You're aware of how the pack bond functions?" Tone light, he nearly succeeded in making me underestimate how critical his connection with the other wargs was to his continued mental health. Without the others sharing his grief over his sister's death, he would revert to the burned-out shell of a man I'd first met not two miles from here. "Each warg is connected to me through a secondary bond that only the alpha can access outside our group. Sharing headspace with the others keeps me level, functional, but it requires an unobstructed connection to work." His voice dipped to a rumble. "When we returned to Georgia, our minds were open books."

"And Bessemer riffled the pages," I finished for him. What secrets had he unearthed that warranted setting Aisha on my trail? "What are you going to do?"

"Close it."

Dread balled, a firm knot twisting my gut. "Your grief will rebound."

The reason for the mental Band-Aid was to grant him a reprieve. Graeson had until the next full moon to get his revenge for Marie's death or Bessemer would announce an open challenge to fill his position, that of beta in the pack. The bond was a temporary fix, one with an expiration date fast approaching. Apparently Bessemer felt it wasn't approaching fast enough.

"Oh, you caught a rabbit. I thought I smelled one." Dell hooked a thumb over her shoulder. "Do you want me to clean it for you?"

In all the excitement, I'd forgotten about what had tempted me outside in the first place.

"I appreciate the offer, but I'll pass." Accepting gifts of unknown origins was not a thing fae did lightly. "I've decided I'm going to give it a proper burial."

"Is there something wrong with it?" Nose wrinkling, Dell flared her nostrils. "Why would you toss dirt over a perfectly good meal?"

"I found it on my steps right before you and Graeson arrived." As much as I hated for even a tiny life to be wasted, that decision had been made when the gift-giver abandoned the kill, well-intended gesture or not. "I don't trust it."

A nearby bush rustled as if a bird had shaken its limbs taking flight, but what prowled forward was no swallow. Thick and muscular, a gunmetal-gray wolf with a gleaming silver streak down its back emerged from the shadowy forest interior, sat on its haunches and inclined its head.

"Get in the house," Graeson said under his breath.

"Wargs are predators." I planted my feet. "If I show weakness now, it'll eat me alive later."

"I have to do this alone." He walked me up the steps backward, shoved me inside and closed the screen door between us, standing close enough to talk through the mesh. "I promise I'll explain everything when I get back."

"I doubt that." I snorted when his eyes twinkled in reward for my sass. "Be careful."

"I'm beta for a reason." He shucked his shirt, hands dipping to his fly and zipping down, holding my gaze the whole time. "Trust me."

"Trust is earned." Graeson had manipulated me one too many times for his own gain. Blindly trusting what he said or did wasn't going to happen. "I expect you back in one piece."

The now-familiar cracking sounds as bone rearranged itself held me captive at the threshold. Graeson embraced the change in steady increments, which must have increased the pain tenfold. Muscle flowed beneath his skin as he went to greet this newest visitor.

This was a statement, a master's show of control over his body, of dominance over his wolf, and I got the feeling whoever waited for him in that clearing was the worst kind of dangerous if Graeson felt the need to show him exactly what sort of adversary he could be.

The shifting pressure became too much. Graeson ruptured, a lush sterling pelt erupting over his quivering flesh all in a blink, as though the beast inside had shredded his humanity in its eagerness to be set free.

Dell pulled on Graeson's discarded T-shirt—for my comfort more than hers since I was the prude visiting what amounted to a nudist colony once the fur started flying—and plopped down in the flattened grass, angled so a cut of her eyes allowed her to watch over both me and Graeson.

Fingers pressed to the cool mesh of the screen door, I marveled at the sinewy wolf shaking out his fur as if being back on four legs was cause for joy. "Are you going to tell me what's really going on here?"

"Cord told you—it's an interpack issue."

"We both know that's not the whole story." I couldn't tear my gaze away from the eerily polite wolves long enough to peg Dell with my patented glare. "Stop giving me the edited version."

"He's going to kill me for this..." a sigh that meant she was caving, "...and I do mean skin me and use my fur to trim the hood of his jacket."

Seeing as how the active secondary bond meant he was aware of Dell at every moment, able to eavesdrop on our conversation through her mind if he chose, I doubted he had murder on the brain. At least where she was concerned. The wolf in the clearing... I wasn't so sure what the deal was there.

"Bessemer met us at the airport and kept us as *guests* in rooms we use for containing the moonsick until about an hour ago." Meaning they had been segregated for something like twelve hours. "Taunting the caged is the kind of thing Aisha lives for, but she was noticeably absent. That lit a fire under Cord to get to you." Busy conducting a one-woman thumb war, Dell scowled at her hands. "She must have wanted to catch you alone, force you to shift and see what makes you tick."

"Force me to—?" I wasn't a shifter, my soul wasn't spliced with an animal's, but I was capable of mimicking one or two aspects of another species for a short burst. Like when I'd used Aisha's blood to borrow her claws, her strength and a touch of aggression. It's not a thing I do on command, and after my first experience with the soothing warmth of the pack bond, not an action I would take lightly with a warg involved. Had Aisha not kept coming for my throat, I wouldn't have given her the satisfaction of feeding off her magic to defend myself. "How does she know what I'm capable of?"

"The reason Bessemer isolated us from the pack was so he could take his time raking through our heads." Her nails dug into her thighs. "We had no choice but to submit. He's our alpha, and shutting down the bond meant Graeson would suffer." Drops of crimson welled. "Bessemer knows you joined with us. He knows what you are. Everything Graeson learned about you Bessemer knows too."

Crap. So that was the point Graeson had been meandering toward when the gray wolf interrupted us.

The violation of the alpha skimming my life's history, gleaning confidences I had never shared with anyone but Graeson, made my skin chill with shame and tingle with fury.

The details of my personal life had made for pillow talk between the alphas.

"You're not a warg. That type of connection shouldn't have been possible." Dell rubbed the wounds with her palm, smearing blood as they sealed before my eyes. "He must have wanted a firsthand accounting of what you're capable of from someone he trusts before allowing you onto pack lands."

"Can you sense him?" Warg politics were foreign to me. Bessemer had sent his mate to get bloodied in the name of curiosity? Was that same interest enough to warrant a front-row seat for the attack, or would he be satisfied sitting at home with his senses perked until I'd made my flickering connection? "Where is he now?"

She jerked her chin toward the imposing gunmetal wolf who stood like a king in the circle of flattened grass, gold eyes shining as he stared at me with hunger that made my skin crawl, and I realized I had made a mistake in assuming Bessemer would want to greet me as a man. His beast had superior reflexes and senses, all the better to assess me. Framed that way, I understood the breadth of the error in judgment I had made. I was thinking like a fae, and that might get me killed if I stayed among the wargs for much longer.

As if thinking of her had conjured her, Aisha appeared at her mate's side. She peeled her lips over her teeth in a wolfy grin for me that Bessemer mirrored. Instinct guided me to ease outside and join Dell, presenting a united front.

Quick to notice the drift in their attention, the silvery wolf that was Graeson shifted to the left and put himself between Dell, my first line of defense, and the alpha mates.

My fingers curled into fists at my sides, my thumb smoothing over my concealed spur. "Are they going to fight?"

She considered their postures. "Not today."

Not today implied *maybe tomorrow* was a distinct possibility. "Graeson would fight his alpha?"

"Over you?" A wild smattering of laughter erupted beside me. *"Yes."*

"I came here for help, not to stir up trouble."

"Where teeth and hearts are involved, men are not rational." She gave my thigh a sympathetic pat. "It's a dominance thing. It's not your fault. Any mate Graeson brought home would face the same firing squad."

"Oh fudge." The implications hit me with the force of a Mack truck, and I dropped my head into my hands. "After Aisha attacked, she called *me* the beta. I thought it was— I don't know—a taunt, but it wasn't, was it?"

The way Dell shrank in on herself told me my hunch was right.

"Aisha is alpha, because she's the female half of the alpha pair." My brain sorted all I knew about wargs and about Graeson's situation into neat little stacks that wouldn't stand taller than a coffee mug if I placed them on my desk. "Graeson is the beta." The wheels kept spinning. "Initiating the pack bond is an intimate act. Inclusion of a new member, I would imagine, must be sanctioned by the alpha."

I read the blossoming dread on Dell's face and knew I was headed in the right direction. "Unless another type of intimate bond was formed that might supersede that of a wolf to his alpha like a—"

"—mate," she finished for me when my mouth and brain got disconnected.

"Bessemer thinks I connected with the pack bond because I'm Graeson's mate." The idea sent shivers cascading down my arms. "Graeson is beta... That makes me beta too?"

No wonder Bessemer had his fur britches in a wad. Betas answered only to their alphas, and his beta had brought home a fae of undetermined strength and origin, one who might jeopardize the running of his pack by weakening his second or sowing discord in the ranks.

Dell twisted hair around her finger and tugged until I was amazed it remained attached. "Yes?"

"We're in trouble, aren't we?" This might not have been the *us* Graeson had hoped for, but I would stand by him in this. The mate thing was big. Huge. Neither of us had signed up for it. Graeson was...confused...about me, and my gift was to blame for that. The same gift that had apparently incensed his alpha. "From what Graeson's told me, your alpha is an eye-for-an-eye kind of guy."

Meaning if he viewed our bond as legitimate, he would also view it as a slap in the face that he was shut out of such a huge decision when I wasn't a warg and therefore couldn't be Graeson's lifemate. Also meaning all the poking and prodding Bessemer would have done to test my fitness prior to welcoming me into the pack would now occur post-bond.

"Bessemer is a hard man." Dell worried the hem of her borrowed shirt. "He has to be."

A wolflike growl rumbled through my chest upon hearing the fear in her voice. Must be the dregs of Aisha's blood yet to be flushed from my system. The fact remained I didn't like how subdued Dell had been acting, as if someone had burst her usually bubbly personality. Her eyes widened at the guttural sound, as if it carried a message she understood. I cleared the tightness from my throat. "So it's fair to say that Bessemer wouldn't mind seeing his beta brought down a few notches."

"More than," she agreed.

Again the silent wolves drew my eye. Too bad the pack bond wasn't a thing I could tap into at will. I would give a lot to know what those two were discussing. Without asking I knew Dell wouldn't tip me off about the content, assuming she could pick up reception for their conversation.

This whole interlude made me wonder if, under normal circumstances, there were distinct channels you could tune into to converse with specific wolves. That would come in handy.

In the clearing, the standoff was ending. Not a drop of blood had been spilled. That was progress, right?

The alpha pair turned and left, the subtext clear: they weren't afraid of turning their backs on Graeson.

I, however, had no trouble admitting my unease. I wasn't taking my eyes off them, not even long enough to retreat inside the trailer. The tip of Graeson's tail flicked my calf as he trotted past, but I kept my stare fixed until

Aisha and Bessemer were gone and not so much as a tree limb swayed to betray their passage.

A nasally chuff sounding suspiciously like a snort drew my attention to Dell, who was staring at a point beyond my shoulder. I finally turned away from the woods just as Graeson ducked around the side of my home. He reared up on the steps and scratched at the door with a pathetic whine in his throat. Dell laughed at his antics, but I resisted his charm. At least until he flopped on the grass, rolled over and showed me his fuzzy white belly just begging for rubs. I opened the door—like a sucker—and he leapt to his paws, darted in and trotted to the rear of the trailer. The jerk leapt onto my made bed where he proceeded to roll until my sheets were a tangled mess.

"Wow." Dell snicker-chuckled. "I can't believe you fell for the old *rub my belly* shtick."

"There's one born every minute," I grumbled, trailing after him. "What does he think he's doing?" Shimmying on his back up and down my bed, paws kicking in the air—that wasn't normal warg behavior. Was it?

"Um, if I had to guess..." she stood and backed a safe distance away, "...I'd say he's marking territory."

"Raise one leg, Graeson. I dare you." I stomped over to my table and rolled up an old sales flyer for a chain store three states away. "One drop on anything that belongs to me, and I'll load you up and drive you to a vet for a few corrective snips. You'll spend the rest of your life squatting when you have to pee."

"It's a good thing your nose isn't better," Dell singsonged.

"What's that supposed to mean?" The sales paper hit the floor. "No. He didn't." I bolted down the steps and really looked at the Airstream's wheels. Liquid glinted on the rubber and glistened on the grass nearby. I leaned closer and inhaled. *Ammonia.* "I can't believe he hosed my trailer." A similar glint drew my eye to the wheels of my truck, which shined. "And my truck?" Sure enough, it too had been splashed with Graeson's golden stamp of ownership. "I'm going to kill him." Standing out here among his conquests, I wrinkled my nose. "As soon as he finishes washing the stink off my stuff."

Cackling merrily, Dell shucked Graeson's shirt, flung it at me and skipped backward toward the woods. "I need to head home and check on Meemaw. Her arthritis is flaring up something awful. See you later."

"Hey," I called after her retreating back. "What are the odds of me arranging a meeting with the Garzas?" The pack witches had performed the divinations to track Charybdis's movements. I would give my eyeteeth to get my hands on that information for my case file. "They live around here too, right?"

"The Garzas are...complicated. I can't guarantee a meeting, but I'll ask." She twisted her bottom lip then released it with a pop. "They made a pit stop on the way back from Mississippi. That much I do know. I'll reach out once they get home."

More delays, but hunting Charybdis was a bunch of *hurry up and wait*. "I appreciate it."

She lifted a hand in farewell. "No problem." Then she was gone, and I was alone with Graeson.

Circling around the trailer, I clomped up the stairs, grabbed the handle on the screen door and pulled. It didn't budge. I jiggled it again. Locked. From the inside. Sitting on the laminate flooring of my entryway, the wolf gazed out the mesh at me through clear, guileless eyes.

"I guess you understood what I said about squatting when you pee, huh?"

CHAPTER THREE

I'm not too proud to admit I bribed my way back into my own home. The cost was a packet of gas station beef jerky from the glove box emergency kit in my truck. Graeson was happy to nudge the door open and take his prize from me with gentle teeth. He was even happier as he trotted to my bedroom and made himself comfortable while smearing drool and meaty juices on my sheets.

I retreated to the table where I could keep an eye on the wolf. I was sitting there, back to the wall and legs stretched out on the cushion in front of me, eating a bowl of soup I didn't taste thanks to the frantic thought loop whirling through my head, when a couple of rapid knocks rang out.

"Cammie," Isaac boomed from the porch. "Groceries." He opened the screen with his pinky then backed through it. "Here. I forgot to tell you. This arrived before we left Three Way." He dropped a bubble mailer on the table with a Wink, Texas return address, and it was all I could do not to snatch it up and tear into it then and there. This could be it. My first real look at Charybdis. Stepping into the kitchen, he dropped off groceries from the list I'd texted him. He froze, one hand in the paper bag. "What the hell?"

A bone-chilling snarl peppered the air.

"Graeson." Hand gripping the back of the bench seat, I scowled at him as he leapt off the bed and prowled closer. "Knock it off."

Armed with the first thing his hand closed over, a carrot, Isaac pointed its tapered orange tip at the slavering wolf. "*That's* Cord Graeson?"

Scooting on my butt, I slid off the booth and between my cousin and my wolf. Not *my* wolf. No one tamed a warg. Graeson. He was just Graeson, and I would do well to remember that.

"This is my favorite cousin, Isaac Cahill." I disarmed him and took a bite out of the raw vegetable. "Isaac, this poodle really is Cord Graeson."

"I've never met a fanged-out warg," Isaac said near my ear. "Is it safe to keep him in the house like this? Should you prop open the door or something in case he wants to go out?"

Twirling the carrot in a *whoop-de-do* motion, I crossed to the entryway and pushed open the screen. With a snort, the wolf sat on his haunches. I cracked the door then returned to Isaac's side in case Graeson got any ideas. He didn't dart for the opening like Isaac appeared to hope he would. In fact, Graeson seemed more than content to sit in the middle of the trailer and block me from being able to put up my groceries.

"He acts so...tame." Isaac placed a hand on my shoulder. "Is this normal?"

The wolf didn't growl, but he did peel his black lips away from his teeth.

Isaac removed his hand, and Graeson pretended the implied threat had been an innocent twitch of his muzzle.

"I'm not sure what's normal for wargs," I admitted. "I'm giving him until bedtime, then I'm unpacking Grandmom's sterling silverware and forking him until he takes the hint and leaves."

The wolf's furry ears perked, but to a new sound or my bluff I wasn't sure.

"Pumpkin, did you get my rhubarb by mistake?" a breezy voice intruded.

"Mom—" Isaac moved to intercept Aunt Dot.

"Don't manhandle me, Izzy." Aunt Dot strolled into the living room, digging bony elbows into our sides as she headed for the kitchen. "I can take care of myself." Seeing the bitten carrot gripped in my fist, she plucked it from my hand and dropped it into my favorite mug where it sat on the counter. "Slice these things first or you'll break your teeth. Next time buy the baby ones or matchsticks for snacking." After patting my cheek, she began sorting the contents of the bag. "Ah. Found it. I'll buy your carrots next time to square the debt, okay, pumpkin?"

The most pathetic whine in the history of wargdom had her pulling out her glasses and slipping them on her nose.

Waiting for her full attention, Graeson sprawled out and then rolled over, exposing his white downy belly to my aunt.

"He's good," Isaac murmured, newfound respect in his tone. At the same time Aunt Dot flung her rhubarb down and hit the floor on her knees, cooing, "What an absolute darling."

"Aunt Dot, this is Cord Graeson." Whose tongue lolled from one side of his mouth. "Graeson, this is my Aunt Dot. Bite her, and you will regret it." Isaac harrumphed. "Bite any member of my family, and you will regret it."

"Camille Annalise Ellis." Aunt Dot glanced up from her vigorous belly-rubbing. "Cord is the first boyfriend you've ever brought home to meet the family—or brought the family to meet him. Don't run him off with your sass."

"Me?" I spluttered. "He's putting on an act."

"Wolves are animals," Aunt Dot chided. "Their emotions and reactions are honest."

"He's not a real wolf." I felt a headache blossoming. "He's a man wearing a fur suit."

"Give it up." Isaac hooked an arm around my waist. "She's already picturing what beautiful grandpups you guys will make together."

I stomped his instep. His groan, coupled with the way he slumped over and rested his forehead on my shoulder while emitting manful whimpers, made me feel a tad bit better about him being right. Aunt Dot probably was imagining all the chew toys she could buy her little grandnieces and grandnephews.

I dropped into the booth, pushed aside my picked-over soup and covered my face with my hands. This was not how I imagined introductions being made.

A cold nose applied behind my ear jerked me upright, and I scooched closer to the wall to escape the source. Except Graeson took it as an invitation and climbed up beside me, going as far as to rest his head on my lap.

"They make such a cute couple." Aunt Dot wiped a tear from the corner of her eye.

This was a milestone moment for me, a new low in a life riddled with dips, realizing my romantic prospects were so pathetic that my aunt, who had raised me like her own child, was thrilled I was shacked up with a wolf.

Shock must have wiped my expression blank, because her saline waterfall dried up between one sniffle and the next. "Pumpkin, what's wrong?" She took the seat opposite me and reached for my hands. "I thought you liked the nice wolfman."

Argh. I resisted the temptation to bang my forehead against the tabletop. I ought to strangle the wolfman in question for announcing to my family we were an item. As cover stories went, it was a good one that kept them safe from knowledge civilians didn't need about the monster we were hunting. But it dovetailed with Bessemer's assumptions too well. Both our families thought we were a couple, if for different reasons. Graeson had trapped me into living a dual-edged lie that was bound to cut one of us sooner rather than later.

"We've got a problem." Since lying wasn't my strong suit, I decided to stick as close to the truth as possible. "The alpha, Bessemer, is under the misconception that Graeson and I are mated, and he's not happy about it."

Isaac dropped down next to his mom, frown in place. "Is his objection to you or to you being fae?"

"Both?" I rubbed Aunt Dot's bony knuckles, worrying the stacked rings covering each of her fingers. "I don't know, and I won't know until Graeson decides to shift and tell me."

The radiant glow drained from Aunt Dot, and cold determination settled over her features. She was shifting from doting aunt to caravan matriarch, and threatening one of hers was a foolish thing to do. "Why does the alpha believe you're mated?"

I noticed that neither Isaac nor Aunt Dot questioned whether the mating *would* occur, only accepted that it hadn't *yet*.

Hope springs eternal.

"I took blood from a pack member, and part of the shift connected me with the pack bond." With a thumbnail I tapped a square-cut ruby that had mesmerized me as a child. "Bessemer doesn't understand—or doesn't want to understand—that it had nothing to do with being mated. It's part of my gift. It was an unconscious action, not a deliberate one."

Isaac studied the faux grain on my tabletop as if mapping the grooves might lead him to an answer. "You barely know Graeson. You should be given time to decide if you two work as a couple before taking on something as complex as navigating pack dynamics." His fingertips started twitching where they rested on the seat behind Aunt Dot. The itch to pick up and leave, to avoid trouble, was as engrained in us as the pattern in the laminate. "Is this—is your wolf—worth fighting for?"

On my lap, the wolf tensed. I don't think he breathed again until I said, "Yes."

My allies were few and far between. I couldn't afford to lose even one.

"Then it's settled." Aunt Dot withdrew from me and patted Isaac's cheek. "We stay."

"This is not our way." The look he gave her was degrees softer. "Do we want to get mixed up with native supernatural politics?"

"This goes beyond our—" I choked it out, "—*relationship*. I need Graeson's help." I hadn't realized I was stroking his fur until I stopped and he nudged me with his wet nose. "He's helping me with a case."

Aunt Dot pierced me with laser focus. "You're on vacation."

As much as I wished that were the case, "A forced leave of absence is not a vacation."

Magistrate Vause felt that between my friendship to Harlow, and my relationship—whatever it was—with Graeson, I was compromised. She no longer trusted me to approach the case with a clear head.

She was right to doubt me. A teen with her whole life ahead of her was missing. And Graeson, he would never stop until Charybdis was dead. He owed his sister that peace in whatever afterlife wargs imagined for their kin.

"As far as the conclave is concerned, the case he and I were working is solved," I continued. "Right now Graeson is one of the few willing to stick his neck out with me, and part of that is because he's a native supernatural and has immunity from prosecution. The conclave can't touch him."

"They can touch you plenty," Isaac pointed out. "You could lose your badge if you get caught. Or worse."

"It's a risk I'm willing to take." The weight of the pearl bracelet I wore, the faint pink orbs carved with intricate designs, demanded it. "The conclave is willing to overlook Harlow's disappearance if it means the case stays closed. I can't let that happen." I rolled the beads with my thumb. "Harlow trusted me to have her back, and I failed her. She was taken right under my nose. It's my responsibility to find her and bring her home to her family."

No one told me to let the conclave do their job. Gemini weren't trusting of outsiders and didn't believe in the conclave's mission to serve faekind without bias. Oh, they believed in policing our own, but not in the establishment created to serve, protect and punish us.

"It doesn't always have to be you," Isaac said quietly. "You have nothing to atone for."

Mournful seagulls cried overhead.

Cool waves broke against a white-sand beach.

A tinkling child's laughter silenced by the froth and foam.

Screams filled the summer night, hers, mine and our parents.

"This isn't about me. Or Lori." I slammed that memory behind as many mental walls as I could erect without shutting myself off from the world completely. Swallowing past the lump in my throat, I wet my lips and focused on the girl I could save, not the one forever lost to me. "This is about doing my job, about taking care of our own. You can't ask me to sit this one out and hope someone else comes along who gives a damn. That's not how this works. That's not how *I* work."

Even the mention of my sister's name turned Aunt Dot's eyes glassy with unshed tears. Isaac was faster to recover, but his voice was strained. "How do we help?"

"You can't, not with this." The less they knew about Charybdis and the grisly details of his murder spree, the easier they would sleep at night. Besides the fact arming them with information made them accomplices. "This is the last time we're going to talk about this. Ignorance is the only way I can protect you."

Graeson might be immune from conclave punishment, but my family was not.

"Camille—" Isaac fisted his hand on the table.

"Tell us what you need, pumpkin." Aunt Dot covered his hand with hers. "We'll play it your way. For now."

"Stay safe. Never go anywhere alone." If Bessemer picked a fight, they would finish it, giving him all the reason he needed to descend on us. As strong as I knew the wards to be, I would rather not test them against a pack of foam-mouthed wargs. "We watch each other's backs and keep inside the wards unless we're escorted by a warg I trust."

The twitch was back in Isaac's fingers, the urge to hit the road and outrun our troubles pulling his skin taut.

"If things get rough with the wargs, we'll go." Giving him a contingency plan was the best way to soothe him. "I have a contact in Texas who's offered her help if I need it."

Gaze tagging the forgotten package, Isaac stilled. "The same friend who sent you this?"

"Yes."

"Fine." He rolled his shoulders. "Mom's agreed to do this your way, and family sticks together, but if we're going to get tangled up in this, then I want your word on something."

"All right." No hesitation. I owed them for standing by me, for trusting me.

"You're going to practice your magic with me. Shifting. Recalling. The works. Every day. No excuses. You've got to get in shape if you want to hold your own with predators. Pack hunters are a whole different animal from the loners you usually track." His expression turned calculating. "Is there anyone here you trust to be a donor?"

The wolf lounging on my lap perked his ears.

"I think so." Dell would think watching Isaac kick my butt was a hoot. "It's just..."

He waggled his finger at me. "No excuses."

"Touching their bond is what started this trouble with the wargs in the first place," I argued. "Bessemer might view it as me rubbing my connection with Graeson in his face. Is that smart?"

"You're serious? We're camping a stone's throw from Chandler pack lands, and you're asking me what's smart? That ship has sailed." He left me no room to maneuver. "Wargs are territorial. There won't be any other fae or native supernaturals you can borrow magic from in the vicinity if you won't use wargs as donors. The damage is done. What more harm can you do here?"

I fisted a clump of Graeson's fur, and he flattened his ears in Isaac's direction. "You don't understand."

The pack bond held the power to shatter me. It flowed across my senses like a molten river of contentment, filling the old wounds to the brim with peace, spilling over the cracks in my heart until I became better, stronger than I was alone. When I lost Lori, I lost that resonance in my soul that came from being so perfectly in tune with another person. The pack bond sang in harmony with me when I neared it, calling me to it, welcoming me home.

After that first taste, I'd feared that taking another warg's blood would shatter the illusion, like maybe I had fooled myself into believing such fulfillment existed or that I could be part of it. Now I understood my reluctance for what it had been. Withdrawal. That inviting warmth was the drug my ravaged heart craved, and all it had taken was one hit to make me an addict.

Each time I touched that awareness, it healed another fissure crisscrossing my soul. Until the connection snapped, and I was thrust back into the emptiness of my own head, alone. All the companionship gone, the loss ripping those fissures open twice as wide, three times as deep, as they had been before I met Graeson.

Gemini weren't meant to live solitary lives. We thrived in pairs, our lives intertwined with our twins, our powers held in check by maintaining balance between two people. I was skewed. I had been since Lori died. The pack bond righted my world, and that terrified me.

"You're making the decision to endanger yourself." Isaac embodied cold logic I had no hope of fighting. "If you're brave enough to stay here, fight for Graeson and buck the system, then you're smart enough to know you don't stand a chance against either while you're this weak."

Weak.

The word had its intended effect. It pricked my heart and made me bleed. It rendered those mental walls to rubble and left me standing exposed to the lash of his intent.

I had failed my sister.

I had let her die.

That was the worst part. Knowing her death proved how weak I had been, how weak I still was.

No wonder my parents left me with Aunt Dot. I would have ditched me and started over too.

"I'll train with you." The voice didn't sound like mine. It was raw, jagged and cut my throat on the way past my lips.

Isaac acknowledged my decision with a grim nod. He'd gotten what he wanted, but it had cost us both.

"I think we've had enough excitement for one night." Aunt Dot shooed him out of the booth, and he kept going until he took the steps. "It's getting late, and I haven't started dinner yet."

I rocked Graeson's shoulder, and he snuffled. There I sat, baring my soul, and he had slept through it all. I wasn't sure if I was grateful or insulted that I had bored him to the point of unconsciousness. Ducking under the table, I hit the floor and crawled into the kitchen on my hands and knees.

"I recognize that expression." Aunt Dot offered me a hand up and pulled me into a hug. "Wipe it off your face right now. Isaac is going to hate himself enough tonight. You don't have to do it for him."

Hating him hadn't occurred to me. No, I despised myself too much to blame him.

A tired sigh deflated her, and she brought my face down to deliver a sound kiss to my cheek.

"I think I'll stay in tonight." I broke away from her gently and used my sleeping guest as the perfect excuse. "I have some research waiting, and I still have to figure out what to do about that."

Silvery legs dipped in white kicked in prey dreams.

"Have fun." A chuckle turned into a smile that crinkled her cheeks. "I'd like to meet him when he's got pants on."

I almost confessed pants didn't happen as often as she might think, but I didn't want to encourage her to hang around until he shifted. "Tomorrow," I promised, ushering her toward the door.

Outside, night had fallen. Isaac had left and flipped on the generator running strings of fairy lights between our trailers. Seeing that glow comforted me all the way to the bone.

The twinkle bouncing off the silver exterior of the trailers painted the closest trees with glimmering stardust.

Figuring the wards and the wolf would keep me safe enough, I scooped up the bubble package and retreated to the rear of the trailer, where I stripped the mattress and sat on the edge. My laptop waited for me on the narrow desk sandwiched between my closet and the bathroom. My luggage stood as sentries beneath it, and I had dumped Harlow's bag there for safekeeping too. After folding my legs under me, I tore open the bubble mailer and popped in the CD.

Time to get to work.

CHAPTER FOUR

The quality of the black-and-white surveillance footage failed to improve with repeated viewings. Tapping the pause button on my laptop, I squinted at the screen, trying to make out useful details. Another tap and the video lurched forward in slow motion. Frame by frame, I watched as a humanoid fae stepped from a closet limned with blinding light into a trashed office at the marshal outpost in Wink, Texas.

Based on the information I had compiled, along with Thierry's statement on her early involvement in the portal breach, I felt safe naming the fae in question as Charybdis. He exited the portal from Faerie and walked straight out the door leading into the hall. The camera was mounted flush against the ceiling in a corner opposite the office door, and that slight crook in the wall made the angle wonky.

Once in the hall, Charybdis stood in plain sight for a full three seconds before cocking his head to the left. This was the part where I wished the video came with an audio accompaniment, but no such luck. The recording was mute. Had I not watched the video a dozen times already, I might have missed the shadowy crease revealing a grainy smile that cut across his mouth as he spoke.

Gooseflesh raced down my arms as a short woman with pale skin paced into view. Between one frame and the next, Charybdis disappeared. At the same instant, the woman jolted as if spooked, rubbed her eyes and exited the screen in a daze. Pen tapping against a pad of paper, I added more notes to the growing pile.

Did the marshal see Charybdis? Is she available for questioning? What is the timeline on this video? Why did she walk past the portal? Did she discover the breach? Or was she a part of the security detail making rounds after the fact?

Eyes dry and itchy, I massaged them with my fingertips, wishing Graeson or Dell could lend me a second pair, but all information pertaining to the video was classified, which meant I was on my own. When I lowered my hand, Graeson stood in the doorway of my bedroom. Hindquarters wiggling, he leaned forward until his wolfy elbows hit the floor while a massive yawn cracked his jaw. I rolled my eyes, and his tail wagged once, as though asking for permission to join me.

"Not on the bed." I made a no-way, no-how gesture. "I only have two sets of sheets, and I'm not doing laundry tonight."

One of the downsides of living in such cozy quarters was the limited closet space. Two sets of sheets—one for the bed and one for the laundry pile—was as luxurious as it got around here.

Polite as could be, he walked over to inspect my desk and laptop. He sniffed the keyboard, dismissed it and dropped his head into my lap instead. Taking the hint, I scratched under his chin until his hind leg twitched. His sudden bark made me jump to my feet, which must have been his point since he darted from the bedroom, blazed through the kitchen and scratched on the screen door's frame until I opened it for him.

He was a pale blur as he leapt from the steps and hit the dirt, initiating his change the second his paws touched earth. This change was slower than others I had witnessed, but in under a minute Graeson sat bare-cheeked in my yard. Careful to keep my eyes north of his collarbone, I gathered his clothes and waited for him to come claim them.

"Did you enjoy your nap?" I called.

With a grunt, he rolled to his feet, and then he was jogging toward me, ignoring the pile of fabric in my hands as he climbed the steps. "I did." He smiled down at me, eyes slumberous. "I haven't slept that well in weeks."

Returning home to the place where his sister had been murdered couldn't have helped his restless nights.

"Is there a reason you decided to introduce yourself to my family while wearing your fur suit?"

"I didn't have a choice. I couldn't shift back." He bent down, leaning close enough the scent of his damp skin filled my head, and reached over my shoulder to caress the doorframe. "It's very subtle magic."

"The wards," I said, distracted by his proximity. "The trailers have dampening wards so that any residual energy is siphoned away from us." His eyebrows climbed. "Retaining magic makes us fidgety. The wards help us sleep. They flush all the foreign energies from our bodies and use it to fuel themselves."

He scratched the stubble on his cheek. "They also prevent wargs from changing."

"I'd have to ask Aunt Dot, but that might explain why you fell asleep." No one outside of my family had been inside my home. Ever. Graeson was my first real guest. "The wards might have been munching on your energy."

"Hmm." The thoughtful sound rising in his throat caused warning bells to ring in my ears. "You think so?"

I shrugged. "Spellwork is her forte, not mine."

For the longest time after coming to live with Aunt Dot I was afraid of the dark. She tried teaching me a spell that manifested in a bouncing sphere of light, but I couldn't so much as conjure a spark. I still can't. Her knack was self-taught using tips from friends she depended on to create our stacked ward system, and they didn't translate to me. My skills tended toward reading magics from touch and being immune to glamour.

"Dell is on her way." Graeson's eyes went distant. "She's watching over you tonight."

A ripple of unease kicked my pulse up a notch. "Do you expect trouble?"

"Oh yes." His nostrils widened as he inhaled the warm night air. "And she's right on time."

Leaning around him, I spotted a pair of golden eyes waiting in the darkness. "Dell?"

"Aisha," he corrected. "I can wait for Dell to arrive before I leave if you want."

Aisha and Graeson. Alone. In the dark. My question came out sharp. "Where are you going?"

"To handle pack business." He reached up and ran his fingers through my much shorter hair. No longer brushing my lower back, it barely tickled the undersides of my shoulder blades now. "I like your hair this length."

Feet cemented in place as he toyed with the frizzy ends, I crushed his clothing tighter against my chest. "Yes, well, I had to get it trimmed." I worked up a scowl. "Someone cut a chunk of my hair off. I couldn't just leave it jagged."

"You donated to a good cause," he assured me, lifting his arm. "See?"

A thick bracelet of black leather circled his wrist, almost melding with the wide bands of ink, the design brightening its center an intricate braid of honey-blonde hair. *My* hair. Of all the things I had imagined him doing with the chunk of hair he'd sliced off with a sharpened nail, turning it into a fashion statement wasn't one of them.

"The wolf wasn't wearing any jewelry." That much I was certain. "How is it you kept it through the change?"

"The stronger the wolf, the more control he has over his change." He let me run my finger across the design. "I can hold on to one or two small items."

I squinted up at him. "Like underwear?"

"Probably." A grin split his cheeks. "But where's the fun in that?"

"Exhibitionist," I grumbled.

"Nudity is part of our culture. I won't say we don't notice each other's bodies, because that would be a lie.

Our souls are spliced with wolves, and wolves have strong mating instincts. We're not immune to the lure of perfect breasts or..." his gaze swept down me, and his tongue darted out to moisten his lips, "...soft curves, but we learn early the difference between nudity and intimacy."

A flush riding my cheeks, I dropped my hand and glanced down at my bare toes.

"Dell's here," he sounded distracted. "I should get going."

"I don't trust her." I didn't have to specify the *her* in question.

He crowded me, smooshing his clothes between us. "Worried about me, Ellis?"

"My interest in your well-being is strictly professional." I managed a cool tone. "I need your help tracking down Charybdis." My throat tightened. "We're running out of time."

Graeson pressed warm lips to my forehead. "We'll find Harlow."

I nodded when the words got stuck in my throat.

"Aisha is waiting," Dell huffed out as she slowed to a walk and leaned against the trailer's exterior.

"Another minute won't hurt her," he said, loud enough it carried.

Dell fidgeted with the buttons on her sleeveless shirt, her lips a flat line. "Be careful tonight."

He palmed her shoulder, bare skin to bare skin, and that contact appeared to soothe the restlessness in her. She left the threadbare buttons alone and sucked in a deep breath that she released in a slow gust.

Physical contact was important to wargs on a level I didn't fully grasp. The thought of Aisha touching Graeson...it did dangerous things to my blood pressure. But the way he was with Dell, and with the other female pack member who had followed him to Mississippi, didn't ruffle my feathers at all. The males slapped backs and bumped shoulders more than humans or most fae did. Those observations helped put our interactions into perspective. What I viewed as an invasion of personal space, he saw as a welcome and necessary part of our social interactions. It made me wonder if he pushed so hard at times because I wasn't fulfilling his need for touch. And then I wondered if that lack was one I wanted to rectify.

Non-warg-to-warg etiquette was something to ask Dell about later, where even if he overheard our conversation through the bond, at least I didn't have to look him in the eye while figuring out if I had to pet him to keep him happy while we worked together.

"Keep Ellis out of trouble." He winked at Dell. "You two stay inside tonight."

"Why?" I had planned to quietly work on my case notes right up until I heard the casual warning in his tone. "Is the pack hunting?"

"Something like that." His gaze lingered on me. "Don't give Dell a hard time, okay?"

I made him no promises.

Turning on his heel, Graeson leapt, and wild magic enveloped him. The change swept over him fever-fast, bones and muscle snapping into place with one decisive crunch. He landed on four graceful paws, glanced over his shoulder with reflective eyes and caught me gaping after him.

"Show-off," Dell called.

The sleek wolf barked once then loped toward Aisha.

"Why doesn't he do that every time?" I marveled. "It seems like it would hurt less—like ripping off a bandage."

"The pain is always the same. Unless it's worse. You can't cheat the wolf." She smoothed her hands down the front of her shirt. "The insta-shift is flashy—not many can execute it and none as well as Graeson—but it's not practical except under dire circumstances."

An intense uneasiness prickled my skin. "What, exactly, is the pack up to tonight?"

The valiant button gave up its struggle to stay attached and popped off in her hand.

"Mom can't find her can opener." Heavy footfalls squished over damp grass. "All I have is a bottle opener." Isaac rounded the corner and drank in the sight of Dell with hungry eyes before blinking away the fledgling spark and replacing it with cool courtesy. "Do you have a spare?"

"I always keep a spare." Aunt Dot wasn't the best cook. She did breakfast well, and she made a mean sandwich, but dinner came safest from the can unless she was supervised. If Isaac was asking for an opener, then they had decided to forego unstrapping the fire extinguisher tonight. "Check the top drawer to the left of the sink."

Blue eyes sharp on Dell, he ran a hand through his dirty-blond hair and approached with caution. The entryway was crowded with all three of us standing there, but Isaac slid past Dell and me into my trailer, where drawers began rattling and thumping. He never listened to me when I told him where I put things.

"That's your cousin?" Dell worried her bottom lip between her teeth. "Which one? You've got two, right?"

"This one's Isaac. The other's Theo." His trailer sat at the rear of our circle, empty. His work carried him around the world, but just like me, he always came back home, wherever home might be. "I doubt you'll see him. Last I heard he was still in Mexico."

"Is Isaac single?" Twisting the tail of her shirt into a knot, she laughed at her nerves and shook out her hands. "How hairy does he like his women?"

"Isaac?" I called.

"I don't see the damn can opener."

"That's not—" I rolled my eyes. "Are you single?"

Something hit the floor, shattered. I hoped it wasn't my favorite mug. I had washed the carroty taste out of it earlier and set it out to dry near the sink.

"Who's asking?" He appeared in the doorway, gaze piercing Dell where she stood.

"This is my friend Dell Preston." I frowned at his coldness. Usually he loved buttering up the ladies. "Dell, this is Isaac Cahill."

"I don't think I've ever met a friend of Camille's before," he said, extending his hand.

Aware of what Gemini were capable of, Dell closed her fingers over his fearlessly.

"Cam's good people." Her Southern accent intensified. "I'm proud to call her my friend."

"You're a warg." Statement of fact. Rubbing his fingertips together as though parsing a confusing texture to her magic, he cocked his head to one side. "You're the donor."

"Yeah. I guess." Tendrils of reddish hair spilled over her shoulder when she ducked her head to peer shyly through the wavy curtain. "I mean, I did the one time."

"About that." I rescued her from the awkward silence following his pronouncement. "A condition of me staying here is an agreement I made with Isaac. I've let my magic go the past few years, and he's going to whip me into shape." Now for the awkward part. "That means I need a blood donor. You're the only warg I trust enough to ask for the favor, but you can say no."

Her head jerked up, all hesitation gone. "I'll do it."

Relief flooded me. "Are you sure? There's no pressure. I can find another source."

"I've seen what you can do. If he can make you better, stronger, then I'm glad to help. Things are tense in the pack right now," she hedged. "You're taking a risk staying here to help your friend. The least I can do is make that stay safer."

"What are your plans for tonight?" Isaac interrupted.

"I, well, Cam..." Her fingers fluttered in an attempt to pluck the right words out of thin air. "Guard duty."

His grunt of approval left her beaming, and he jabbed me in the side with his elbow. "How would you feel about getting in some practice?"

"Right now?" Even I heard the plaintive note in my voice.

The surveillance footage called to me, its siren song whispering I would unlock its mystery on the one hundred and first viewing, but a promise was a promise. The best thing I could do for Harlow today, right this very minute, was to keep an ear to the ground for any news hinting Charybdis had resurfaced while I got myself in fighting shape. The next time we met, he would pay for what he'd done.

"Yes." He glanced at Dell. "Unless you two have something better to do."

"Nope," she chirped, inching closer to him. "I'm game for whatever you want to do."

Oh brother.

Or maybe that should be *oh cousin*?

CHAPTER FIVE

Dell bounded after Isaac, leaving me to chew over whether their introduction was a wise one while I changed into yoga pants and a T-shirt. Dell was a good girl, and pack life meant she came with deep roots and ties to her community. Isaac was a drifter bound by honor to stay at his mother's side, even while her own sense of duty demanded she accommodate me and my odd lifestyle. But Aunt Dell was no spring chicken, and Geminis lived a roughly human lifetime. One day the tethers binding him to me and my seminomadic lifestyle would be severed, and he would stretch his heart's wings at last. The wanderlust in his soul was present in each twitch of his fingers, and I didn't want Dell pinning hopes on him that would clatter to the ground when we left.

"This isn't a date," Isaac called when he spotted me. "You didn't have to get all dolled up for me."

Shadows flickered in his eyes, and I lifted an eyebrow. What had ruffled his feathers? His gaze speared Dell, a twitch in his jaw. His cheeks were flush, and hers were too. She wiped her lips with her thumb and shot me a wink.

My eyebrow climbed higher. Usually Isaac tore a page from Theo's book and toyed with his women. Gave them flowery words and shored up the hope they might be the one who settled him. For once the shoe appeared to be on the other foot—paw? Dell was making her interest clear.

She was ready to play the game, and Isaac appeared unnerved to find himself the prize.

The pair squared off against one another in the center of the backyard created by circling our Airstreams. Twinkling lights strung between each trailer bathed the area in a soft glow and made Dell's eyes sparkle.

Isaac couldn't turn his back on her fast enough. "Have you been doing your stretches?"

As flat and hard as an open-handed slap, his voice jarred me to attention.

"I'll take that as a *no.*" He anchored his hands at his hips. "When was the last time you took magic into yourself for the purpose of shifting aspects?"

"This afternoon." As he well knew.

"That was a gut reaction. Acting in self-defense doesn't count. That's not skill, it's not choice, it's your fight-or-flight reflex," he lectured. "When was the last time you purposefully used your magic to instigate a change for reasons other than saving your neck?"

Thinking back over the past few weeks, I worried my bottom lip with my teeth.

"Okay, let's try this another way." A hearty sigh heralded his disappointment in me, but that was nothing new. I was an old pro at disappointing those I loved. "When was the last time you shifted prior to today, period?"

"Two days ago, and once a day for several days before that."

His shoulders relaxed. "How many sources?"

"Three, I think."

He rolled one of his hands, expecting a recitation.

"A kraken, a legacy and a warg." It felt like I was missing one, and it came to me. "A witch."

"Four shifts." Amazement wreathed his face. It had been a tough week. "And your reset?"

I flinched, but he kept waiting for an answer. This was part of his bargain, I realized, forcing me to talk about my sister, a thing I rarely did, a name no one spoke within my hearing at home. For a trickle of seconds, I wasn't sure the deal was worth it.

The pearl bracelet glinted a reminder at me, and I shored up my resolve.

"I didn't..." I croaked. "I didn't need the reset." *The reset.* Harsh as it was, I was grateful for the reprieve, glad he wasn't calling her by name. "I initiated the change of my own free will."

Mostly.

Hand extended to offer me comfort, he caught himself mid-step and turned the move into a widening of his stance. "Why would you?"

"That's classified." I almost found a smile to make light of those circumstances, but *almost* wouldn't fool him.

Ever the puppeteer, Vause had pulled my strings and made me dance. I had shifted into Lori and used the memory of my sister to interrogate the only one of Charybdis's victims to survive. Painful as it had been, the intel we had gained from the McKenna girl was worth the cost to me.

"Okay." Letting the remark slide, he brought his hands together in front of him and cracked his knuckles. "I can respect that."

Face quirked in an odd expression, Dell glanced between us, either attempting to read the tension thrumming between us or playing spymaster for Graeson, I wasn't sure.

"I used seven donors this past week," Isaac informed us without a hint of bravado.

No surprise there when he made a point to never use the same source twice, to always stretch the limits of his abilities by choosing the rarest or most difficult magics to imbibe. Oh the hearts those experiments had broken. As the lone man in our caravan, except for the rare occasions when Theo condescended to join us, he pushed himself hard to hone the edge of his skill.

"Do you want the honors," he said, shaking out his hands, "or should I go first?"

"You can go first," Dell chimed in.

He shot me a glance to see if I minded.

"Knock yourself out." I wasn't about to fight him for the privilege. His recalls were stunning.

"One." Left arm extended, he coaxed the change forth until his skin turned a sunburned hue. The fingers of that hand stuck together, the thumb popping out of alignment as his melded digits flattened, curved. Bands of white striped his joints, and peculiar, bristly hairs sprung from his hardening carapace. In under thirty seconds, he wielded a giant crab pincher. A grunt of effort, and he spun into a flying kick that ended with him snapping his claw an inch from my nose. *Pagurus armatus.*"

"Where did you run into a giant hermit crab?" Tennessee was a landlocked state.

Click-clacking his weapon, he shrugged. "She rented lot 4B." The appendage dissolved in a ripple of magic and pink skin. "I noticed her species on her renter's form and got curious."

Maybe Dell was just biting her tongue to avoid cracking a really good joke about getting crabs from hooking up with a stranger in a trailer park, but the barely audible growl vibrating in the air around her at the mention of a previous lover reminded me of what curiosity did to the cat.

For his sake I hoped none of his recalls were feline.

The Three Ways from Sunday RV Park in Three Way, Tennessee had been our home for the past year. Aunt Dot enjoyed running parks, and she owned or had owned at least a dozen. The way she traded property with friends made tracking her properties impossible. I was glad that headache fell to Isaac. Keeping tabs on tenants was tough, too, but the steady arrivals and departures distracted her from getting too itchy to relocate. The influx of talent also kept Isaac occupied, though crablike fae had to be a first.

A spark of interest in Dell's reaction lit his eyes before he veiled them. "Number two..."

The rest of his changes flowed faster, and each was as unique and distinct from the last as the pincher had contrasted his natural hand. The transition was so smooth from donor to reset to the next donor that, had I not known Isaac as well as I did, I might have mistaken his arrogant scowl while performing his impression of Theo for the real thing.

By the time he worked through all seven of his reserves, an impressive number even for him, a sheen of sweat dampened his shirt.

Wiping the back of his arm across his forehead, he gestured me forward. "All right. Let's see what you've got."

Hours had passed since I tasted Aisha's blood. In theory, I should be able to summon her black pelt and claws, repeating my earlier performance. The reality was less impressive. I reached down deep, into the core of my magic, and stirred the dying embers. A tiny flicker took pity on me, and I sprouted patchy black fur down my right arm. Even that much effort left me shaking and sweaty.

"Not bad." He bestowed a proud smile on me. "You did better than the last time we tried this." That had been almost a year ago. "Your talents are like muscles. You have to isolate and exercise them to build strength."

"That's it?" Dell walked over, smoothed her hand down my arm, and the clumpy fur shed.

Innocent as her rebuke was, it still stung my pride. "It's the best I can do."

"For now," Isaac corrected, cutting Dell a sour glare. "You'll get better with practice."

The sentiment reminded me of one Magistrate Vause had shared not too long ago, preaching how I could only get better with dedication while ignoring the reason I let these "muscles" atrophy.

"I should have gone first." I shook out the tingles of lingering magic. "It's impossible to follow up Isaac."

"You'll be kicking his ass in no time." Ever the supportive girlfriend, she slung her arm around my shoulders. "With my grade-A warg juice pumping through your veins, how could you not?"

"Are you strong enough to continue?" Isaac intruded on my vigorous eye-rolling. "I don't want you to overexert yourself."

"I'm good." To my surprise, it was the truth. The past week had limbered me up, making me flexible in ways I hadn't been in years. "Let's keep going."

"All right." A brief grin split his cheeks. "Say the word, and we stop."

My few minutes of exertion were nothing compared to his, but the burn felt good. "Okay, Grade A, this is where you and your juice come in."

"I want to see transformation to the elbow. Full transformation. Not a single hair past." Isaac dragged his finger across the crease in my arm like I'd failed basic anatomy. "Hold it for sixty seconds and then release it."

I puffed out my cheeks with a sharp exhale. "Okay."

My most extensive transformations had been fueled by adrenaline. Shifting cold was harder, which was the point of the exercise. That didn't make me any more eager for the attempt.

I stuck out my arm, and Dell clasped hands with me. The nail on my right hand's middle finger wiggled loose, pushed free by the emergence of my spur. Quick as a flash, I pierced the back of her hand and tasted her rich blood in the back of my throat.

Golden fur sprouted down my arm, and Dell squeaked with glee as the now-familiar static trickled into my head. My fingers extended, the nails lengthening and sharpening. My vision wavered, caught between what I saw and what my mind perceived. I saw nothing when I looked at Isaac, but Dell... She glowed with subtle light, her resonance as distinctive to me as her voice.

"Hiya."

The greeting pinged around in my skull.

I felt my lips curving upward and couldn't have stopped the smile from blossoming if I'd tried. *"Hi."*

Between one heartbeat and the next, Dell vanished, ducking underneath the giant claw Isaac brandished. His swing went over her head and almost gutted me. I swiped my nails over his carapace, and the screech made my back teeth ache.

"What are you..." I ducked another swing, "...doing?"

"This isn't a game, Cammie." He sucked in a hiss when I sliced his shirt to ribbons, drawing thin lines of blood from the shallow cuts. "It's not enough to summon the aspects. You must learn how to wield them to your advantage."

A vicious snarl quivered in Dell's lips. The quality of her light shifted, altered. She was changing. *Oh crap.*

"Dell," I snapped. "No." I winced when his pincher snipped off two of my claws like he wielded a pair of overgrown nail clippers. "Let me handle this."

Her glow pulsed once and then leveled, but the snarl kept coming, a steady reminder she was there to help if I needed her. The show of support bolstered me, and even as my arm muscles trembled with the strain of holding the magic to my skin, I tensed for another blow. Isaac aimed for my soft middle again, not holding back, but blood was rushing in my ears, and I was ready for him. My shaggy forearm batted away his claw, the sound like nails raking a chalkboard, yet somehow over the screech I heard a single word, a thought, really.

"Ellis?"

I shook my head, but the tendril remained. *"Graeson?"*

The blinding white light I associated with his mental presence splashed red.

Spine stiffening, I spoke aloud. "Graeson?"

"Watch out," Dell cried.

Too late to duck the blow I hadn't seen Isaac launch, I grunted when his punch landed, and my teeth clacked together. At least his pinchers had been closed. Knocked backward, I hit the dirt on my butt and brought the tail of my shirt up to wipe my lip. Sparring match or not, he wouldn't hit me while I was down.

I winced at my tender nose, searching out Dell. "Can you sense Graeson?"

A short pause lapsed while she dug her toes in the dirt. "Yes."

"What's wrong with him?" I spat blood. "His light— aura—whatever—it's wrong. It's not as bright as it used to be. Was he injured in the hunt?"

Dell shifted her weight onto her heels before slapping the balls of her feet to the ground. "I can't."

"Can't what?" The tug of fear caused the magic to slip away from me, and the pack bond evaporated in a whirl of crimson voices. I pushed to my feet. "What's going on, Dell?"

"Let it go. Please." She peered through her lashes at me. "You can't help him." Her gaze latched on to Isaac as if he might side with her, but he was Switzerland. "Let's keep practicing. Or maybe go try some of that soup you were making earlier."

Things were bad if she was suggesting we all go eat mushy vegetables together.

"Show me," was all I had to say.

A quiver ran through her. "Screw it," she muttered, then bolted for the trees.

Dell sailed through the forest as though she were an extension of it. Limbs glided over her skin to rake mine. Leaves that held their silence in her passing crackled under my feet. Insects chirped as if saying hello, greetings cut short by my passage. The earth and its children were her domain, her presence welcome here. Me, the woods seemed eager to betray with noise and injury.

Lost to the duck low, leap high, dodge left—no right!— obstacle course that was our flight through the woods, I was paying attention to my feet and not Dell when she flung out her arm. The difference in our heights meant she nearly clotheslined me.

Panting hard, I leaned back against rough bark and gained my bearings. Something about this place set my hairs on end, the intense sensation requiring me to rub my arms to ease the prickling awareness. This spot was familiar, but not, the memory wispy like a forgotten photo glimpsed upside down that would come into focus when righted.

I smelled water before I saw it. The earthy scents of decomposition and mold, decaying fish and leaves dissolving into a new layer of silt, burned my sinuses. Above us, the towering longleaf pines leaned forward as if admiring their reflections.

Acid splashed the back of my throat, and I almost toppled sideways when the puzzle of our location solved itself in my head.

This was Pilcher's Pond.

Marie Graeson's body had been found here. I had first met Graeson in this spot, too, the grieving brother who searched for his sibling until locating her remains, who had joined in the hunt for Charybdis to avenge her. This was…the last place I expected to find him. Unless…

Whisper-soft, unsure why the quiet felt so absolute, I asked her, "Has his grief rebounded?"

The selfish hope that I was wrong, that he was still fit to help me work the case, warred with a tremulous fear that the desperate man I had first met would reemerge and that I would have no way to haul him back from the precipice, to teach him how to balance the same edge I walked daily.

Dell lifted a finger to her lips.

Those concerns flittered away to be replaced with new ones once the thunderous rush of blood in my ears receded.

Snapping teeth. Yelps. A short howl muffled.

Those sounds led me in a clockwise circle, until the full breadth of the lake revealed itself step by step. What I saw at the water's edge chilled me to my marrow. The wolf I recognized as Graeson was ringed by four others whose colors and patterns were vaguely familiar. Two more lay on their sides, panting heavily, their flanks slick with what the moon revealed as blood.

Dell hooked her arm through mine at the same time I stepped forward, and she clamped her hand over my mouth. I hadn't realized I was about to speak, but the words burned up my throat now.

Graeson needed our help. He was outnumbered. Aisha must have tricked him into coming out here and then sicced the other wolves on him. I summoned the dregs of magic still in my system, managing to sprout a layer of fine golden hair down my arms. The renewed strength allowed me to pry Dell's hand away, but it fizzled before the pack bond rushed me.

Disappointment sifted through me. No. Not disappointment. Relief. I was grateful to be spared that intimacy twice in one night, right? That thrum of belonging, the warm feedback that hummed in the back of my mind like a lullaby sung to me as a child.

Fingers tight on Dell's wrist, I was about to light into her when Graeson charged, his form a blur to my eyes as he attacked one of the wolves. The wrongness of it left me holding on to Dell for different reasons. This wasn't right, wasn't fair, wasn't Graeson.

The four remaining wargs made no move to engage him. Unless they were blasting mental threats at him, the vicious attacks were unprovoked. A thin, brown wolf with ribs exposed hung limp from Graeson's jaws, yet he didn't twitch a paw in retribution. He took it, everything Graeson dished out, without a whimper to betray the gruesome damage inflicted upon him.

Fight, damn you, I willed the wolf, but the words bounced in my skull. I wasn't pack. The bond didn't hum for me without a fresh drop of their kin's blood in my system.

Tired of his prey not giving him the fight he clearly hungered for, Graeson spat out the brown wolf and turned an eye to the next warg. This time when I strained against Dell's hold, the effort was feebler. A final shake of her head was as good as a confession. There was no panic to rush in and help, only grim acceptance and stone-cold resolve not to interfere. She had known this was happening, and she hadn't told me. For her to be so calm, Graeson must have known what he was walking into and prepared her for what might spill over the bond. No wonder she had jumped right in and distracted me with practice.

As the outsider, viewing the spectacle without being able to sift through Graeson's head to find a reason for this calculated brutality, I tired of the scene quickly. The precise cruelty of his attacks disabled his opponents—or was that victims?—and watching him embrace his role as beta soured my stomach. I had seen enough.

Turning on my heel, I picked my way back home, not caring if Dell followed.

Isaac leaned against my trailer, sharpening a pocketknife against a whetstone, and glanced behind me with a frown pinching his brow when I returned alone. "Well?"

"I'm turning in early." I breezed past him before he got a chance to respond. "Night."

Slumping against the door, I locked myself inside, just like Graeson had wanted.

CHAPTER SIX

A short buzz caused my phone to vibrate across the table, and the incoming notification made me hesitate with my spoon halfway to my mouth. I hadn't seen Graeson all morning, and I hadn't gone to the door when Dell knocked thirty minutes ago. Not to be deterred, she'd plopped on the steps to wait me out or play sentry. I didn't care either way. But seeing as how wargs aren't keen on technology, I caved to impulse and unlocked my cell.

A text from an unfamiliar number lit up the screen, a quick promise to discuss the surveillance footage after the unknown sender slept off the nightshift.

Thierry. It had to be.

The promise of an eight-hour delay made me twitchy. The footage was the only promising angle I had uncovered. The marshal onscreen had answers. She must. The other feelers I had sent out had been met with dead air, and a creeping suspicion made me question if Vause was directly involved in the radio silence. It wouldn't surprise me. Being the pet project of a powerful magistrate came with strings attached. One wrong move and those slender filaments became the garrote that strangled you.

Setting the phone on the table, I resumed the eating of my breakfast, half wishing Aunt Dot would misplace her reading glasses or her paperback, anything to warrant a quick visit. But she rose with the sun each day. No exceptions. By the time I had climbed out of bed, she and

Isaac had already eaten and returned to their respective trailers. Her to watch soaps. Him to resume tapping away at his keyboard.

Tempted as I was to seek out their company, I didn't want to explain my bleak mood last night to Isaac, and I didn't want to go another round with him either. Not when it meant borrowing from Dell and giving her—and Graeson—access to my headspace.

Writing off my soggy flakes as a lost cause, I dumped them in the trash then washed and dried my bowl before trudging back to bed. I sat on the edge of the mattress, arm extended, about to watch the Charybdis video for the one hundred and second time, when a knock on the door saved my eyeballs from the repetitive strain.

Still dressed in my sleep shorts and tank top, I opened the door without checking to see who had arrived, figuring if it was anyone or anything dangerous, Dell would have taken care of them. Except there was no Dell. The steps had been vacated, and the yard stood quiet and empty. Drawn by a flash of color, my gaze dipped. A scrunchie sat in the dead center of the top step, its edges fluffed and then smoothed. Rose fabric with lemon dots and gold threads that caught the sun. Had someone pulled down a ponytail, the tie would be bunched up with a few strands of hair stuck in for good measure. This wasn't that random. It had been neatly arranged, almost like a presentation. Almost like a gift.

That or Dell suffered from scrunchie OCD.

The low rustle of voices had me searching for the source. "Dell?"

A reddish-blond head poked around the corner. She spotted me standing in the doorway and called to the person behind her. She walked out carrying a bucket of sudsy water, and Aunt Dot followed holding a dripping squeegee. Aunt Dot must have spotted Dell moping around and put her to work. That was how it worked when we were kids too. Tell her you were bored, and she found ten ways for you not to be. We learned quick to never use the B word around her.

Setting the bucket on the ground, Dell wiped her hands on her pants. "What's up?" she asked at the same time as Aunt Dot said, "Is something the matter, pumpkin?"

"It's probably nothing, Aunt Dot." Eyeing Dell, I pointed down. "Is that yours?"

"Nope." She ruffled her wild tumble of curls. "Nothing helps with this, so I let it hang loose."

Each glossy twist was perfect, as though fairies had spent the night curling her hair on rollers forged by moonlight, and here she was complaining about them. Some things transcended species, I suppose. All women wanted the hair they didn't have. Mine was wheat-blonde and just wavy enough I had to straighten it to wear it down but not so wavy that I could scrunch it and have soft curls.

Scooping up the hair tie, I held it up so they could both get a look. "Did either of you see anyone else out here?"

"No, and I didn't pass anyone on the way." Dell tilted her head back and inhaled. "I smell pack and your family. That's it."

"There's something familiar about it." Aunt Dot dunked the squeegee in the bucket, crossed to me and took the hair tie from my hand. "I can't quite put my finger on what it is." She got the oddest expression and lifted the fabric to her nose. "This smells like..." She shook her head. "No, that's not possible."

"What is it?" I joined her in the grass. "What's not possible?"

"For a minute there, I thought..." She shook her head and passed it back to me. "You might have been too young, but your mom loved this herbal shampoo made by a pixie in South Carolina. It turned even the coarsest hair into silk. I've never smelled anything like it, and it might be all the pollen clogging my sinuses right now, but this reminds me of it." A small laugh shook her shoulders. "The crazy thing is, when I saw it in your hand, I thought immediately of Diane. It's exactly like those hairbands she used to wear all the time. Your momma had the craziest obsession with matching them to her socks. Do you remember that?"

"I remember," I murmured. "She did the same thing with me and Lori." I almost smiled. "We hated it." Unable to resist, I brought the material to my nose and breathed in a peppery-mint fragrance that sparked instant recognition. "Mom never let us use that shampoo except on special occasions." Those were few, far between and usually involved family portraits. "One night Lori used it as bubble bath. Dad laughed. Mom didn't think it was funny. She bought a lock for her bathroom door the next day."

Aunt Dot chuckled. "That sounds about right."

"Where did it come from?" Who could it belong to? Not Mom, surely. I hadn't seen her in years. "Could it have—I don't know—fallen out of something in your trailer and gotten tracked over here?"

I was grasping at straws, and I knew it, but it was the only logical scenario.

"Anything is possible." A frown touched her mouth. "I was doing some spring cleaning, as you can see. I might have dropped it outside and—" her shrug encompassed the area, "—someone might have picked it up and put it there."

"Who?" I stretched the elastic. "If not us, then maybe Isaac?" My gaze went to the trees. "Unless someone from the pack came for a visit."

The look I shared with Dell told her what I thought of that possibility.

"I'm going to grab a water." Aunt Dot wiped her forehead with the back of her arm. "Can I get you girls anything?"

"No," Dell and I said in concert.

With a chortle at us like she found us precious, Aunt Dot retreated to her trailer.

Beside me, Dell resumed excavating dirt with her toes. "Do you want me to tell—?"

"No." I crushed the fabric in my hand. "He's the last person I want to see right now."

"What you saw last night..." She dragged her fingers through her hair, leaving it artfully tousled. "You don't get it. We aren't like you." She slapped her chest. "There's an animal inside us, right under the skin, and if we aren't careful, it can do horrible things. There's a reason why packs are ruled by alphas. We need that guiding hand to keep us in line."

"What I saw last night was a powerful warg tearing into lesser wolves." After replaying the scene over and over in my head, I remembered why some of them looked familiar. "Those were the wolves Graeson brought with him to Mississippi. They were the ones he said were his best." I cringed as she wilted before me, but I kept going. "Is that why they're loyal to him? He's beaten it into them?"

Dell's shoulders ratcheted up to her ears. "You don't understand."

"No." I shoved the scrunchie into my pocket to investigate later. "And guess what? That's because neither you nor Graeson have made any attempt to educate me. He's doing what he does. He's blocking me out because he thinks he's always right."

"He didn't want to do it," she said, lips barely moving.

"Then he shouldn't have done it." Problem solved.

Her body shook, close to tears. "You don't—"

"Don't tell me that again." I sighed, exhausted by her defense of him. "It's a weak excuse, and I'm tired of hearing it."

I was wrong.

Dell hadn't been about to cry.

She exploded.

Her hands trembled with rage as she fisted my shirt, lifted me and pinned me to the wall of my trailer. "You said it yourself. Those were Cord's best wolves. His. Not

Bessemer's. *His*." She thumped my head on the metal. "When Cord needed them, they left the pack. They *left*. He didn't ask them to. He would never endanger them like that. They lied to him, told him Bessemer gave permission for them to go, and he believed them because he's still so twisted up on the inside he can't see straight. By the time they reached Abbeville and he could read the truth for himself, it was too late. The damage had been done."

An unsettling calm stole over me. "The wolves in the clearing were being punished."

A single tear rolled down her cheek.

"It was Bessemer's idea, wasn't it?" My throat tightened. "He made Graeson punish those who trusted him."

"No." A watery smile. "The wounds he inflicted were healed by sunup." She dropped me and swiped her fingers under her eyes. "They weren't ever the targets. Not really."

Graeson. Bessemer had been gunning for him when he orchestrated the beating of those loyal deserters.

A fragment of doubt lodged itself in my breast. One thing I knew well was how to snuggle up with blame every night like a warm blanket that would tangle around your throat and choke you in your sleep. Graeson blamed himself for his sister's death. He was so like me in that respect—and yet so unlike me. He was confident, a leader. He never doubted, didn't hesitate. He acted, not reacted. Even when his first impulse wasn't the best solution, he still rolled with his gut. And I, being the worst fake girlfriend ever, had leapt to conclusions based on my own sense of morality, without giving him or Dell a chance to explain. I hadn't spared a single thought for how he was coping after last night, because I hadn't understood that living with his actions was the true punishment.

Suddenly, the surveillance marathon could wait. "Take me to him."

Deep into Chandler pack land, skin crawling under the watchful eyes of unseen wargs, I came to a standstill beneath a massive oak tree that dominated this section of forest.

"This is as far as I should go." Dell rested a hand on a wooden slat nailed to the tree trunk. "Are you good with heights?"

Squinting into the sun, I tilted my head back. Way back. Far above us, I glimpsed the base of a platform built around the thick cedar's upper branches. "I'm not not-good with heights." Though this climb might test those limits. "Is this safe?"

She patted the bark covering his hideaway. "If it held Cord, it'll hold you."

With those words to recommend it, I gripped my first handhold, tested my first toehold and hauled myself up three feet off the ground.

Only twenty or thirty left to go.

"You can do it." Dell popped my bottom and winked at me. "I'll be right here to catch you if you fall."

"Let's hope it doesn't come to that." She might be supernaturally strong and fast, but I would be a hundred and thirty-eight pounds of dead weight if I lost my grip. Huffing out a breath, I found my next grip. "Here we go."

I made the rest of the climb in silence. Each step was as sturdy as any ladder, and though the tree had begun claiming the slats, growing over the edges anchored against its trunk, each remained clean and treated. The platform above me, when I reached it, also appeared to be solid and free of mold or warping.

This, I knew before reaching the top, was Graeson's sanctuary. Too much care had been taken for it to be labeled as anything else.

A generous square had been cut where tree met platform, but I hesitated, unsure how to climb through the gap without losing my grip. The concern was wrested from me when a corded forearm, wrapped with cypress ink, extended toward me. I clasped his warm, strong hand and risked gripping a handle near Graeson's foot. Somewhat certain I wasn't about to plummet to my grisly end, I half-climbed, was half-hauled up, onto the platform.

"Give me a minute," I panted. The exertion wasn't as bad as my nerves. "This is my first time pretending I'm a squirrel."

He squatted before me, hazel eyes heavy with shadows, and brushed a few stray hairs from my eyes that had been annoying me but not enough to chance sweeping them away while on the move.

"You didn't have to come all the way up here." His legs folded under him, and he sat beside me. "Dell could have asked me to climb down to you." He tapped the side of his head. "Pack bond, remember?"

No. Actually I had forgotten their two-way head radio in my haste to ensure he was all right. Dell would have remembered, though, and we were going to have a chat about manipulating me into Graeson's path very soon.

"Well, I'm here now." And finding him whole left me full of adrenaline with nowhere to go. "The question is— why are you?"

"I come here to think." He swept out his hand. "Elevation lends clarity, or something profound like that."

Not once had I peeked down on my way up, and if I hadn't had the solid reassurance of his body close to mine, I doubt I would have risked it now. But he was here, and I felt safe, so I forced my gaze past him and sucked in a gasp. "Wow."

A grin cracked his cheeks. "Wow works too."

Tucked away in the verdant canopy, I admired the pack lands rolling as far as the eye could see. Nothing but trees and earth and sky. Glitter in the distance hinted at water, but even that failed to dull my thrill. "I can see why you come up here to—" I almost said *escape*, "—think."

"I built this for Marie when she was maybe three or four. I brought her up here every night, had tea parties, the whole nine yards. This was her favorite place. We held her birthday party right here every year." He draped his arm over his knee. "She told me seven months ago she was too old for tree houses and wanted me to rent the roller rink in town." He shook his head. "Kids grow up so damn fast."

Unsure what to make of his somber mood, I rested my hand on his shoulder, figuring the touch would do him more good than words.

"You didn't stay home last night," he said, broaching the reason for my visit.

"No." I admitted, "I'm not much good at taking orders."

The truth of that statement was a fresh revelation. I liked to think of myself as one of the good guys, a cog in the conclave machine that turned the wheels of justice, but enduring my first corrective punishment since joining their ranks had shed new light on my thoughts on the organization. Until being shut out of the Charybdis case and forced to skirt the edge of the law, I hadn't known I had a rebellious bone in my body. Apparently I had several.

His focus went distant. "So I'm beginning to see."

"Bessemer put you up to it." It was as good a starting point as any. "It wasn't your fault."

"You don't believe that." His gaze cut to me. "I can smell the lie."

"If you had asked me this morning, I would call bullshit." I rolled a shoulder. "People are responsible for the choices they make. No one can force you to act outside your character." But some concessions had to be made. We might live in a human world, but neither of us were one. "There's a lot about warg society I don't understand, but bullying and corruption of absolute power transcends species."

A flash of teeth winked as though I had amused him. "You realize you're implying I'm being abused?"

"You are." I swept my hand out, indicating not the vista but those living below us. "They all are."

I startled when his knuckle smoothed down my cheek, the scars white and thick against his sun-kissed skin.

"Keep talking like that, and I'll start thinking you care about me." He tilted his head. "About us."

"I didn't come to Georgia for any of this." I soaked up his caress when I should have snapped my teeth at his hand. "I have a job to do, a job I thought you could help me do."

"I didn't expect Bessemer to react this way. He can be cooperative with fae when he must. Being in my head, reading my feelings for you and learning you accessed the pack bond lit his fuse. He thinks I've betrayed him, with you and with the others." His hand lowered until his fingers teased mine where they rested against the planks. "This isn't what I offered you. I've been putting out fires with the pack instead of helping, and I can't promise that will change in the next few days. It might get worse." He traced the smooth curve of my thumbnail. "I never would have invited you or your family into this if I'd had any idea how it would all play out. I hope you know that."

"You expected the pack to close ranks around us because you told them to, because they respect you and this is what you wanted." I spotted the damning flaw in that expectation as soon as the words left my mouth. "Do you ever think this beta gig isn't enough for you?"

From what I had seen of Graeson, he was driven to protect those he called his own. Even when they didn't need protecting. His biggest flaw was in failing to see how his calculated machinations pushed away the very people he tried to keep close. He had been willing to sacrifice me to protect his greater good, to bring down Charybdis, but somewhere along the line his prerogative changed. I was now one of the protected, and that meant he felt he had total control over our not-exactly-a-relationship.

"It used to be." His fingers tapped mine absently. "A switch has been flipped in my head, and I can't seem to unflip it."

"Sometimes trauma can cause radical changes in behavior."

"I can't blame Marie's death for this." He rubbed a white smudge on his wrist. "I was already getting twitchy. The older I get, the worse it becomes, the more Bessemer and I clash over what's right for the pack."

I cocked my head at the pale spot, but he kept it covered. "What is that?" I'd noticed it the first time we met, but I had yet to ask what it meant. "Can I see?"

His fingers peeled aside, and I got my first clear look at the full design of his tattoo.

A tiny figure in white ink stood in the pitch black forest with her head tilted back and hair spilling down her back. She stared up at the sky, where the moon ought to be.

"I had it done days before she went missing," he said softly. "It was her idea. She never did like how dark and lonely the woods looked on my arms, so I promised to ink some life into them, starting with her."

Throat tightening in sympathy—how could he stand living where his sister had been murdered when I couldn't stomach the sight of water not inside a bottle?—I nudged the topic away from his loss and back to warg business. "Is it normal for betas to evolve?"

"Yes." The change in topic relaxed him and chased the pallor from his cheeks. "It makes for a difficult transition, because it means more clashes with the alpha as those same primal urges to protect and lead emerge."

I scoffed. "From where I'm sitting I don't see Bessemer doing much of either."

"The alpha tendencies manifest in us all differently, and he's a power among our kin." A breeze ruffled his hair. "He wants the best for his people, I still believe that, but he doesn't see that strangling their free will makes them weaker, not stronger."

"Hmm." I cut my eyes toward him. "You don't say."

Delicious irony would have made me laugh if not for the circumstances of our rendezvous.

His lips flattened in a mulish line. "Everything I do, I do to protect the pack."

I drew my knees to my chest and rested my chin on top of them. "Wouldn't Bessemer say the same if I asked him?"

He twisted so he faced me head-on. "You just accused him of being a tyrant, and now you're comparing us?"

"Yes."

"I want to be insulted that you think I'm a dictator in the making, but I doubt you would have made that climb for Bessemer." His eyes narrowed. "Yet you made it for me."

"I know what it's like to blame yourself for the choices you've made, to doubt they were the right ones even when you felt there were no other options at the time." I hugged my legs closer. "I didn't want you to be alone." I bit my lip to keep from adding, *Like I was.*

That tiny crack in my armor allowed the fingers of the past to dig into my memory and pry it wide open.

"You're too slow." Trilling laughter. "Hurry up."

"My foot hurts." I limped as sand clotted the wound and salt stung my eyes. "I want to go home."

"Don't be a baby." Lori twirled under the moonlight. "I'm going in the water. Yell if you see Mom or Dad coming."

"No." I crossed my arms over my chest, shifting foot to foot, wishing she would get her toes wet already so we could get back before our parents noticed us missing. "Let's just go back. Before something bad happens."

"Ellis."

I snapped to attention. "Sorry."

The weight of his arm blanketed my shoulders. I wasn't sure when he had gotten so close, but I didn't pull away when he tucked me against his side, or when he urged my head onto his shoulder so he could rest his cheek on my hair. I sat there, stunned, and allowed him to hold me.

Aunt Dot tried to comfort me when the past rode me hard, but I pushed her away, not feeling I deserved for her to make everything okay when Lori would never be held or touched by a loved one again. Isaac got in a hug here or a squeeze there, short and fast enough I didn't have time to register what he was doing until he was gone.

I'm not sure why, but for the first time since the night I lost my sister and cried myself to sleep on my mother's lap, I entrusted another person with a portion of my sorrow. This man who mourned his own loss, so sharp and fresh, he was unable to endure it without the pack's support. That gaping hole in him should have made him weak, should have made me handle him with more care, but our negative spaces called to one another.

Both of us had made decisions we regretted, both of us had taken actions we couldn't undo, and both of us would live with those burdens. Ours was an isolated punishment, self-inflicted as all the deepest wounds were, but in this moment, trapped against the warmth of his body and breathing the scent of his skin, relishing the strength in his hands and marveling at the contented sigh he released, I wondered if perhaps the way to lessen guilt and grief was to share them.

Gods knew nothing else I had tried worked.

Forcing my muscles to loosen until I was cozied up to Graeson and he trusted me to stay put enough to link his arms around me, I tipped back my head and found his hazel eyes inches from mine, the pupils dilated and the striking emerald striations in his irises made more vivid by the greenery surrounding us.

"Tell me about your sister."

Tension ricocheted through him, tightening his jaw where it rested against me. Feeling awkward, I started to pull away, but he held on to me as though I was the one thing anchoring him against the swell of his heartache.

"Mom died in childbirth, and Dad never recovered. He was broken. Too broken to run a pack. That's when

Bessemer made his bid for alpha. He bled my dad and took over." Old bitterness without much bite laced his words. "A few weeks later, Dad picked a fight with a warg a few rungs up the new dominance ladder and lost. I was seventeen. Marie was three. The pack let me hold on to the house, helped me find work so I could support my sister. A chain of mothers organized sitters for the days I was in school and the nights I was at work." He sat there for a while, so long I thought he was finished. "Her favorite color was vermillion, because she said it was a million times better than the plain old green I liked."

Heart a wounded thing in my chest, I did for him what I hadn't allowed others to do for me.

I sat.

I listened.

And I held him as he told me the story of how his world ended.

CHAPTER SEVEN

"We've got company" were the first words past Dell's lips when my feet hit the sweet, sweet ground. Graeson leapt from the makeshift ladder and landed in a crouch behind me. He rose and dusted his palms before placing one at the small of my back and pushing me in the general direction of the trailers.

"Why the rush?" a woman possessing a rich Southern accent called. "I only wanted to say hello."

"Keep walking," Graeson ordered under his breath.

"She's following." Dell grimaced. "You're going to have to talk to her eventually."

"Cord." Petulance sat heavy in the new voice. Clearly she was one of those women used to pouting and getting her way. "You know my legs aren't that long. Slow down. We haven't talked since you got home. I'm starting to think you're avoiding me."

Graeson, who kept to my back, remained unreadable. Dell I saw clearly out of the corner of my eye, and her wrinkled nose told me what she thought of the woman dogging our heels.

A muttered curse brought his warm breath across my nape in the same instant as a hand closed over my arm. A petite woman with wide eyes and curves for days smiled up at me through straight white teeth as her magic prickled my skin.

"You must be Ellen." She beamed. "I'm Imogen." A bashful shrug as authentic as her white-blonde curls bounced her thin shoulders. "Cord and I dated in high school. You know how that goes. I like to keep tabs on him is all, make sure he's being treated right."

The jealous ex-girlfriend experience was one I had never had, and I wasn't thrilled to be having it now. I didn't bother correcting her about my name. She knew it. I could tell. That hard glint in her eyes some might mistake for a personable sparkle masked lethal intelligence. I bet she knew more about me than most of my coworkers ever bothered learning.

"Nice to meet you." I stared at the point where her hand touched me, and she blushed as she released my elbow. "You two were childhood friends? How sweet that you've kept up for so long."

Her eyes narrowed slightly as she filtered the words, searching for insult. "Well, you know how first loves are." She gazed up at him with caked-on adoration. "You never quite get them out of your system."

No, actually, I didn't. I had never let a man get that close to me. I pasted on a smile and let her read agreement in it.

"It's early and all, cart before the horse and such," she continued, "but I wanted to meet you before the selection begins and tell you it's nothing personal. Cord is a beta, and you don't understand what that means, but it's a big deal to us wargs. He needs a strong mate by his side if he's going to hold his position, and you're just not it." She glanced over my shoulder at Graeson. "You know the rules. I'll have to participate. I don't have a choice."

Had glee not suffused her being, I might have believed her based on the slight rounding of her doe eyes. As it was, the widening of those dark, liquid pools reminded me of a black hole seeking to consume all which thrived around it.

Admitting my ignorance as to what the selection was or why it mattered one way or another if Imogen participated would only have earned me a pitying glance. I avoided the play in favor of asking Dell about it later, figuring the truth would be easier to pin down with her than Graeson.

A shrill ring sent my hand diving into my pocket, eager for an excuse to extricate myself from this awkwardness. "Ellis."

"Long story short, a drunk elf picked a fight with a dwarf in a holding cell at the marshal's office." Thierry's yawn made my jaw twitch in sympathy. "I drew the short end of the straw, so I'm awake—sort of—earlier than expected. Can you talk?"

"Hold on a minute." I muted the call. "I have to take this call. It's for work."

"What do you do?" Imogen pretended interest. "The suit you wore when you arrived on the property screamed *secretary*." She batted her lashes at Graeson. "Not that there's anything wrong with wanting to service a man in a powerful position."

I bit the inside of my lip. *Service a man*? Really? Why didn't she strip naked and start humping his leg? It would have been subtler.

No harm in telling her since the news would make the rounds fast enough. Bessemer knew thanks to his fishing expedition inside Graeson's skull, and if he knew, then Aisha must know too. I wasn't sure what degree of access the rest of the pack had to his thoughts and memories, but I was willing to bet Aisha would love nothing more than to share a cup of coffee and gossip with Imogen.

"I'm an agent with the Earthen Conclave." The absent weight of my badge reminded me this side trip to Villanow wasn't sanctioned. "It was nice meeting you, Imogen. I'm sure I'll see you around."

"The Earthen Conclave." She paled a fraction before smothering the momentary glimpse of panic with a smile as she looped her arm through Graeson's. "That's quite progressive of you." She gave him a squeeze. "Why don't you run along home and handle your business? I can take care of Graeson for you."

I just bet she could.

Spending the morning on the shade-dappled platform with Graeson had talked me out. I flicked my fingers in a wave at him, not trying to spare him from the cruel fate of small-talking his way out of Imogen's clutches.

I set out for home, and Dell trailed at a respectful distance. I liked her, enjoyed her company, but I wondered why, if she was truly a submissive warg, Graeson had seemingly assigned her to my guard detail. It was more than consideration for companionship. I was fast learning he didn't have those tender leanings. His thought processes were ruthlessly efficient. Dell was with me because he trusted her, because she was capable, and as evidenced by Aisha and Imogen's total dismissal of her, because no one except Graeson appeared aware of the ferocity hidden behind her stooped shoulders and bowed head.

Shaking off those thoughts, I focused on what I hoped was the first good news I'd heard all week.

"All right," I spoke into the phone. "What have you got for me?"

Three hours later, I was wearing a track in the floor of my living room while clutching a rolled-up printout of a mental health facility in my fist. The call from Thierry confirmed that, as far as she knew, Charybdis hadn't resurfaced. No new drownings fitting his MO had been reported, no new kills that might hint at sinister intent had been discovered. The loss of his avatar seemed to have slowed him down. I held tight to the thin hope that loss didn't mean Harlow had gotten promoted to fill the spot.

The downside to no new crimes was no new direction either. Time kept ticking, and I had no clue where to look.

"Well?" Dell poked her head inside the trailer. "Did your friend have good news?"

"Yes. Well, maybe." I hadn't decided yet. "How is Meemaw?"

Dell had dropped me off then zipped home after a ripple in the pack bond set her on edge.

"Meemaw is fine. She took a spill while she was gardening and sprained her ankle. It was already healed by the time I got there." She put a hand to her chest. "She'll probably outlive me, but you know how it goes."

I was more prone to fearing life than death but could appreciate the sentiment.

"Have you seen Graeson?" Hours had passed since I'd abandoned him to the clutches of his ex, and I hadn't seen or heard from him. "I expected him to stop by with questions." Eager for fresh leads, he would be curious about anything newsworthy I unearthed. "Dell?"

"He went home with Imogen." She kept seesawing her front teeth over her bottom lip. "I saw him go inside her cabin on my way to Meemaw's."

"Oh." A brittle thing fractured in my chest, and my voice came out broken. "I see."

"They were probably talking," she told her toes, unable to meet my eyes.

"You're hardwired together," I pointed out. "You know what he's doing." Which probably explained the guilt seeping from her pores. "It's okay, Dell, really."

But that crackle over my heart kept spreading as the ridiculous impulse to grab her hand, take her blood and see for myself how he was spending his afternoon shivered through me. Graeson wasn't my mate or my boyfriend. Not really. To willfully believe in a lie is to welcome hurt. We were…friends. People who had bonded over shared pain. I liked him as often as I wanted to choke him. The ability to resist murdering one's partner wasn't a solid basis for a relationship. Even when I didn't want to kill him, he frustrated me with his constant scheming and truth-twisting.

"I can feel him." Her bottom lip reddened to the point of bleeding. "Right now he's—"

"I don't want to know." I whapped the roll of paper across my palm for emphasis. "Let's just forget I asked, okay?"

"Okay," she agreed readily. "What's with the map?"

I tapped her on the shoulder with it. "This is the most solid lead I've got."

Cabin trysts forgotten, her eyes brightened. "That's great." She poked it with a finger. "What is it?"

"Blueprints for a mental institution in Kermit, Texas." I elaborated as her eyes rounded. "One person was present when he—"

The tingle of magic suppressed what I had been about to say. I had made a blood oath to Thierry, and certain facts were off the table except where others who were already in on the secret were concerned.

"This person may have interacted with Charybdis prior to his killing spree," I amended. "All attempts to question her failed because she fell off the grid that same day."

"She got herself locked up." Dell mulled over the implications. "Did she have a history of mental illness?"

"No. She was a highly decorated marshal who lived for her job." I unrolled the printout for her inspection. "My source says her family is also free of mental illness, meaning there's a possibility that whatever nudged her to commit herself two weeks later might be connected to that chance meeting."

"Has your source spoken to her yet?" Dell frowned as she studied the layout.

"No." Thierry walked a fine line just by feeding me this much information. If I wanted that interview, I would have to conduct it myself. "Marshal Ayer isn't accepting visitors. Her doctors forbid it. She's practically living in isolation. They say the presence of others upsets her too much."

Warm fingers curled over my forearm. "Tell me you're not thinking what I think you're thinking."

"Crap." I rolled the paper and dropped it on the table. "I keep forgetting that talking to you is the same as talking to Graeson."

"Sorry." Her shrug conveyed sheepishness and a hint of what I hazarded to label as relief. "It's not like he can hear every conversation every pack member is having at any given time. He has to tune in to get the right channel, and there are seven of us so…"

"Seven?" That couldn't be right. "That's not the whole pack. There were that many wolves in Mississippi."

"We're separate from the rest until we release Graeson," she explained. "It's like we're operating on another frequency, and all the others hear is static around us."

"Hmm." That explained how packs kept their business secret from other wargs. Different frequencies. "So Bessemer is the only one who can listen in?"

"Yes." She shivered. "He's the alpha."

That tremor in her voice grew stronger with every mention of Bessemer and made my back teeth ache. A week ago—two weeks ago—I wasn't this person. I did my job and went home. I waved to colleagues who didn't know my name any more than I remembered theirs. I smiled and made small talk when forced, but I couldn't tell you details of a single conversation once it ended. Part of that was my job. Earthen Conclave agents drifted from conclave outpost to outpost as needed. We usually ended up with a spot at the local marshal's office, but we weren't part of the team. We were outsiders looking in on the tight-knit units that called those outposts home. And part of it was my nature. Gemini tended to look homeward for companionship. And yet another part, the largest part, was the lack in me that I felt certain everyone saw. I know I did every time I met my gaze in a mirror.

Being alone had suited me fine until I met a sometimes-mermaid with cotton candy-pink hair who had teased me out of my shell. She had watched over me when I was drained from expending too much borrowed magic and put her trust in me so completely that her faith staggered me. Harlow, in the short time I had known her, had pried a fine crack open in my armor, and Dell had wiggled through.

I might not be a warg, but there was nothing right or normal in fearing the man whose duty it was to protect you. There was nothing noble or proud in causing those under your care to cower at the mention of your name.

I didn't know Bessemer, had never met the man, but his actions had imprinted his pack in such a way I could tell that for the first time in ages, I had room in my heart to hate someone other than myself. He was a bad man. Of that, I had no doubt. His taste in mates didn't bolster confidence either. Aisha was more of a spitting cobra than a wolf, and her venom corroded all she touched.

Dell, with her big heart, deserved better than to be resigned to a life of skulking behind Graeson in the hopes she could hide in his shadow. She ought to be like that bold and sassy woman who kidnapped me in an SUV every day, not this pale echo of her true self.

"I'm going to Kermit," I announced, not doubting for an instant Graeson would manage to pick that out of Dell's head. "Will my family be safe while I'm gone?" They could defend themselves, but I hoped it wouldn't come to a show of force. "Or would it be better if they moved on?"

"Cord secured guest rights for your family. They're allowed to remain on the fringe of the pack's lands as long as they don't cross over without an escort." Her forehead scrunched, and I wondered if she wasn't speaking with Graeson right now. "The punishment for breaking the alpha's oath is death."

In that, the fae and earthborn agreed. There were strict rules for hospitality that fae believed must be observed in order to maintain honor while acting as a guest or while entertaining guests in one's home. Once past the threshold…well…that was another matter.

"Good." That was one less worry for me. Aunt Dot and Isaac were used to me leaving for extended periods of time. They wouldn't bat an eye at an overnight trip. "Aunt Dot still hasn't met Graeson sans fur, and it would be hard on her to relocate so soon. A Gemini is never out of practice when it comes to roaming, but it's been a peaceful year for us. I would like to spend more time here— another week at least—before uprooting her again."

"We'll protect your kin," she vowed, soft tone laced with steel. "I promise you that."

"Dell." The fact I wasn't included in any of her declarations niggled the back of my mind enough that Imogen's words drifted back to me. "What is the selection?"

A subtle flush rose up her cheeks. "Cord wants to talk to you about that. Tonight."

"He does?" Doubt weighted my voice. "Are you sure you're not exaggerating?"

Snorted laughter crinkled her cheeks until her eyes vanished. "It's his idea." She crossed a finger over her heart. "I swear."

I narrowed my eyes. "Did he have this brilliant idea before or after I told you I was going to Kermit?"

She mimed zipping her lips.

A sigh escaped me. "That's what I thought."

CHAPTER EIGHT

Graeson arrived on my doorstep wearing a faded green button-down shirt, which still managed to complement his eyes, tucked into jeans with a crease in them. Even his scuffed boots had been dusted clean. His hair, always falling forward into his face, was slicked back and neat as a pin.

Either he was trying to impress me—mission accomplished—or Imogen had dressed him like a doll in a nice shirt of his she'd probably hung on to since high school, and pants she'd starched and ironed on his way out of her bed—I mean, house.

One person wasn't conflicted about his sudden appearance. Aunt Dot was a blur as she streaked past me then tackled him with a hug and a kiss on the cheek. Her giddy smile made my stomach curl in on itself. Isaac was right. Grandpuppies were dancing in baby pink and blue clouds over her head while she drank in the sight of Graeson.

"You must be Cord." She patted his cheek. "You're a pretty thing, I'll give you that. No wonder you turned my little pumpkin's head." She stepped back to admire all six feet plus of him. "You clean up nice too." Laser eyes swiped over me. "Why didn't you dress up, hon?" She wiggled her eyebrows. "Playing hard to get?"

I slapped a palm over my face, but my neck broiled with a flush. "I didn't realize this was a dress up kind of occasion."

Or that it was an occasion at all. I thought we were meeting to discuss my findings and get to the bottom of this selection nonsense.

The fact he was putting so much effort into looking the part of a man calling on a date twisted my heart. I couldn't help thinking how nice it must be to greet a handsome man who looked forward to spending an evening with you. Maybe, once Charybdis was behind me and Harlow was safe, I could dip my toe back in the Gemini dating pool, the analogy as close to water as I ever wanted to get outside of a shower stall.

"It's my fault, Aunt Dot," Graeson rumbled. "Can I call you Aunt Dot, or would you prefer Ms. Cahill?"

"Oh, you." She swatted his chest playfully. "You can call me anything you want, sweetie. I'm not picky."

"Aunt Dot it is then," he said, sounding pleased. "Ellis is right. Tonight is a surprise. I didn't want to spook her by tipping my hand." His gaze, when it raked over me, raised chill bumps. "Besides, she's beautiful. She doesn't need to dress up for me to see that."

I squirmed, pinned to the spot by his compliment and the hungry glint in his eyes. Had Dell not told me how he spent his afternoon, I might have been taken in by the pretty package as easily as Aunt Dot appeared to be. But I hesitated, afraid that stepping close to him would bring a possessive tendril of Imogen's perfume tickling my nose.

"I don't understand you kids." She shook her head. "Why not call each other Camille and Cord? It's so catchy."

I could have told her first names implied an intimacy lacking between us, a privilege granted to friends or lovers when I wasn't sure we were or would ever be either, but I played the game I had committed to and smiled. "It keeps the relationship fresh."

"All right." She tapped her cheek, and I dutifully bent to kiss it. "I'll get this laundry put up for you, okay?" She shuffled back to the basket that had brought her visiting.

"This is the first time I've ever had to wash wolf fur out of your sheets."

The sting in my neck intensified to noonday-sun proportions. "I can put them up when I get home."

"Nah. I have time." She lifted a pair of sheer black panties in a scandalous cut in front of her and began folding them into a tiny square before our eyes. "My shows don't start for another hour."

My jaw dropped open in tandem with Graeson's. His throat worked over a hard lump, and he wiped a hand over his mouth. All I could do was goggle at her while she hummed, pretending not to notice our stares.

Gods help us.

Those weren't even mine.

Where had they come from? Surely they weren't...? No. I didn't want to know. As they say, ignorance is bliss.

"I won't be long." I shoved Graeson out into the cool night. "I'll call when I get home."

"Take your time," she called after me. "There's no need to rush back on my account."

I scooted down the steps, shut the door behind me and slumped against the trailer with my eyes shut. "I've never seen her like this."

"It's cute," came a voice much too close to my ear.

My eyes popped wide open, and I flattened myself against the siding. "You need to step back."

Breaths coming in short pants, I sucked in the smell of him, but his personal cologne was all his. Not a hint of Imogen lingered on his skin or in his clothes. For that I was grateful, even if I didn't want to examine why.

"Scared?" He rubbed his cheek against mine.

"Of what I might do to you?" I breathed. "Yes. I don't want to go to prison for murder."

A husky chuckle escaped him as he withdrew. "We need to talk." He extended his hand, but I couldn't take it. I thought of wargs as being defined by their soul mate culture, but Dell—and now Graeson—had proven the hunt for Mr. *or* Mrs. Right wasn't forefront in all their minds. "I thought we could discuss the new developments in the case you mentioned to Dell over dinner. At my house."

"Your...house." Not until Dell mentioned Imogen's cabin had I wondered where the wargs called home. The entire forest was their domain, no structure capable of containing their wild spirits, but they were half-human. I should have put more than a passing thought into where and how they might live. "I— Sure. Okay."

His fingers slid down my arm without purchase, accepting I didn't want to hold his hand but unable to resist stealing a light touch. "Come on." Hands shoved into his pockets, he strolled toward the dense pines. "Let me show you my home."

Entering the forest at night brought chills coasting over my skin. The sensation of keen eyes peering from the underbrush had me rubbing my hands up and down my arms. Moonlight cast a silver path through the trees, and Graeson walked it with confidence, his heavy steps managing to land time and time again without so much as snapping a twig. By comparison, I felt like an elephant stamping after him, or like the merry calliope piping at the top of my lungs that the circus was in town. After all, whoever those flickers of gold belonged to had come to watch a show.

"Welcome to Silverback Lane. Not everyone lives here full-time. Most work in human cities during the week and return home for the weekends, celebrations and hunts, but each member is assigned their own cabin." Graeson distracted me from my thoughts. "The alpha lives there, on the rise."

Twin floor-to-ceiling windows lit with harsh yellow light glared down at us from a slight elevation in the distance, the symbolism clear. The eyes of the alpha were always watching.

Shaking off that creeping sensation, I picked up my pace. "How many wargs are here at any given time?"

"It's forbidden to share that information with your kind." He walked on. "It's dangerous for fae, for the conclave, to be aware of our numbers."

Another woman might have called him paranoid, but rivalries between species were cutthroat. Should the fae ever set their sights to procuring pack land, and were they aware of how many—or few—wargs were present at any given time, the coups would be bloody and swift.

"I didn't mean to pry." There were more wargs here than I could fight off alone, and that was all that mattered to me. "I was just making small talk."

"I trust you, Ellis." He glanced back at me, and his lips quirked. "There isn't anything I wouldn't tell you if you truly wanted to know."

I got the unsettling feeling he was challenging me. All I could think of was Imogen.

Did you go home with her?

Home being not what I meant at all.

I didn't ask. My throat tightened painfully when I tried.

Slowing until I reached him, he brushed his hand down my arm. "I've always been honest with you."

Unable to isolate a particular untruth to hurtle at him, I swatted his hand. "You befriended me under false pretenses."

"Are we friends?" He caught my hand in his. "Is that all this is?"

"*This* is a job. We're hunting a serial killer, remember?" I scraped him off me. "You seem to be forgetting that."

"This is a job," he allowed, in a way that made it seem like he was agreeing to something I hadn't said.

All the years of emotional isolation hadn't equipped me to deal with the masculine enigma in front of me. The urge to snap off a branch and whack him with it couldn't be normal, but what was? My parents had an easy love. They laughed and traveled and marveled at the world together. Aunt Dot had never married and never dated after her longtime lover passed more than a year before I was born. Isaac didn't date so much as plow through available women in a quest to satisfy his drive to discover the limits of his talents in the most pleasurable way possible. His heart wasn't involved in those transactions. They were calculated and sterile in a way that left him holed up for days after each interlude. Theo, well, his philosophy was much the same as Isaac's, minus the curiosity and the guilt. So what was normal? The sneaking tendrils of envy that curled into my chest when I thought of Graeson with someone else? With Imogen?

This thing with Graeson wasn't love or simple lust. It was undefinable, and a thing without definition that technically couldn't exist without such parameters shouldn't hurt so much. But it did.

The trees didn't part to reveal civilization so much as log cabins appeared to emerge from the very pines used to construct them. Despite what I'd said earlier, I was curious and counted as many as I could spot, some homesteads blending with the surrounding elements until they all but disappeared into nature.

"This is us."

He gestured toward a cabin whose flawless symmetry spoke to me. Built of thick, hand-hewn pine logs, its bright white chinking reflected the faint light. The steps leading onto the porch included a handrail that boasted an antler collage instead of spindles. The squat staircase brushed a massive stone chimney that I ran my hand along as we ascended. Rockers nestled either side of a square table covered by a woven red-and-black quilt. Someone had used one of the oversized checkers that completed the set as a coaster to hold a glass half full of what appeared to be sweet tea.

The front door swung open under his hand. Apparently the residents of Silverback Lane didn't lock their doors. Expecting the heavy treated ceiling beams to make the house dark and cramped, I was surprised by the use of light wall colors to brighten the space. The open floor plan exposed the cozy living room, the casual dining room and a kitchen boasting state-of-the-art appliances at a glance.

Wide-plank floors shone under my feet, and stepping inside felt a little like entering the Three Bears' house. Shoes three sizes too small lined one short wall beside boots three sizes too large. The contrast of young girl and grown man was a theme continued through every room I examined.

Marie might be gone from this world, but she was not forgotten in this house.

"It's beautiful." Rustic had never appealed to me—I enjoyed the sleek shine of my trailer too much for that— but the sense of permanence about this place warmed me. *Welcome home.* That was what the cabin whispered when you entered. Love had soaked into these walls, and I was tempted to touch them. See if I could read the magic of it, perhaps glean some understanding of the man standing silently beside me. "Nice kitchen. Do you know how to use it?"

A proud grin stretched his cheeks. "You'll just have to wait and find out, won't you?"

"Are you serious?" I laughed, nervous. "You're not cooking." His smile kicked up a notch. "Are you?"

"Steaks are marinating in the fridge, and there's a baked potato with your name on it."

Nice clothes. Buttering up Aunt Dot. Bringing me home. Cooking for me. "What are you up to?"

"I'm just being neighborly," he protested on his way to the stainless monstrosity that was his refrigerator. "Would you like a drink, *neighbor?*"

"Yes." I could use something to wet my throat for when the arguing started.

"Have a seat." He pointed to a pair of tall stools tucked under a bar built into the granite-topped island. "We can talk while I work, if that's okay with you."

Having never been cooked for by a man, I wasn't sure what protocol dictated, but I slid onto a stool just the same. "This is fine."

"You look ready to bolt for the door." He snagged a tumbler from a glass-fronted cabinet then used the controls set into the fridge's door to pour ice and filtered water. "Should I lock it, or can I trust you to hang around?" He offered me the drink, our hands brushing as I took it. A smile quirked his mouth, and he snapped his fingers. "Oh. Almost forgot."

While he dug through the contents of a paper bag on the counter, I accepted my fate. I wasn't going anywhere. Not yet. "We need to talk." I took a sip, wincing where he couldn't see it. Plain water was just so...plain. "You owe me some answers."

"There." He presented six curvy plastic bottles settled across his palm labeled with names like *kiwi strawberry* and *berry medley*. "I wasn't sure what flavor you liked best, and the store here doesn't carry your usual brand, so I grabbed one of everything."

"My usual brand?" It was like he was speaking in tongues. "How do you know my usual brand?"

"I have eyes." He dipped a hand into the front pocket of his pants. "I also have this." He held up an empty bottle and wiggled it. "You never used the same flavor twice, and the cashier had never heard of orange-pineapple flavor enhancer, so I winged it. Is this okay? Will one of these work?"

I accepted the bottles and lined them up on the counter. Several of my favorites were present. "This is perfect." I tore off the safety seal and squirted a few streams of crimson into my cup. "I appreciate your thoughtfulness."

He rubbed his cheek with his thumb. "You couldn't just say *thank you?*"

"No." The way he asked made me think he was well aware of that fact.

"Huh." He strode to the sink and washed his hands then donned an apron. *Women want me, cows fear me* was written in bold red letters on a black background. "I'd heard fae were funny about thanks, but you're the first I've really spent time around."

82

HAILEY EDWARDS

He'd befriended a water sprite as a young man, but she was gone now, and she hadn't survived so long among wolves by giving away her secrets.

"Oh, it's very real." I had collected several and had yet to use any of them. "Thanking the fae is never a good idea. Avoid it at all costs."

"Thanks for the tip." He screwed up his face. "Didn't take long to break that rule." A curious expression crossed his face. "Does this mean I owe you a favor?"

Laughing at his wariness, I stirred my drink with a finger. "This makes us even."

He returned to his food prep, back facing me, hauling out steaks and dashing them with spices. Watching him fascinated me. Where my family assaulted the kitchen, Graeson moved through it with practiced ease, comfortable in his space, revealing a new facet of his personality.

"You like to cook." More than having a fancy preparation area, he knew how to use it.

"Wargs like to eat." He popped a slice of zucchini in his mouth to illustrate the point. "With Marie, it was either learn to cook or accept I'd be driving into town to pick up chicken nugget meals for dinner every night until she was old enough to drive herself."

I held my breath, expecting his fluid motions to stutter or his voice to catch, but his tone remained rich and amused. He was healing. It was a beautiful thing to witness.

"So," he said casually, "I hear you're going to Kermit."

Right to the punch. "My, what big ears you have, Grandma."

"You know how the pack bond works." He made it sound like any eavesdropping on his part was accidental. "I can't help what filters through."

"Mmm-hmm."

"Were you going to mention you were leaving, or was I going to knock on your door one morning and find you gone?"

Ah. Here we grappled with the root of the problem. "I would have mentioned it to you for the sake of my family."

The knife in his hand thunked to the cutting board. "What about my sake?"

"I wasn't going to ask for your permission, if that's what you're insinuating should have happened."

Giving up on the vegetables he was slicing, he turned back to me and planted his palms on the bar top. "What has your panties in a twist? You've got that look in your eye like you're spoiling for a fight." He huffed. "What did I do this time?"

"You went home with Imogen." I hadn't meant to say it, was horrified as soon as the words left my mouth, but there was no calling them back.

He hung his head and shook it like he couldn't believe I'd called him out on it either. "You don't think much of me, do you?"

"She was creeping up your leg like a poisonous vine when I left you, and you went home with her."

Funny thing about anger. It lubricated me until things I never would have said out loud to another man slid right past my filters.

"You left me to fend for myself." His head lifted, expression cool and unreadable. "I thought you didn't care she was pawing me."

I jerked up my chin. "I don't."

"Ellis, you don't get to throw down the gauntlet and then decide to pick it right back up and dust it off."

"You're supposed to be my mate." He'd said it himself, that his current disagreement with Bessemer stemmed from confusion over how my talent interacted with pack magic. "Don't you think what you did was disrespectful?"

"I walked a beautiful woman home who was having trouble with the word *no*." Imogen's tenacity didn't appear to surprise him. "I did go inside. I drank sweet tea and chatted, and then I left once the glass was empty. I'm polite, not disloyal."

Had Dell known that was all there was to it? Or had she retreated from that intimacy before getting stuck with mental images she couldn't shake of a man she admired? She had assumed the worst because there was history between them, and I had too. Was it too much to hope both of us had underestimated him?

"That's the problem." I flipped the cap open on the squeeze bottle, snapped it shut. "We aren't mated. If you want to be with Imogen—"

"Then I wouldn't be here with you."

Flip. Snap. Flip. Snap. "We aren't real."

He reached over and cupped my cheek in his warm palm. "You feel plenty real to me."

The melting sensation in my chest left me scrambling for a new topic. "What is the selection?"

"It's exactly what the name implies." He withdrew and snaked his arms across his chest. "The top three wargs in a pack get one chance to pick their mate. There are laws about soul mates, but that's a separate item. The most dominant wargs can bring home a mate of their choosing for inspection by the alpha. If he deems him or her worthy, the mating becomes official in the eyes of their peers, the new member is folded into the pack, and that's the end of it."

I got a bad feeling about where this was headed. "If the alpha doesn't approve?"

"The pack member becomes a petitioner and the proposed mate becomes an aspirant. The aspirant then has to earn their title—their right—to stand beside their chosen partner."

Earn by tooth and claw no doubt. "What happens if the aspirant fails?"

"The alpha grants the victor the right to claim the petitioner as their own."

I waved my hand. "What victor?"

"The aspirant must secure rank within the pack. Dominance fights mostly. They are required to rack up an equal standing to the petitioner." He blew out a short breath. "Should the aspirant fail, the warg who defeats them becomes the victor and has the option of choosing to claim the petitioner as their own *if* they're of equal dominance."

The interlude by the platform in the woods suddenly made a lot more sense. "Bessemer has named me an aspirant." Graeson didn't dispute the assessment. "That's what Imogen meant. She's going to challenge me, and when I lose, she's going to claim you as her mate because she's a high-ranking pack member."

"That's her plan."

He sounded so calm about it while I wanted to poke Imogen in the eye. "You're okay with that?"

"No." Emotions cascaded over his face too quickly for me to parse. "I'm also not okay with you getting hurt. This isn't your culture. These aren't your laws. I won't allow you to be punished to assuage Bessemer's pride."

I linked my hands in my lap. "You sound certain I would lose."

The lack of faith shouldn't have bothered me, not when I doubted I could win a fight against a mature warg female frothing to mate with the next best thing to an alpha, but he deserved better. Bessemer clearly prized viciousness and mean-spiritedness in women. That kind of mate would break Graeson. He was strong but emotionally raw. Saddling him with a woman who would pick him apart piece by piece in this stage of his healing process was a mistake. It wouldn't take long for her to get through the meat to the bone.

He cocked his head, lips twitching. "You sound ready to fight."

I didn't dignify that with a response. "How do I get disqualified?"

"You throw a match." His gaze dipped. "The winner claims her prize and you walk away."

"Just like that." A lifetime commitment cemented in blood.

"Just like that," he agreed.

"That's why you went home with Imogen." It all clicked into place. No wonder Dell had sounded so grim. It wasn't what he had done, but what he planned to do. "You think she's most likely to win, the one people will expect to win, and you made a deal with her."

"This isn't your fight, Ellis." He swept out a hand, indicating his home or the state or the pack. "You don't want this." He brought that same hand to his chest and thumped it. "Or this."

In typical Graeson style, he didn't ask my opinion. He assumed, because he had decided it was best for me, that I didn't want him when even *I* didn't know if I did. His instincts told him once that I belonged to him. What did that mean? I wasn't a warg. I knew the lifemate bond wasn't possible. But for him to give up on pursuing me in the span of a few days... It stung my pride.

How did I explain to Aunt Dot that I lost my man, who wasn't really mine in the first place, in a fight? Like he was some sort of prize to be awarded to the winner. Which, according to Graeson, was exactly his place in this scenario.

Wishing my water was something stronger, I took a sip to give me precious seconds to string together a cohesive sentence that didn't boil down to *grr*. "When is this fight scheduled?"

He pushed away from the counter. "It can wait until you and Dell get back from Kermit."

I choked on my next sip of water. "Dell's going with me?"

"A beta's mate can't travel alone, even as an aspirant." He didn't sound sorry about sending me a babysitter at all. "Besides, she worries about you. She'll feel better if you've got backup, and so will I."

"Will Bessemer let her go?" Aiding and abetting a fae seemed tantamount to high treason with him.

"We came to an agreement." Muscles ticked in his jaw. "Please don't fight me on this."

"Okay." I raised my hands in a gesture of peace. "I won't."

Dell was a willing donor, and her power was one I was familiar with harnessing. She would be an asset, and she made for good company.

Eyeing me like my acquiescence was some kind of trick, he resumed his food preparations, casting a wary glance over his shoulder now and again, but I only had eyes for the bottles of liquid flavoring.

What kind of man paid this sort of attention to a woman? What did those six tiny bottles truly represent?

I didn't hang around long enough for people to learn what I liked. Most folks didn't care to know.

The empty bottle Graeson set down looked worn, like he had been carrying it around in his jeans since the day he pocketed it. The label was faded and peeling as though he had worried it with his thumb while thinking. Of me? What did it mean that I would never see those bottles again without thinking of the ink-stained warg with ghosts in his eyes who had combed a grocery store and emptied a dispenser in search of my favorite flavor?

Such an insignificant thing, but not so insignificant at all.

CHAPTER NINE

Graeson set a small plate with a homemade brownie square and scoop of vanilla ice cream on top in front of me. Dinner was over, the steak devoured and the baked potato inhaled. I could barely lift my fork to take a bite, but when the chocolate hit my tongue, I moaned.

This right here was what made a man worth keeping, worth fighting for, I was sure of it.

"You approve?" He snapped the lid on the carton of ice cream, the only premade item on tonight's menu.

"This is the best meal I've ever had in my entire life." He deserved the compliment, and I had no trouble paying it. "Have you considered giving up pack life and opening a restaurant?"

His rich chuckle warmed me as much as the heated fudge drizzle. "No, but I'm flattered you have that kind of faith in my cooking skills."

We finished the meal in silence, and when he offered me a hand, I took it and let him haul me to my feet. My palm came to rest over my stomach, which threatened to burst at the seams, and I winced inwardly at the thought of the long walk home.

Dropping to his knees, Graeson slid my boots onto my feet. I had discarded them at some point while trying to make room for more food. I couldn't very well unsnap my jeans, so I kicked off what was most convenient. Not that it had helped me down that last rich, chocolaty bite. Sadly, I had no choice but to leave it on my plate.

I groaned when he jostled me while strapping me in, and he patted my thigh. "Regretting that second potato?"

I braced my hands on his shoulders. "I have no regrets."

"I'm glad to hear it." He pushed to his feet and scooped a plastic container off the counter. "Then you won't mind if I purge my kitchen of temptation."

"Are those the rest of the brownies?" My fingers curled with the urge to either grab them or swat them away, I wasn't sure which.

"I would send the ice cream, but there's not much left." He pushed the brownies into my hands. "It would be mush by the time you got home with it anyway."

"Are you sure you don't want to keep some?" I shoved them back.

He dropped his arms, forcing me to hold the container, and patted his firm stomach. "I don't want to risk losing my girlish figure."

My eyes rolled, giving me a visual tour of the thick beams crisscrossing his ceiling. "I should get home."

I had stayed later than I meant to, and Aunt Dot would wait up until I called. She might fake a yawn or muffle her voice, but I knew better. The odds were good she would have her nose pressed to the glass and the phone at her ear to make sure she didn't miss any juicy goodbye-ing on our part.

"Do I get to know the reason behind all this?" We hadn't accomplished much except enjoying each other's company.

"I wanted to know how it would feel to pick you up and take you somewhere nice, just the two of us." A rueful smile bent his lips. "This was as nice as I could manage under the circumstances."

"And?" I gripped the plastic container until it crinkled. "How was it?"

"Perfect," he said without hesitation. "Thanks for tonight. I need this so I'll remember..."

"Remember what?" I prompted when he went quiet.

"Come on. It's late." He opened the door and nudged me past the threshold. "I need to get you home before Aunt Dot comes looking for me with a rifle slung over her shoulder."

"She's a Gemini," I reminded him, not missing the fact he hadn't answered me. "She's all the weapon she needs."

The warm night caressed my cheeks when we stepped outside. The scent of pine hung in the air, and the chirp of crickets blanketed the yard with comforting sounds. I gripped the rail with one hand and took my time crossing to the well-worn trail we had taken. Now that I was full and relaxed, I noticed there were no cars or trucks, none of the SUVs I knew the pack owned. The only transportation visible were a few Mule ATVs parked under porches and a pair of cherry-red go-karts snuggled on a flatbed compact, enough for one of the Mules to haul with ease.

I made it all of three steps before white-hot pain blazed up my left side. Holding the brownies in front of me, I glanced down as Graeson yelled. Thanks to the heads-up, I spun aside in time to avoid the second furious swipe of claws. When the dirty-brown wolf lunged again, I whacked it in the face with the plastic container, and baked goods went flying. A whimper escaped the wolf as Graeson reached me, and the standoff came to a standstill.

"You know the rules. You can't interfere," a darkly masculine voice intoned. "Let your aspirant face her challenger."

"This is not what we agreed," Graeson snapped. "Ellis isn't prepared." His gaze cut to the wolf, and disgust curled his lip. "Ambushing her in the dark was cowardly, Becca."

"I was alpha last time I checked." A tall man stacked with muscles stepped into the light cast by the cabin's windows. "I stand as witness to the first challenge of the selection." His moss-bright eyes gleamed with liquid gold. "If your aspirant is too weak to compete, she's welcome to bow out now and save herself the pain and shame of losing."

A quiver started in my gut, the first stirrings of fear. This was real. This was happening. No sooner had I learned about the selection, than its first round slapped me in the face. The small wolf snarling under her breath glared hatred at me. I had no idea who she was, but I doubted it was coincidence she showed up at the same time as the alpha put in an appearance. This was a choreographed move, and it seemed I was the only one unaware of the proper steps.

"You don't have to do this." Graeson's cold hands clamped down on my upper arms. "You can walk away."

"I'm not a coward." I covered his hands with mine. "You deserve more than this. You deserve someone who cares about *you*. Not your status in the pack."

"Ellis, you know what accepting her challenge means."

"Yes." I wet my lips, well aware of what I was doing. Claiming him. The alternative? Losing him? Not an option. "It means all the brownies I can eat for as long as we both shall live."

A softness warmed his eyes, and he nuzzled my cheek. "I'll even throw in homemade ice cream for free."

Sucking in a tight breath, I tried smiling at his joke. Mostly the mention of food and fighting made me want to vomit. "I'll need your help."

He understood and gripped my hand tighter. "Take what you need."

The nail covering my right hand's middle finger popped off as my spur emerged. I pierced his skin and braced for the snap of connection, my breath held in anticipation. I wanted it, craved it, and a drop of his blood thrust me into familiar headspace.

His presence was a brilliant warmth in my thoughts, his fury a broiling sea beneath his skin. Through the static hum of the pack bond, I identified one voice, one light that was somehow both heard and seen, that burned brighter in my mind's eye than all the others combined.

To me, Graeson was a creature of light, the mental image superimposed over the physical, and he was glorious.

My forearms stung as lush fur rippled down them. Practicing with Isaac had helped, because the magic splintered, shifting both my arms into thickly muscled wargish limbs. Blinking, I tried clearing the glare from my vision only to realize I wasn't seeing things. My adopted pelt wasn't the silver I'd expected, nor was it Aisha's black or Dell's golden blond. The hairs were platinum with black tips, a meld of all three.

"Are you sure this is what you want?"

Graeson was a whisper of strength amid the soul-crushing doubt churning my thoughts, his question exposing an insecurity I had never glimpsed in him. It humanized him and reminded me that at the end of the day, with his ego checked at the door, he was just a man. I had given him no reason to hope this relationship was what I wanted, because I hadn't known myself until a slavering warg dared to stake her claim on what was mine.

"This is the rest of your life we're talking about." I glowered at Bessemer. *"It's worth fighting for. You are worth fighting for."*

An audible sigh passed his lips, and he bent his head, placing his lips at my ear. That heated brush of his skin solidified him, shook the sparkle from my eyes and allowed my vision to readjust to the darkness. "Sometimes I think all that's holding me together is you, not the pack bond. *You.*" His warm breath tickled my throat. "Be careful. If Bessemer gets you killed playing his games, I'll snap his neck."

The violence of his vow thrilled me on a primal level—it must be the warg blood—and when I pulled back, his eyes were twenty-four karat. His wolf was riding him, making promises that quivered beneath his skin with the urge to shift. I gripped his arm hard. *"Don't get yourself killed."*

"There's that faith in me again." A lazy smile curved his lips. "Do you trust anything about me outside of the kitchen?"

I didn't dignify him with a response.

"I don't have all night." The alpha circled me and sat on the topmost step of the nearest cabin. "This won't last long. Let's get it over with so we can all go home."

Having him at my back made my spine tingle, but Graeson flanked me, and I forgot about the alpha to focus on the bristling wolf in front of me. Here I was trusting him and without a kitchen in sight.

I flexed my hands, razor nails clacking, and that was all the invitation the she-wolf required. She darted in lightning quick and snapped at my calf. I swiped at her, but she danced out of reach. She repeated the move, and I missed again. The third time ended with thick laughter from the spectator behind me.

"Stop playing, Becca," he chastised, sounding not at all peeved by her advantage.

The truth hit me like a two-by-four to the forehead. Becca was wearing me out. Either she knew I couldn't hold on to the magic for long periods of time, which Bessemer could have skimmed from Graeson, or it was an instinctive warg defense to even the playing field for smaller predators like herself.

Confident in her speed, she charged me, teeth snapping. This time I was ready. I braced my feet apart and swung my arm outward like a baseball bat, connecting with her jaw and startling a yelp from her. She walked off, shaking her head to regroup.

Mentally, I was doing the same. *What do I have to do to win?*

"Knock her out," Graeson answered a beat later. *"When she stops getting up, it's over."*

Becca wasn't as spry or as ruthless as Aisha had been. She circled me once, searching for vulnerabilities, before a low growl from Bessemer told her to quit stalling and get on with it. Bunching her hindquarters, she leapt for my throat. I flung up one arm at neck height to block her jaws from clamping down on my vital parts and threw my shoulder behind a punch that sent her flying. She hit the dirt on her back and lay there a moment, breaths coming fast and heavy, eyes shut. For a second I thought she might not get back up, and I relaxed my stance.

"Is it over?" I sent the question to Graeson.

Cheek mashed to the ground, Becca cut her gaze toward me as if she'd heard me. She blinked once, twice, then panted through the effort of forcing her legs under her.

"How much longer can you hold your shift?" was his answer.

"I don't know." I was fine now, but soon my limits would be stretched. *"She looks ready to drop."*

Movement caught my eye. Becca on the prowl.

"This isn't right." I sent to Graeson. *"I shouldn't have to hurt her to end this."*

"No. It's not, but she won't hold back. You can't either. Not if you want to win." His fists strained at his sides. *"Finish this before it goes too far."*

A leaden weight settled in my gut. We'd passed *too far* when she drew first blood. Becca didn't deserve what I was about to do to her, but she could heal in a day what took me a week to mend. I couldn't let her wear me down until I made a deadly mistake. The fight was on. Unlike Graeson's Imogen proposal, this match wasn't rigged. No. That wasn't true. This late-night brawl had Bessemer's name written all over it.

Becca's next attack was the least graceful yet, and I steeled my heart against what I had to do. Her small stature and the boost of having beta blood fueling my magic allowed me to withstand the impact of her furry body slamming into my chest hard enough to empty my lungs. Muscles quivering from the strain, I clutched her ruff and held her out at arm's length while I severed her Achilles tendons, one after the other, with the tapered edge of my claw.

Frantically kicking her legs, she transformed her agony into a heartbreaking howl that raised bile up my throat.

I set her on the ground as gently as I could with my muscles screaming and magic ebbing then backed away in case she caught a second wind. Breaths regulating, I spread my hands so Bessemer saw the crimson slicking them. "Are you satisfied?"

"Are you implying that I enjoy seeing a female of my pack reduced to this?" He gestured toward Becca's shaking form. "I don't." He stood with fluid grace. "Her blood is on your hands, not mine."

A touch from Graeson anchored me enough to notice our tiff had attracted an audience. Most were female, sizing up the competition, I guessed. My gaze collided with his, and I wondered how I would survive the selection if new challengers tapped my shoulder at every turn. Were there rules? One fight each night? Two? Three?

I might have asked if the pack bond were more solid, but it was faltering. I sensed him, but I didn't hear him, and I didn't want to risk pushing out thoughts Bessemer might overhear.

The rough pad of his thumb stroked over my pulse, calming me. "Come on." He didn't shy away from taking my hand in his, despite the fur and the blood. "I'll walk you home."

Nodding, I held on tight and hardened my gaze to a killing edge before raking it across the crowd.

Respect brightened several faces. Calculation sharpened others.

I had to wonder what weaknesses I had exposed and who would be the first to exploit them.

Graeson opened the door of my trailer and led me inside like a gentleman, but I think he was more concerned about my claws shredding the metal than politeness. Adrenaline kept me furry to the elbows, and I couldn't shake off my nerves enough to trigger a change.

He eased me into the booth, and his gaze swung wide. "The wards will help drain the magic so you can shift back, right?"

"It will." I hissed out a sharp breath. "I'll give it another minute to fade, but if it doesn't…"

I would have to reset, and we both knew my reset was broken. No, that wasn't right. I could shift into Lori. Maybe it wasn't busted so much as it broke me a little every time I used it.

The soothing energies of the dampening wards embedded in the walls of the trailer began nibbling on the residual magic floating in my system, and I relaxed as best I could. I pressed a hand to my side, and it came away smeared with blood from where Becca had sucker-punched me. With her claws.

"We need to get you patched up." He went to the sink, grabbed a cloth and dampened it. "Do you want me to get Aunt Dot or Isaac?"

"No." Gingerly, I pulled the fabric away from the clotting wound. "It hurts too much for me to think of a good excuse as to why dinner with my 'boyfriend' ended with his family taking chunks out of my hide."

"Okay. Then we handle it ourselves." He strode toward the bathroom, which he must have scouted in wolf form, and called back to me, "Take off your shirt."

Dumbstruck, I sat there staining my furniture and gawping up at him. "What?"

"Your shirt. It's ruined. Take it off." He spread his supplies on the table in front of me. "I'll clean you up and get you a new one."

The ridiculous urge to cross my arms over my chest made my voice snap. "Casual nudity is part of your culture, not mine."

He eyed my breasts appreciatively. "Are you wearing a bra?"

"I don't see why that's any of your— Hey." I popped his hand when he shoved the neck of my shirt aside in search of straps. "Stop that."

"Ellis, either take off the shirt and let me clean you, or I'm going to wake up Aunt Dot." He drummed his fingers on the bench behind me. "It's just a shirt. There's still a bra on under there. You've still got pants on. You won't be naked. You'll be halfway to a bikini."

"I've never worn a bikini," I grumbled, hooking my thumbs in the hem of the shirt and peeling it over my head.

"No." Apology tightened his expression. "I don't suppose you have."

I gritted my teeth to stop the rush of blood in my temples from transforming to the crash of waves. A ribbon of girlish laughter echoed through my thoughts before I clamped down on the memories. I didn't want to lose it in front of Graeson. I preferred confronting the specter of my sister alone.

"Here." I offered him the ruined T-shirt. "You can toss it in the trash can under the sink."

He did, then brought the damp cloth and knelt in front of me. I sat sideways on the seat, with one arm braced on the table and the other on its back. My feet were planted on the linoleum, knees tight together until he nudged them apart with a firm hand. Cupping my shoulder, he twisted me just enough to invigorate the burn.

"The cuts aren't deep." He gave each mark his full attention. "There's more blood than wound, honestly." He applied the warm cloth, and for a second the wet heat felt divine. "How fast do Gemini heal?"

I winced as he shifted the nubby fabric. "Slightly faster than humans."

"Does whatever ability you've absorbed at the time augment that at all?"

"It's possible." I considered the question. "We don't have absolute control over what qualities we skim from the blood of our donors. Usually it's their most striking feature or their most dangerous asset, since it's a defense mechanism for us. Even though we tend to absorb only one or two facets of a donor's gift, extras crop up from time to time."

"Extras?"

"Once, when I was a kid, before..." I pressed my lips together. "Isaac and his brother, Theo, hitched a ride with one of Aunt Dot's renters into town. I caught them at the edge of the park and begged to go. They hated when I tagged along, so I should have been suspicious when they welcomed me into the car."

Graeson moved his hand a fraction, and I sucked in air between my teeth.

"Once we got to town, they dared me to borrow magic from the guy. I was five, and I didn't know what he was when I took his blood." But those two had known exactly what was about to happen. "It made me faster, my senses keener, and..." I put it out there. "I sprouted this muscular bald tail—like a possum's—as long as my arm. It popped out inside my jeans and hurt so badly being cramped up in there I stripped right on the street. I was so freaked out by it that I couldn't shift back. Then they started to panic, because they knew they were going to get in big trouble, so they ditched me. I had to walk home in my panties, because the elastic allowed me to tuck the waistband under the base of the tail."

It had been the first of many such walks of shame.

The corners of Graeson's eyes creased, and I knew he wanted to laugh. I guess in hindsight it was kind of... No. It still wasn't funny to me.

"I'm no doctor, but here's my two cents." He grabbed a tube of antibiotic ointment, squirted a generous amount on his fingertips and smoothed it gently over the scratches. "It's safe to say you absorbed some of my healing ability. You're healing almost as fast as I do. You should be as good as new by morning at this rate."

I risked a glance, expecting gaping flesh despite his diagnosis, but he was right. A pissed-off house cat could do the amount of damage I saw. "That's amazing." I flexed my still furry hands. "This—not so much."

"Do you need to reset?" He kept it casual as he finished up and wiped his hands clean. "Is that something you want to do alone? Or would you like me to stay?"

At first I didn't know how to answer. He knew better than most why using my reset gutted me. Shifting to my other form jarred me back into Lori's skin, ripping open a different kind of wound as I went.

I surprised myself by saying, "I wouldn't say no to company." I fisted my hands in my lap. "I just... Could you give me a few minutes? Alone?"

"I'll wait on the steps." He cocked his head, listening. "Dell's worried about you. She's on her way over. I'll head her off and explain things unless..." His thumb smoothed a crease in my jeans. "Do you want me to go? She could hang out with you."

"No." I winced at the volume of my voice. "Dell is great, but I don't want to see her tonight." I would have set a hand on his shoulder if both mine weren't still half-changed. *I need you,* was what I meant to say. What came out was, "Please, don't go."

"Okay. I'll give her an update and send her home." He gave my upper thighs a reassuring squeeze. "Call if you need me."

I ducked my head in a halfhearted nod and listened as he exited the trailer and shut the door behind him. The knob barely had time to click before I heard muffled voices pitched low in an earnest discussion.

Gripping the medical supplies in an awkward hold, I shuffled toward the bathroom and put things back in their place. There was no room for clutter, and I didn't want a mess to clean up later. Figuring this was as good a place as any, I nudged the door closed to give me room, lowered the lid on the toilet and sat.

With a moment to myself, I studied the fur covering my arms. The coloration mystified me. Gemini mimic that which already exists—we don't alter it beyond the changes required to adapt a borrowed talent to our bodies. There was no reason why I didn't share Graeson's sterling silver pelt down to the hair.

Isaac might know, and if he didn't, Aunt Dot would.

"Enough procrastinating," I chided myself, the faint echo a lonely contrast to the conversation happening outside.

Cupping my elbows with my palms, I hugged myself and cracked open the lid on my memories. The deeper they cut, the better. The more agonizing the recollection, the less physical pain the change wrought from me. But instead of the beach of my nightmares, I found myself remembering those summer trips to the Great Smoky Mountains, comparing those forests and mountains to these.

A ripple of magic slipped over my skin, and I submersed myself deeper in the past.

One of Lori's favorite places had been a tiered waterfall hidden from the trails. The hike had left our short legs burning, and we whined every step of the way. Dad was ready to turn back, but Mom spun the endless trek into a game to see which of us could collect the most oak leaves. Each had to be fallen—no picking them off the limbs—and there could be no tears or holes or spotting. Soon we carried armfuls of leaves we flung at each other as we ran. By the time we stumbled upon the falls, we were all smiles.

I'll never forget how it resembled the most perfect layered cake, the frothy falls white like icing as the water flowed down the ever-widening expanse of rocks before crashing into an otherwise-calm basin.

I'll also never forget how Lori took one step, slipped on a moss-covered stone and fell on her butt into the ice-cold water. Or how she'd climbed out, shook off and shoved me in face-first to get even with me for mocking her.

The undercurrent of laughter shook my shoulders, and I smiled as warm magic twisted around me. The stirrings of the change contracted my stomach, tensed my muscles, and that flicker of amusement vanished with the first hard cramp. I gasped through clenched teeth, locked my elbows and held tight. Being compressed into the body of an eight-year-old made me painfully aware of every inch taller and wider I'd grown since Lori passed. My essence, tamped down into that tiny container, stretched me taut until my new skin threatened to burst.

The roller coaster of agony lasted forever, and when I could breathe again, I sensed Graeson standing outside the bathroom door.

I stretched out my arms. They were chubby with baby fat that Lori never shed. The platinum fur was gone. The razor edges of my claws had dulled and shrunk into plump fingers with chipped purple nail polish adorning the tips. The jeans and boots I'd worn earlier had vanished, replaced by a nightgown sprinkled with fat moons and grinning stars that brushed my bare ankles.

A sink basin sat next to my elbow, the compact shower stall beside that. If I had guts enough, I could stand in front of that counter, stare into that mirror and see Lori's face reflected as mine. But her smiles and mannerisms were her own. There was no copying those. All I accomplished by studying her was refreshing the mental pictures I kept that would never fade so long as I had a means of punishing myself by wearing her skin.

"I told you to wait outside." Soft and breathless, chest wound too tight, I sounded like a kid panting through a hundred jumping jacks challenge. "I don't want you to see me like this."

Had he not been there, I realized, I would have looked into that mirror. I would have gripped the metaphorical knife lodged in my heart with both hands and twisted until I couldn't stand and collapsed on the floor.

"You were screaming." His muffled voice held an edge.

Had I cried out? I couldn't remember. So much of the change was mental, it was hard keeping up with the physical.

"I shook off the wolf." I studied my nubby toes and wiggled them. "I need to shift back. Just give me a minute."

The shadow under the door didn't budge, but he didn't try the handle either. With Graeson, who had problems with hearing *no* and tended to do what he wanted, it was a small victory.

The change took longer than a minute, but Camille unfurled from Lori's shell in record time, and again I wondered if that wasn't due to the knowledge that Graeson was there, waiting, a whisper away if I needed him.

Back in my own body, I was still covered with blood. I showered before exiting the bathroom wearing pajama pants and a matching tank top. I found a large silver wolf curled up in my bed and realized he must have gone outside to shift while I was washing the blood of his pack mate down the drain. His change relieved pressure I hadn't realized was coiling ever tighter in my gut as I pondered our sleeping arrangements. When I hesitated in the doorway, the wolf whined low in his throat, rested his head on his paws and gave me liquescent puppy eyes that should have looked absurd on a warg his size.

"You expect me to sleep with you?" He took up half the bed, and I wasn't even in it yet. I'd never had a pet, never slept with an animal, and he was getting fur all over everything. Was it too late to ask for the man back? "You aren't serious."

His tail thumped once.

I huffed as I pulled back the covers, flipping the light off as I went. I crawled into bed and grumbled as I settled in on the sliver of mattress he'd left for me. I lay there—stiff and not really comfortable at all as I wondered if wargs got ticks or fleas and if that's why my skin suddenly itched—and had about decided to sleep on the floor when he rested his large head over my stomach, pinning me to the bed under its weight. He released a gusty sigh, licked his lips and didn't move again.

Positive he was sleeping, I risked rubbing one of his ears through my fingers then stroked down his spine. His fur was a contrast of downy soft and coarse hairs, and petting him soothed me. I drifted to sleep with a hand fisted in his ruff, lulled by his warmth and the sound of his breathing.

CHAPTER TEN

The bed was empty when I woke except for the hairs stuck to my sheets and clinging to my top. Unsure if I still had company, I fumbled my way into the kitchen and found Graeson seconds from cracking eggs I hadn't bought into a skillet I didn't own.

I rose on my tiptoes, arms reaching high overhead, fingertips almost brushing the ceiling. "Am I still dreaming?"

He turned in time to catch my yawn. "Do you often dream about men cooking you breakfast?"

The heat of his gaze traveled over my navel, exposed by my morning stretch session, and my skin tingled.

"No." I inhaled on a blissful sigh. "This would be a first."

"Good. I don't like competition." He used a knife—that one I did recognize—and slashed open a package of bacon. "So…" Voice calm, reasonable, he drew out the pause. "Do you dream of me outside of cooking you breakfast?"

"First of all, you're the only person not related to me who's ever cooked for me." I went to the fridge and poured myself a glass of orange juice, but he stuck a mug smelling of chai in my hand, and my insides melted as the heat ebbed into my palm. "And secondly, I'm not about to admit to what happens when my eyes close."

"So that's a yes." He sounded pleased.

"This must be a dream." I sat on the bench and scooted close to the wall so I could rest my head against it. "It's too surreal."

A masculine chuckle overlaid the sizzle of bacon. "I hope you don't mind. I invited Dell over."

"Not at all." Any minute now I would wake up and find myself alone in a cold bed instead of breathing in the warm scents of Graeson's efforts. I wanted to enjoy this fantasy right up until my alarm blared. "As long as you keep doing what you're doing."

A clink of sound jolted me upright from my slouch as Graeson thunked down a plate in front of me. A mountain of home-style potatoes sizzled, all crispy and browned. My mouth watered, and my stomach gurgled loud enough to embarrass. I'd burned a lot of calories shifting last night, and I'd been too stunned and heartsick to replace any of them. If Graeson hadn't stuffed me prior to my first challenge, I might not have woken until late afternoon or even tonight.

One thing was for sure. Until Graeson, I hadn't realized what poor care I was taking of myself. Then again, until Charybdis brought us together, I hadn't had much need for shifting or practicing self-defense that didn't involve reflecting catty comments from temporary coworkers.

"If I'd known the way to your heart was through your stomach—" he picked a promising spud off the top and pressed it against my lips, "—I would have cooked for you sooner."

I snagged the morsel with my teeth, and he growled appreciatively while I chewed. "Is all this for me?"

"Well," he said on a laugh, "Dell is expecting food at breakfast. Maybe save her a bite?"

I ate a second potato and considered my answer. "How have you managed to stay single this long?"

"Easy. I didn't settle." The pan hissed and crackled as he flipped the crisping strips of bliss some called bacon. "I wanted to set a good example for Marie."

"So you ascribe to the soul-mate theory." Even to my own ears, I sounded flat.

"I don't believe souls are split down the middle before they're stuffed into our bodies, or that it's our life's goal to hunt down the missing half of ourselves, if that's what you mean." He tapped his tongs against the fryer. "I do believe that sometimes—whether it's fate or accidental— we cross paths with someone who shatters us on a fundamental level and remakes us into a better version of ourselves."

I ate another potato. "That sounds painful."

"Love is a series of small hurts," he agreed. "Even when everything goes right, your heart gets bruised." Carrying a plate of bacon draining on a paper towel, he set it out of my reach. "Some people are worth it, some people are not, and I doubt any of that has anything to do with fate or divine intervention."

"Dell said something similar to me once." I darted out my hand and snagged a strip of perfectly cooked bacon before he could catch my wrist. "She doesn't believe in fated mates either."

"Dell is a progressive woman." He rubbed his jaw. "It's just as likely fated mates are a product of the very prejudices you and I are facing now. Most warg females have fertility issues when it comes to interbreeding. The result is few pureblood children being born, and those pure bloodlines being prized."

"Ah." I crunched thoughtfully. "You think fated mates are cautionary tales." I could see that. "So if a male is in a relationship with a female who isn't getting pregnant, he can ditch her in favor of another one and blame it on fate. Or vice versa, I suppose."

"I've seen happy couples who've been together for years busted up by a male scenting a female in true heat and being unable to control himself. Same for females going through their cycle multiple times and failing to get pregnant. Males who already have a child—or multiple children—are a temptation some can't resist. Those are rare scenarios." He pointed his finger at me and pulled the trigger. "But fated mates are supposed to be rare, right?"

I leaned forward, fully engaged. "What about half-bloods?"

"It's much easier for wargs to breed with humans. Those children have a fifty-fifty shot at being able to shift at puberty. You get a few cases of latent wolves several generations removed, but those are almost myth they're so rare. Usually a child with less than half warg blood has no chance of shifting." He shook his head. "It's a hard choice, but with our species shrinking with each generation, it's one being made more and more often. Half a chance is still half a chance more than what they had."

"What about you?" I couldn't resist asking. "Do you want kids?"

"I'm a dominant, which usually means a stronger, purer bloodline." He kept it light, like it meant nothing. "I've got a good chance at having full-blooded kids."

No wonder Becca was willing to have a go at me. A union with Graeson offered more than status, he represented the possibility of something far more precious. Babies. The future of the pack. Of their species.

Another thread of doubt wriggled through my mind, the fear I was standing between him and a thing he might want, an opportunity he might feel obligated to explore. Biological urges were strong, but his conscious needs and wants factored into his choice, right?

Plenty of people—fae and human—had children with partners they didn't like or downright despised. Who benefited from those unions? The children growing up in divided households? Or worse, in homes where resentment polluted their every breath from infancy? The mothers with their dull eyes or fathers with the collar of duty strangling the life from them?

Instead of accepting his brush-off, I had to know. I told myself his answer would decide for me whether fighting for his hand like some twisted fairy tale was the right thing to do or if it was my own stubborn refusal to allow tradition to swallow him whole, but I wasn't entirely convinced that was the truth. It was hard sitting in my kitchen eating the man's bacon while denying the heat coiled in my belly wasn't from the rendered pork but his proximity.

I chewed thoughtfully. "That's not an answer."

Fabric whispered as he slid into the booth opposite me, took my hands in his and linked our fingers. "What if I said I want blond-haired girls or boys with storm-cloud eyes that roll with thunder like their mother's?"

Children who, if he got his wish, would bear an uncanny resemblance to me, and to the sister I had lost. Gemini birthed twins. Always. How painful would it be to look into the faces of my daughters and see Lori's shadow? Would I be able to endure it? Could I view them as individuals, or would I only see her ghost and flee from the pain the way my mother and father had? Leaving Graeson, once again, to raise children on his own?

Honesty was the most I could offer. "I would say I don't know if I can give that to you."

His thumbs rolled over my knuckles. "I understand."

And the worst part was, I knew he did. He had an uncanny way of reading me as though the pack bond was always strung between us. I wished I understood him half as well.

A couple of raps on the door announced Dell's arrival. Graeson didn't react, so I figured she had given a mental knock before the physical one.

"Come in," I called, unable to stand because my fingers were meshed with an unmovable object's.

"You guys look...tense." She stalled out in the kitchen. "Should I come back later?"

"No." Graeson stood and hauled me from the booth with him. "I was just leaving."

"What about breakfast?" There was so much food, and he hadn't eaten any of it. "You aren't staying?"

"I can't." Using our linked hands, he tugged me closer and folded his arms behind him. Mine followed, linking my arms around his waist. "When are you leaving?"

"This afternoon. Isaac is driving us to the airport." I wanted him back inside the safety of the wards before sundown. "Will I see you before I go?"

Graeson ducked his head, pressing his nose against the point where my neck met shoulder. A long, slow inhale lifted the hairs down my arms. He exhaled through his mouth, and his breath rippled down the front of my shirt, tightening my stomach.

"I'll do my best," he said, and I heard the lie.

I turned my face so our cheeks brushed, the stubble of his chin scoring me when he tilted his jaw. "Will I have to worry about another challenge before I leave?"

"No." That one word rang with truth. "The pack will be otherwise occupied."

I drew back to look into his face. "I don't suppose you'll enlighten me?"

"I don't mean to break up this beautiful moment," Dell said, scooting past me and closer to the bacon, "but it's not as good once the grease congeals. You gotta eat this stuff hot."

"She's right. You should eat and pack." His fingers slipped from mine, and after patting my arms to keep them in place, he cupped my face in his hands. "Learn all you can, but be careful."

"We'll talk when I get back." My fingers wormed into his belt loops. "This woman, she might have some of the answers we need to pinpoint Charybdis's next move. If I can figure out how—" My lips burned in silent warning, the blood oath at work. "All I'm saying is this is the best lead we've got. I'm keeping my fingers crossed she's the key to figuring out where Charybdis might have gone to lick his wounds."

Fresh worry creased his forehead. "I should be the one going with you."

"You've got your hands busy here." Cleaning up the mess I had helped create. "Don't worry about it. I can handle this."

"I know you can. I have faith in you." A tight grin thinned his lips, but it didn't reach his eyes. "I just wish you didn't have to do it alone."

Before I realized his intent, he ducked his head and captured my lips with his. The soft pressure vanished before his taste registered, before I could decide if I should yank him closer or bring my knee up between his legs. Somehow he stood across the trailer by the time my brain gained traction.

Graeson had kissed me. *Kissed me.* And it started the room spinning.

"Take care of her, Dell." They shared a grim look that set my arms prickling. "Check in before you leave Kermit."

With those enigmatic words, he exited the trailer. The resignation in his posture sent alarm bells clanging in my head. Dell caught me by the wrist before I turned the front doorknob. I hadn't even realized I was following him on unsteady legs.

That kiss had clearly fried my brain. He was a grown warg. He could take care of himself for twenty-four hours, less than if we got lucky with our timing.

"Let him go." She tugged me to the booth and pushed me back in my spot. "We need to eat and nail down our agenda. Cord will be fine."

Despite her reassuring toast, made with my forgotten glass of orange juice, deep in my gut I didn't believe her.

⁙ ⌇

"I don't get it." Dell leaned forward in the passenger seat of the rental car we'd picked up after our flight dumped us near Kermit, Texas. Almost pressing her nose to the windshield, she squinted into the full darkness beyond the glass. "Are you sure your GPS isn't busted?"

"Hmm?" I stopped drumming my fingers on the steering wheel.

"That's a cow pasture, not a mental institution."

I followed her line of sight to where a grandiose five-story structure rose from a manicured lawn, more country estate than sterile institution. Warmth glowed behind its elegant arched windows, and spotlights illuminated white stone statues and spiral topiaries scattered artfully across the grounds. Despite the late hour, a patient could stroll the sprawling garden even if they weren't one of the nocturnal fae species.

"Don't worry." I had that covered. "We're in the right place."

"Are you okay?" She squeezed my forearm. "You looked like you were a million miles away."

Villanow was closer to twelve hundred miles away from Kermit, but I wasn't one for splitting hairs.

"I was just thinking." About how Graeson never came back. He kissed me and vanished, and I got the queasiest sensation low in my gut when I thought about the finality of that moment. "Our contact should be here any minute now."

Thierry was bringing a trusted friend along, and that woman would be responsible for getting us inside the facility.

Accepting my excuse with a raised eyebrow, Dell resumed staring ahead. "So how do you know we're in the right place?"

"The conclave uses glamour to conceal its bases, buildings and properties." Her blank stare prompted me to continue. "It's illusionary magic. It makes one thing look like another. Some fae use personal glamour to hide their inhuman attributes so they can blend with humans. Others use terrestrial glamour to manipulate houses, buildings, property. Some of the more talented fae can make it feel real too, to a certain extent, but in most cases it doesn't have to pass more than the look test. Terrestrial glamours tend to be used to hide things, meaning there are enchantments layered in the magic that push against the minds of anyone who gets too close. It says: *Keep walking. There's nothing to see here.*"

"Huh." She cocked her head. "It doesn't fool you, though?"

"I have a knack for reading glamour." It helped Geminis gauge the strength of a potential donor, as well as allowing us to see exactly what we were getting ourselves into by borrowing from a source. "With personal glamour, I have to touch it to read it, but terrestrial glamour is in the air. I can breathe it in, make contact that way, and unravel it."

"You know all the cool tricks."

"Shifting into a wolf is a pretty cool trick too."

"Maybe. I guess." She shrugged. "I've been a wolf, been raised with wolves, my whole life. Furred and fanged is my normal."

I caught myself worrying the pearl bracelet Harlow had given me and twisted in my seat. "Any word on the Garzas?"

"They aren't returning my calls." With her thumb and finger, she flicked the plastic notice warning passengers to wear seat belts. "Either they're back and not ready for company or they're still traveling and don't want to be disturbed."

Hearing they embraced technology was promising at least. "There's no way to be sure?"

"Only if you want to piss them off." She half-smiled. "Trust me. When they're ready, they'll let us know."

Flashing headlights in the rearview mirror tugged my attention away from her. "We've got company."

No cars had passed since we pulled off the side of the road to wait. That we saw motion now set my nerves chiming with anticipation. This could be it.

A sporty car, an eye-catching shade of light green even in the dark, grew larger as it neared, and at the last minute it swerved off the road and squealed to a stop behind us. I powered down my window and waited.

Two women sat in the car. The one with a hand clamped over her mouth like she might be carsick I recognized. The other woman rolled her eyes, stepped out of the car and set about smoothing her pantsuit.

Average height and wafer thin, she wore her expensive ensemble well. Her chestnut hair twisted in an elegant topknot on her head was held in place by lacquered chopsticks in a nod to her Asian ancestry. Her warm brown eyes sparkled as she watched Thierry climb from the car with a wobble in her step.

"My driving isn't that bad," the newcomer assured me, spinning her keys around her pointer. "Thierry is overly dramatic."

"Let's get this done. I need to organize a search party." Thierry put a hand over her gut. "I think I left my stomach back there."

I got out and met them on the shoulder of the road, and Dell ghosted from the car, a silent threat behind me.

"Thierry, good to see you again." I stuck out my hand, braced for the burn of potent magic that raced up my arm. "This is Dell Preston of the Chandler Pack."

"Good to see you too. Nice to meet you, Dell." She bumped shoulders with the woman beside her. "Mai, this is Camille Ellis." To us, she said, "Ladies, this is Mai Hayashi, my best friend who thinks she's a NASCAR driver, and your ticket inside the Edelweiss Institution."

"I work for the conclave." Mai extended her hand toward me. "I'm interning for a counselor who specializes in displaced fae youth. I'm sad to say several of the parents responsible for the rise in abandoned kids are locked up here and in other places like this. Some can't cope with this side of the veil but can't go home either. Others are locked up before they can become a danger to themselves or others." Her cool fingers closed over mine. "Either way, no one will look twice at me being here. I usually work third-shift hours and deal with the nocturnal fae, so I can pass this off as routine."

The rush of wild magic in her touch sang to me, a gentler note than that of the wargs. "You're a kitsune."

Thierry coughed into her fist then snapped her fingers.

"Hold your horses." Mai reached in her pocket, removed a slim wallet and passed Thierry a twenty-dollar bill. "There. Extortionist." She crossed her arms and studied me. "How'd you guess?"

"It's a talent of mine." Another weapon in the Gemini tool kit to help us identify creatures with complementary magic that we could use as our own. "Legacies are the only fae I have trouble reading."

"Legacies?" Understanding sparked behind her eyes. "You mean like Thierry. It's a bloodline thing?" She narrowed her eyes at her friend. "You're a dirty cheat."

"Showered this morning, thank you very much." She snapped the cash between her fingers. "Would you feel better if I used my winnings to buy us some Thai food on the way home?"

Mai scowled. "Why do I feel like you just tricked me into buying you dinner?"

"Probably because I did." She pocketed the cash. "Sucker."

A throat cleared behind me, and Dell shifted her weight. "The night's not getting any younger."

"Sorry," they said in unison.

"We don't get much girl time these days," Mai explained. "Our mates are overprotective, and we had to bribe them to sit this one out." She slung an arm around Thierry's waist. "Breaking the law is more fun with a girlfriend, am I right?"

"Right," I said at the same time as Dell murmured, "Sure."

"Let's get this show on the road." Thierry clapped her hands. "Dell, we're holding down the fort."

"Camille, you're with me." Mai jingled her keys. "We need to get moving, though. I have to cover my tracks once I leave here to keep the conclave off my back, and I need time to make that happen."

"Hold up." Dell gripped my elbow when I stepped forward, and held on tight. "Cam's not going anywhere without me."

"Getting in one extra person is hard enough." Mai glanced between us. "I won't risk two."

"You're not fae," Thierry pointed out. "If you walk in there without ID and a damn good excuse, you'll all three be detained. Camille works for the conclave, and she consults. It makes more sense to let her go with Mai."

"I don't like this," Dell growled. "Cord wanted me to stick by you. He'll be pissed when he finds out I let you go alone."

"He'll get over it." I walked to the passenger side of the coupe. "What will you two be doing?"

"Playing damsels in distress." Thierry opened the driver door, leaned in, and the hazard lights started flashing. "Not much traffic comes out this way. We should be able to twiddle our thumbs in relative peace. Should anyone ask, Mai and I stopped to offer assistance. Cell reception out here is crap. Her car is a two-seater. We'll stretch the truth and say she drove you up the road to make a call while I waited with your friend."

With our lies rehearsed, Mai and I climbed into her car.

A whisper of unease slid over me as I noticed Dell sizing up Thierry. A distinctly predatory gleam lit her eyes, and Mai's headlights reflected gold back at us. Apparently Dell had no trouble drawing on her inner she-wolf when there were no other wargs around to temper her instincts.

"Here's the deal." Mai shifted into reverse and stomped the pedal. "There's a paper trail a mile long linking you to the Charybdis file."

That answered the question of how much Mai knew about our mission. *All of it.*

"The best lies are half-truths," she continued. "Our cover story is that you need to talk to the patient in connection with a case. Since she checked herself in, and the level where she's being held is non-secure, we should be able to zip in and out without raising any eyebrows."

The car stopped on a dime, and I caught my breath before she pressed the accelerator flat to the floorboard. She wiped a stray hair from her eye, and my heart stuttered when her hand left the wheel. Thierry must have a cast-iron stomach compared to mine. I was about to lose the bag of chips I ate at the airport.

"You're risking a lot to help us." There was no guarantee this lead would pan out.

"I was there at the portal breach," she said quietly. "I...froze." Her lips mashed together. "Fae here are tame, young, compared to what's in Faerie. If I hadn't been so afraid, I might have made a difference. I might have stopped this thing—whatever he is—from breaking through."

This was atonement for her, setting right a perceived wrong at great risk to herself, half-believing if things fell apart, she deserved it. That I understood.

"Were you there when he crossed?" I hadn't seen her on the footage, and I had it memorized.

"No." Her eyes shut for a heart-stopping second. "After the initial blowout, Tee packed me up and sent me home where I'd be safe. Like a coward, I tucked tail and went."

A thread of unease sifted through me. "Thierry was there too?"

"So." She flashed a blinding smile at me. "Your job must be exciting, huh? Chasing bad guys cross-country."

"You didn't answer my question." It felt important to know where Thierry fit into this whole timeline.

More teeth, wider smile. "No, I didn't."

The niggling sense of unease kept prodding the back of my mind. "You're not going to tell me."

"Nope." The playful mien she wore so casually lifted to reveal stone-cold determination. "There's a lot about Thierry that's need-to-know. As the saying goes—you don't need to know. Don't pick at that string because it's wriggling in front of you. Do it, and you'll regret it. You'll unravel a whole heap of trouble that's got nothing to do with you or the killer you're tracking."

I leaned back in the seat and watched the institution loom as we neared the circular drive. "That sounded almost like a threat."

A quick jerk of the wheel, and Mai all but stood on the brake. Gravel spun as we slid into a parking space marked *Employees Only*. Twisting sideways, she studied me with the same barely leashed ferocity Dell wore when we left her with Thierry.

"Tee has a savior complex. She can't help getting involved. It's a sickness." She huffed out an exasperated breath. "That said, you should know that if tonight blows back on her, I will hunt you down, point my manicured finger in your face and tell the magistrates everything I know about you and what you're doing."

Thinking of Harlow, my anger rose a notch. "Even if it condemns an innocent woman to death?"

"For Thierry?" An airy growl vibrated her throat. "Yes."

I dipped my head, wondering if I would say the same in her place. I was risking my job, possibly jail time, by pulling this stunt to save a friend. But was I as willing as Mai to exchange a life for a life? I hoped to never have to answer that question.

"How good is your acting?" Half twisting in the seat, Mai raked her gaze up and down me. "Can you pull off cool professional, or are you the nervous, babbling type?"

I bent my lips to approximate a smile. "I can act."

After all, I played the role of well-adjusted conclave agent every day, even when the eight-year-old girl trapped inside me was screaming.

CHAPTER ELEVEN

Getting inside Edelweiss was as simple as Mai signing a sheet pinned to a clipboard at the receptionist's desk thanks to the fact said receptionist was nowhere to be seen. The exterior's sweeping architecture had me hypothesizing the building had once been a private residence. Most likely it had been left in a trust for conclave use. From there, they must have converted it into a mental health facility while maintaining its elegant appearance. The interior, however, had been gutted of luxury. There was no difference between walking its halls and strolling any sterilized corridor in a major hospital.

Pity if this had once been a home. It was a cutting-edge medical prison now.

Mai waved me on toward a set of double doors. We pushed through, and a curvy woman with a pin-tight bun snagged us on the other side.

"Ms. Hayashi." A warm smile brightened her face. "What can I help you with tonight?"

"I'm here to see Marshal Ayer." She gestured toward me. "My associate is consulting on a case involving Ms. Ayer. I volunteered to escort her down here since I'm familiar with Edelweiss and its exemplary staff."

Preening, the woman tittered. "I've got a minute. Why don't I walk you there myself?"

Mai beamed. "That would be great."

The orderly turned on her heel, white Crocs squeaking on the shiny floor, keys jingling where they bounced against her ample hip. We followed her through single doorways and double doorways, down long halls and past short alcoves, until my sense of direction muddled. Thank the gods for Mai's familiarity with the complex. The place was a labyrinth.

"Here we are." The orderly pulled a clipboard from a bin screwed into the door of a room on a hall lined with such bins. "Ms. Ayer has been sedated, but she's capable of holding a short conversation. I can allow you ten minutes, then I'm afraid the patient needs her rest."

"Gotcha." Mai signed her name then passed the board back. "We'll try to keep this as low-key as possible."

After plucking a key from the wide ring attached to her belt loop, the woman opened the door and stepped away so we could enter. Once we were shut inside the room, I shivered.

There was no doubting this was the same woman from the grainy surveillance video, but she managed to appear more washed out in person than on the black-and-white recording. The healthy grayish—for an Unseelie—cast to her skin had paled. She sat in a wingback chair positioned in front of a tall window. Soft pink pajamas swallowed her, washing out her complexion. Her wispy hair settled in gentle waves across her shoulders. She didn't turn to look at us. I'm not sure she knew we were there.

Fingers tingling with nerves, I advanced on Marshal Ayer. "I'm not here to hurt you. I just need to touch your skin."

Glassy brown eyes stared forward in answer.

I pressed two fingers against her forearm, and a corresponding *ping* of magic told me several things. She was a dhampir, half fae and half vampire. Most damning was that even all this time later her skin held the signature I associated with waterlogged corpses and amputated children.

"She didn't just see him," I told Mai. "He touched her, infected her with his magical signature."

"Is that a good thing or a bad thing?"

"I'm not sure." I waved a hand in front of Ayer's face. "On the video, he steps into the hall and vanishes. She flinches, like maybe she saw him pull his disappearing trick, rubs her eyes as if it's been a long night, then leaves the frame."

"Marshal Ayer." Mai came around and squatted in front of her. "We'd like to ask you a few questions, if you don't mind."

Ayer kept her gaze fixed on the moonlit horizon.

I took point questioning her. "What can you tell us about the night of the portal breach?"

A tic developed beneath her left eye.

"Did you see someone step from the portal?" I circled her. "Did he touch you? Speak to you?"

The marshal kept staring ahead.

"This is getting us nowhere." I restrained the urge to kick the wall. "She's too sedated—or too far gone—to be of any use."

"I've got an idea." Mai removed a tube of lipstick from her pocket. A nasty comment about her primping readied itself then died when she removed the cap, twisted the base and a short blade extended. She cut her eyes toward me as she sliced a gash across her wrist. "This will either jumpstart her metabolism or make a mess. You ready?"

Unsure what I was agreeing to, I nodded and moved closer as Mai brought her wound against the woman's lips. Being half vampire meant Ayer required blood, but I wasn't sure how much sway its siren song held with her fae half.

A soft rumble vibrated in Ayer's throat, seeming to come from hundreds of miles away. Mai's blood hit her tongue, and her eyes dilated. Black voids latched on to that fresh source of blood, and Ayer lunged, knocking over her chair and tackling Mai to the floor.

I gripped Ayer by the nape and hauled her off the bleeding kitsune. Weakened as Ayer was from her time here, I had no trouble restraining her. "Feel up to answering our questions now?"

Snarled words almost below my hearing told me she was revived enough to curse at us.

Mai stood and cupped her hand against the shallow cut she'd given herself. "We don't have much time."

With minimal effort, I righted the chair and dumped Ayer in the seat. I uttered a universal restraining Word, one I'd learned during marshal academy, and experienced the satisfaction of hearing her yelp as her wrists snapped together, bound by magic.

"Let's try this again." I rounded on her. "Did you see someone step from the portal?"

Blood smearing her mouth, she curled her lip. "Yes."

A brief thrill zinged through me. "Did he touch you? Talk to you?"

"He took me." Her feral expression crumpled. "I didn't want him to. I said no."

That fast my high flatlined. "He raped you?"

"Yes." Her brow puckered. "No. He was inside me, but not that way. He was under my skin, in my head. He told me what to do, and I did it. I couldn't stop myself. I lost control." Her throat flexed when she swallowed. "He taunted me with things no one knows. *No one.*"

Treading carefully over her pain, I had to press for answers. "How did he get to you?"

"He..." Her eyelids fluttered.

"Marshal Ayer?" I shook her shoulder gently. "How did he take control of you?"

The adrenaline rush was fading, and Ayer was too weak to climb back out of her stupor. Mai could try a few more drops of blood, but we only had minutes left, and I wasn't convinced the trick would work twice. She slumped back, lids heavy, mouth gone slack.

"Stay with me," I gritted out while shaking Ayer, whose eyes closed.

"She's done." Mai touched my shoulder. "All that shaking is going to give her brain damage."

"Do you think she was lucid?" Or had it been the drugs, the sensory deprivation talking? "Do you think we can trust anything she said?"

"I don't know."

A snapping sound lifted my head as Mai clasped a wide leather bracelet around her wrist, covering the cut. I leaned over to take a better look. "Are you okay?"

"The best way to cover tracks is not to leave any in the first place." She examined her wrist then clothes before pulling out a compact to check her face. All the blood from the attack was gone. "Vamp saliva coagulates to clot blood so their prey doesn't bleed out. Dhampirs don't have it, and whatever they pumped her full of is causing me to heal slower than usual."

I got on my feet and posed Ayer into comfortable lines. "I wish we'd found her sooner."

The door opened on a breath of fresh air, and the orderly greeted us with a smile. "It's time for Ms. Ayer's bath. I'm going to have to ask you to leave." She waited as we filed out in the hall. "I hope you got what you needed."

What we got was more questions than answers. There was no doubt he had touched her, violated her, but how? What was at the root of the infection? Until I figured that part out, Ayer had no clues left to offer us.

"We did." Mai beamed as she signed out. "Thanks for your help."

At the receptionist's desk, Mai greeted a slight brunette with buns pinned to either side of her head. Pen in hand, Mai scribbled her name and turned to go.

"Ms. Hayashi." The receptionist stood. "You're good to go, but I don't see where your friend signed in." She eyeballed the sheet. "Or out." She extended the clipboard. "I have to ask you to sign in, ma'am. I'll also need to see some ID."

"I left my wallet in the car." Not a lie. I hadn't planned on needing ID since the whole idea was to get in and out without leaving a trace. "I can go get it if you like."

"Wait there." She sat and reached for the phone. "I'll have security escort you."

"Isn't that a little extreme?" Mai chuckled. "You know my car, and I parked right outside."

The woman paled, proof she was indeed familiar with Mai's vehicular prowess. "You know the rules, Ms. Hayashi."

"Of course." She caught my eye. "I have to use the little fox's room." She winked at me. "I'll meet you—" *wink wink*, "—at the car, okay?"

"Sure thing," I said, masking my irritation for the receptionist's benefit.

Left to fend for myself, I awaited my escort's arrival. Threats aside, I hadn't expected Mai to abandon me the first chance she got. Showing my ID wouldn't have raised red flags, at least not tonight. When the guard realized I had none, they would ask me to call in and get a copy faxed over for their records. That shot past red flags and blasted straight into pyrotechnics.

If Vause had tagged my file, she'd know within minutes where I was and demand I put in an appearance to explain my actions. That would sink me and drag Mai down too, not to mention it was a short hop from Mai to Thierry. Without Thierry's access to conclave resources, I would be forced to sit on my hands and wait out my suspension.

This whole night was turning into a lost cause. Any hopes I had of following up with Ayer burst.

"This is Officer Lam," the receptionist chimed. "He'll be escorting you."

The lanky young man who breezed into the lobby wearing aviator sunglasses flung a grin my way. "It would be my pleasure."

Heart thumping, I headed for the doors. Things were about to go downhill fast.

The guard beat me to them and held one side open. "After you, miss."

Outside, the night air teased hairs into my eyes. We reached the coup, and I stalled. "I don't have the keys. We'll have to wait for Mai."

"No need." He reached into his pocket and brought out a sleek fob that made the car chirp. "Get in there and pretend you're searching your purse. We need to buy her some time."

I caught the fob when he tossed it to me. "Who are you?"

"A friend. Mai helped out my kid brother and me when our mom... It doesn't matter." He folded his arms and made a show of being impatient while I got in and pretended to search the car. "When Mai gets here, strap in and hold on tight. She's going to be in a hurry."

"What about the receptionist?"

He tipped his shades down his nose, revealing mercurial eyes that swirled with power. "I'll handle it."

That brief glimpse made my bones melt the way a hot bath at the end of a long day might. Assuming the bath also involved a glass of chilled wine, a tray of decadent chocolates and a blindfolded cellist serenading away your cares while a masseuse gave you the foot massage of your life.

My spine had dissolved, leaving me in a puddle. "Wow."

"I aim to please." He nudged the glasses back into place. "Trust me now?"

"Mmm-hmm."

"Lam," Mai snapped. "Tell me you didn't whammy her."

"Whammy? Really? That's the best you can do?" His lips twisted. "It cheapens the experience."

"So that's a *yes*. Wonderful." She huffed. "I hope her friend knows how to drive."

"She does," I replied helpfully. "Dell kidnapped me once. In a black SUV."

Both of them turned to look at me.

Mai flung a disgusted sound in Lam's direction then tossed a plastic bag at my chest. "Do what you do, and be careful. Call if you hit any snags." She slanted a glance at my dopey grin. "Did you wipe her too?"

"I'm a self-preservationist. What do you think?" He tipped an imaginary hat and grinned at me. "Hold on, Blondie."

The car shifted when Mai slid behind the wheel. She leaned over, snapped my seat belt and hauled the door shut, jarring my elbow. "We have to be long gone by the time he works his mojo."

"Mojo," I agreed dazedly, wondering who she was talking about.

Seat belt on, Mai cranked the car and revved the engine. The tiny car spun out, and my head hit the seat rest. That warm, fuzzy feeling lapping over me evaporated in the nine-point-three seconds it took her to go from zero to sixty.

Clutching the plastic bag to my chest, I reevaluated my religious beliefs as we sped back to where we'd left Dell and Thierry. My weight slammed forward, eyes squinching as we came to a gut-lurching stop. No sooner had I caught my breath than the door wrenched open and Thierry gripped my arm.

"Something's wrong with Dell." She took the bag and helped me out. "One minute she was pacing the road, the next she hit the asphalt screaming *Ellis.*"

Dell didn't call me Ellis. She never had. But there was one warg who did, and he was plugged into her head.

I bolted for the rental. The rear doors were open, and Dell's tall frame spilled out either end. I ducked inside and checked her pulse. Steady. She groaned and stirred, curling around my arm.

"Cord," she moaned. "He's gone."

Ice encased my spine. "What do you mean *gone*? Gone where?" I pushed tangled hairs off her damp face. "Dell, what's wrong with Graeson?"

"I don't feel him." Rocking, she pressed her face against me. "The pack bond... It's gone."

My spur emerged without thought, and I barely restrained myself long enough to get permission before taking Dell's blood. The shift ripped through me, and I gasped as platinum hairs dipped in inky blackness sprung from my fingertips to shoulders. Never had the change swept over me so far so fast.

A hazy golden glow encased Dell, and her stream of consciousness fed into mine. That was the only indication I had the pack bond was active. There were no other voices, no other lights, no other thoughts.

"Graeson." I sent a thought reaching for him only to have it smash against a mental wall and rebound on me. "Where are the others?" I focused on Dell. "Why can't I hear them?"

"We're too far away." She whimpered. "Without Cord to anchor the bond, it can't stretch over such a long distance."

"He broke the bond." Why would he cripple himself now when he needed his strength the most?

"No." A shudder wracked her. "His mind was ripped out of it, torn out of us."

"Bessemer."

A slight nod twitched her neck.

Was this what Graeson meant when he said the pack would be otherwise occupied? A second, gut-rending thought popped into my head. Had he known this was coming and planned for it?

He was Graeson. Of course he had. And, in typical Graeson fashion, he had decided my time was better spent tracking Charybdis and had faced Bessemer alone, without giving me the choice to stand by him. The damn stubborn man was going to get himself killed one of these days. If he hadn't already.

"Is she all right?" Thierry's voice came from over my shoulder.

"No." Dell was a hot mess, her thoughts a frantic blur. "But she will be."

"Tell me what I can do to help."

"Nothing." I straightened. "I have to get her home. She needs her pack to recover from this."

Thierry absorbed the news with a nod. "Did you learn anything back there?"

I hesitated. "I'm not sure."

"Think on it, and let me know. Here." She returned the plastic bag to me. "These are Ayer's belongings. It's the clothes she showed up in and the contents of her purse."

New respect zipped through me when I looked to Mai, who leaned against her door, foot tapping. She was one sly fox. "I'll sort through this and let you know what I find."

"Pop it in a mailer when you're done," Mai called. "I'll smuggle it back in before anyone notices it's gone."

"Will do." Turning to Thierry, I yanked her in for a quick hug that took us both by surprise. "Thank you. For everything."

Magic zinged across my tongue, sealing the favor I owed her.

Her eyes widened at the knowledge I had granted her a boon. "You're welcome."

"Guys, we need to roll out." Mai checked her phone's display. "Tee and I have an appointment in a half hour. We need to be on time to maintain our cover."

"Touch base with me when you can." Thierry backed toward Mai. "I hope your friend recovers quickly."

"Me too," I said, hands shaking as I fumbled for the keys. "Me too."

CHAPTER TWELVE

Hauling a semiconscious warg through airport checkpoints was an exercise in frustration. The smart thing to do would have been to drive straight to Georgia, but I wasn't sure Dell had that kind of time, and Graeson... I was trying hard not to think about what this meant for him.

Hair tangled and skin waxy, Dell resembled a flu victim in full bloom who'd been creamed by a bus on her way through the parking lot. Getting on the plane turned out to be the easy part. Keeping our seats was harder. Polite to a fault, our flight attendant suggested we might want to disembark and exchange our tickets for ones later in the day.

Teeth clamped together, I insisted Dell was fine, that nerves were to blame. I even smiled when she brought Dell a chilly mimosa, while wearing a white mask that covered the lower half of her face, and downed it once her back turned. It was early for alcohol, the sun was just thinking about rising, but I figured there was orange juice in the mix, and that counted as breakfast.

Graeson, who I suspected might fresh squeeze his own OJ, would have been properly horrified by the use of concentrate and the general lack of bacon.

Once Texas dropped beneath our feet, I shot a quick text to Isaac. It went unanswered, of course, but he was waiting in the lobby when we landed. He took one look at Dell, set his jaw and gathered her in his arms. She curled against his chest, and he opted to ride in the backseat of his crew cab truck with her tucked in his arms while I drove us back to Villanow.

The first thing I noticed when I pulled into the clearing was Aunt Dot pacing inside the wards that extended to the front yard. When she spotted us, she clasped her hands and ran for us.

"Isaac said that sweet little Dell isn't feeling well." She hauled me out of the cab and into her arms. "Is she okay? Are you all right? What can I do? Do you need anything?"

"I'm fine, and Dell will be too." I gave her a squeeze. "We have to get her home. Her family will know what to do about this."

"I'm coming with you." Isaac joined us on the grass, leaving Dell curled on the seat. "I don't want you out there alone."

A second's hesitation made me wonder if his was general paranoia or if something had happened while I was gone. There would be time for questions later. Right now I had to focus on locating Graeson's house. A sinking feeling in my gut made me doubt it would be so easy as to find him there waiting for me. He had neighbors, though, and they would know how to get Dell to her meemaw's house.

"I'm coming too." Aunt Dot rolled up the sleeves of her floral-print blouse. "Something happened last night that made those wolves go nuts. They were barking and yapping and howling all night long."

"Graeson said there was a gathering." Implied it more like. "That must be what caused the ruckus."

"Not another word, missy." She pointed a finger at me. "I'm old, not senile, and I will sit you in the corner until you're my age if you try and lie to me."

I ducked my head. "Yes, ma'am."

"I've got her." Isaac had scooped up Dell while Aunt Dot dressed me down. "Let's get moving."

I set out in the general direction where Graeson had taken me, wishing I had a warg's keen sense of smell to help me navigate the woods. Trails forked off the main one, and I had no idea if I was leading my family toward Silverback Lane or on a wild-goose chase.

Until we turned a bend and found ourselves staring at four silver bullet-shaped trailers all huddled in a tight circle.

"We don't have time for this." Isaac shifted Dell in his arms. "I can't hold her forever."

Dell was lean and muscular and leggy, which meant she was also heavy. Unconscious, she was dead weight.

"She's a donor." Isaac speared me with a glare. "Take her blood and tap into that bond you mentioned."

"The bond shattered." I glared right back. "That's what's causing this."

Aunt Dot rested a hand on my shoulder. "Can you reach her through the blood connection?"

"Yes. Sort of." I rubbed my face. "It's confusing. It's quieter and not as strong without Graeson."

"Give it a try," she urged. "Otherwise we'll have to put her inside and wander around until we find someone willing to help."

The idea of bumping into Imogen or Aisha curdled my gut. All I needed was another fight on my hands while Graeson was nowhere to be found.

"I'm sorry, Dell." I took her hand and pierced her with my spur. Pelt sprouted almost the instant her taste registered in the back of my throat. The mental connection hummed between us, a familiar, unlit path I tread carefully. *Can you hear me?*

"Cam?" Her body jerked hard once. *"I want to go home."*

"We're trying to get you there, but I got us lost. Can you help?"

More fevered judders as her mind rose to wakefulness. *"Follow the pictures."*

Before I could ask what she meant, a barrage of images flooded my mind. Each shot leapt several yards forward like an album being flipped. The knowledge settled, and I lined up the first shot with the trees ringing the clearing.

Facing straight ahead, I waved my family on. "I've got it."

Walking while two images superimposed one another kept me stumbling. The difference in our heights meant the mental pictures taken from her perspective were off just enough to make coordinating my feet and thoughts almost impossible.

Silverback Lane came into view at long last, and I blinked away the tumble of snippets Dell had shared with me. Vision cleared, I found myself standing in front of an ancient cabin covered with moss. The structure sagged and leaned to one side, but the path was well tended and the scent of baking bread made my mouth water.

"You shouldn't be here. The alpha has ordered everyone indoors until Cord is apprehended."

I whirled toward the creaking voice, the sound like unoiled hinges protesting, and found myself squaring off with a woman who might have topped four feet on a good day. This was not a good day. She appeared shrunken over the shaft of her walking stick, her skin layered in heavy wrinkles, her eyes all but lost to the folds of tanned skin.

"I had to get Dell home." Behind her, Isaac and Aunt Dot waited for my cue. "She's not well." I tracked the short woman's progress as she circled me. "Is this it? Are you Meemaw?"

"Who else would I be?" She fluffed her wire-hard gray hair. "Don't you see the family resemblance?"

"Yes," I lied with a straight face. "I do."

"Poor child is a fool." She squinted up at me. "I see why she enjoys keeping your company. You've a like temperament." She jabbed me with a wizened finger. "Cord has lost his mind, girl. Were I you, I wouldn't want to be in these woods when he catches your scent."

My pulse stuttered. "Where is he?"

"I haven't seen him since the bonfire last night. Bessemer reached into his head and—" she mimed snapping a stick, "—broke him. He's not himself. He's not a man at all. He's all wolf." The layers of cloth in her skirt rustled when she stepped forward. "Haden had just brought his mother to visit me when the bond recoiled. He hit my floor convulsing and screaming the name *Ellis*."

Haden. I skimmed the surface of my memory for why his name sounded familiar. Of course. He was one of Graeson's six. I'd met him at the bait shop turned base camp. He was the warg who'd griped when I claimed a bucket of fried chicken for Dell.

Meemaw's account of Haden's collapse mirrored Thierry's version of Dell's reaction to the bond severing.

"The woman with Dell when she collapsed said she cried out for me too." I rubbed my arms. "She doesn't call me Ellis. Only one person does."

"They were still acting as conduits." Her knuckles whitened as her fingers clamped her rough-hewn walking stick. "It was Cord's final thoughts blasting through their minds and out their mouths. It was Cord who thought of you as Bessemer ripped his mind apart. It was Cord who was desperate to get to you, to protect you. And that means it's you the wolf is frothing at the mouth to find." Pity touched her gaze. "All the wolf knows is the want of you. Not the why."

"What about the others?" I rasped. "How are they?"

"They'll recover in a few days, but they won't open their heads for a long time yet. Minds are tender meat before the jaws of a slavering wolf."

The slavering wolf being Bessemer.

"Your family is safe here. With me." Meemaw at last went to her granddaughter and smoothed a gnarled hand over her hair. "My sweet child." To me, she said, "You've done her a world of good. You've given her purpose, hope. She wouldn't forgive me if I let you get caught."

"Purpose?" So far it seemed all I'd done was get her into trouble.

"She has you fooled too." A rusty chuckle moved through her. "Good."

Pitched high and loud, a soul-rending howl rolled through the forest.

Meemaw's amusement fled, and she paled beneath her tan. "Run," she barked at me. *"Run."*

I stumbled back. "I can't leave my family."

"I can protect them." She waved her stick at me. "You have my word, it's not them he wants."

Another throaty call, this one closer, the plaintive song raising chills down my arms.

She ushered an overburdened Isaac and a protesting Aunt Dot inside before pleading with me, "Go. Run. *Now.*"

My feet knew what to do without being told. I flew down the path, flipping those mental pictures in reverse to get me home again. I left Silverback Lane in the dust. The urge to glance back was a twitch in my neck, but I kept my eyes forward and my legs pumping hard.

Imogen stepped casually into my path, unconcerned to find me barreling toward her. I altered course to run past, but she flung out her arms, corralling me on the trail. I slammed into her and bounced off, hitting my shoulder on a tree trunk.

"What are you doing?" I panted, rubbing the tender spot. "Get out of my way."

"Sorry, shug, not happening." Her lips peeled back to reveal gleaming white teeth. "Cord's wolf has gone haywire. No one can reach him, not even the alpha."

"And your first thought when realizing a rabid wolf was prowling the woods was to take a walk?"

"No." Her razor laughter sliced at me. "My first thought was how grateful I was he brought you here and how perfect life will be when you're gone."

Fear curdled my gut. "You're hoping if we stand here long enough he'll catch up and maul me."

Didn't she get it? If Graeson had truly lost his mind, she would be next.

"No wonder you work for the conclave with smarts like those." She blocked my feint to the left, and I gasped as pain radiated through my shoulder. "You're his chosen mate. This should thrill you. Your sacrifice will be the making of him."

She was off her rocker. "If he kills me in a blind rage, he'll never forgive himself."

"He'll never trust his wolf again." Delight sparkled in her eyes. "Finally, after all these years, the pissing match with Bessemer will end. Cord will accept his position and settle down."

"You want him broken." A thready rumble pumped through my chest. "Why did you make that deal with him if this was what you wanted?"

"I made that deal, because having children raises my status in the pack. Having them with a beta? That puts me second only to Aisha, and she's childless." A curious expression twisted her features. "You really care, don't you? I thought..." She laughed. "I don't know what I thought. That you're fae, and fae always have an agenda, but not you."

"I won't let you do this to him." Graeson had enough demons riding him. I wasn't letting this she-devil she-wolf climb aboard too. "He deserves better than this, better than you."

Muscles tensed, I lunged for her, ramming my good shoulder into her chest, crying out when agony radiated across my upper back. My spur emerged, and I raked it down her jugular. She gurgled and staggered back, clutching the raw meat of her throat. Blood oozed through her fingers as I gaped at her.

This was not right. Something was wrong. A spur didn't cause that kind of damage. Her hand slipped, and I saw them.

Claw marks.

Numb, I glanced at my hands. Silver-white fur covered my arms and tickled my nape, the magic climbing higher than ever. Crimson stained the fingers of my right hand. The taste of her blood tightened my throat a beat later.

Recalled magic, it must be. But how? One practice session did not a master make.

Another howl rent the air, this time in a different direction. Gods have mercy. He was circling us.

"Don't...go," Imogen wheezed, dropping to one knee. "He'll...kill...me when he...smells your blood..."

Rubbing the heels of my palms into my eyes, I struggled to find the images Dell had loaned me. They were my memories now, but fear kept them blurry and out of focus. No use. I reached for the source and smashed into a barrier.

"Dell." I chanted her name over and over in my head. *"Are you there?"*

A trickle of light glimmered behind my eyes, and I felt Dell's arrival. *"I'm here."*

Relief made me giddy. *"Give me directions to Graeson's tree house."*

Another stack of pictures cascaded through my mind, and I overlaid those where this path crossed that one.

"Get up." I hauled Imogen to her feet. She wobbled and leaned against me. "Come on. We have to get moving."

Hooking her arm around my shoulders, I tightened my grip around her back and hauled her down the trail ghosting my vision. Warg strength suffused my limbs, not enough to pick her up and carry her, but enough I managed to half-drag, half-hobble with her to the platform where Graeson had bared his soul to me.

At the base of the tree, I gripped the first wooden slat and groaned. "This is impossible." Imogen was healing, but she needed to keep pressure on the wound. She couldn't do that and climb, and neither could I. "Take off your shirt."

Too weak to comply, she turned wide eyes on me. I sighed and cut through the fabric with a claw. Once off her body, I tore the shirt into one long strip, knocked her hand aside and bound her throat. She cried out in pain, and the noise tapered into a growl. A deep, rumbling sound that didn't vibrate her throat.

Because it came from behind us.

I glanced over my shoulder, and my knees turned to water. The silver wolf taking his time approaching us was covered in blood. His muzzle dripped with it and his paws were splashed with it, the kill was so recent.

Please let that be from a bunny.

"Climb." I knotted the shirt around Imogen's throat and shoved her behind me. "Get as high as you can."

"What about you?" She didn't wait for my answer.

"I'm just waiting on you," I snapped. *"Move."*

Trembling as she climbed, Imogen wasn't going fast enough. She was tipsy from the blood loss, and fear clouded her like rank perfume. I breathed it in over my tongue and wanted to spit out the taste. Graeson, though, smelled of the woods, of coppery wildness that made my stomach taut with hunger for a taste of the freedom he experienced on four legs.

He lifted his head and sucked in air until his sides rounded.

"Camille." Imogen grunted. "Hurry."

I risked a glance behind me and spotted Imogen high enough I could start climbing. Pulse thrumming in my ears, I waited seconds longer. I needed more room, or all the wolf had to do was jump up and latch on to my leg to haul me down to the ground under him.

Movement from the wolf snagged my attention. He sauntered closer, head cocked at an angle as he watched Imogen climb as though confused about why prey would do such a thing. I checked Imogen's progress and all but crossed my fingers the wargish limbs would help me scuttle up to the platform.

"Graeson." The mental touch slid off his mind like water off a duck's back. There would be no reasoning with him when he was like this.

Heart a wild thing fluttering in my chest, I spun and grasped the first rung. I made it up three before teeth closed over my ankle. I blessed my leather boot, fisted the wooden slats and kicked out with my other foot. Graeson whined and hit the ground. The precious seconds it took me to establish a new foothold was all he needed. He leapt again, and his teeth pierced my lower calf and ripped. I kicked him off a second time but barely, his fangs shredding meat as he fell.

"Hold on." Imogen reached down for me. "Take my hand."

I flung my arm up, and our wrists clasped. My ruined foot found purchase, and I hauled myself up higher. The wolf below me howled with rage. The tension in my chest released a fraction. I'd made it. I was higher than he could reach. I could take my time and—

Steel jaws clamped over my heel and hung on tight. At once Imogen and I supported our weight...and the couple hundred pounds of snarling adult male warg dangling from my foot. Together we held our position. His grip slipping, Graeson began swinging his body and shredding my boot through to my flesh. The taste of blood incited him, and he struggled with renewed vigor. Warm moisture plinked onto my cheeks. The strain was ripping open Imogen's wounds.

"You have to let me go." I heaved a sharp breath. "I can't hold on."

"Camille." Her hand clamped down over mine.

"You wanted this, remember?" I let my hand go slack. "Save yourself."

Her expression twisted, a decision being made. "No."

A moment of clarity cooled my fevered thoughts. She was too weak. She couldn't save me. I was too far gone to rescue myself. All she could do was fall with me, and what was the point in both of us dying?

Breaking her grip was easy. I twisted my wrist, and Graeson's weight did the rest.

The wolf dropped like a stone, and I tumbled after him, landing on my back so hard I lost my breath. Catlike, he landed on his feet and limped a circle around me.

"Camille," Imogen called.

I didn't dare respond, not with the wild-eyed beast so close to my head. I lay there in the grass, in the same spot where Graeson had shared his secrets with me, and knew that if he did this, if he killed me, I would be the last to ever be fed those morsels of his soul. The death of an innocent, *my* death, would break the man who had teetered on the edge of the abyss. The wolf, though, seemed to have no such reservations.

I was prey, naughty prey who ran from him, prey who—Graeson once said—smelled like I belonged to him.

Having never specifically asked if the wolf was a separate entity or merely a facet of Graeson's personality, I wasn't counting on the man's views to sway the beast.

Tense seconds passed while Graeson sniffed, first my hair and then across my soft belly. My gut knotted as his muzzle nudged my shirt up above my navel, and he breathed in the scent of my skin. The pelt on my arms delighted him, and he rubbed his face against my fur. Satisfied with that, he continued his inspection until his nose brushed the mangled flesh of my calf. He lapped at the warm blood spilling out, and a low whine surged in the back of his throat.

I didn't breathe until his sharp teeth were out of biting range.

Head lowered, he sat on the ground beside me, as though pondering what he ought to do with me now that he'd caught me.

I hoped that decision involved not being eaten.

Seeming to come to some conclusion, he lowered his belly to the grass, rested his head on his front legs and simply stared at me.

With no place to go, I released the magic stinging my arms. It was half gone already, and holding on to it only made me weaker. I could steal a drop from Graeson if I had to shift again. His blood was more potent than Imogen's, and I needed every advantage if he came at me with teeth bared.

An eternity later, my eyelids began to flutter. Too much magic spent, too much blood lost.

The solemn eyes of a wolf locked with mine, and then there was darkness.

CHAPTER THIRTEEN

My bladder woke me. More to the point, the leaden wolf's head pressing down on the swollen organ woke me. I came awake to find the promise of midday had burned off to twilight. The radiating pain in my calf slammed into me a second later, and a gasp punched past my lips.

I had a choice to make. Risk the wolf's wrath and find a toilet, or lay there and let nature take its course. I made up my mind not to die in wet jeans, and the rest went easier from there.

Palms braced on the ground, I levered myself up into a sitting position. Graeson eyed me and slid his head lower, until his chin rested on my thigh.

"Oh thank God." A voice drifted down to me. "You're alive."

"For now." I tested my injured leg, and stars exploded behind my eyes. "Let's see how long it lasts."

"Your family is nearby." Imogen peered over the platform's edge. "Cord wouldn't let them anywhere near you."

A flutter of panic that they might be close enough for him to take notice winged through me. "I'm going home."

"Are you sure that's smart?" Her tone screamed I was suicidal. "You're injured, and he's..."

"I don't have much choice. I'm not staying out here forever, and he seems calm enough now." My fingers curled into my palms, the urge to stroke his fur and find some shred of Graeson lingering in his eyes overwhelming. "Tell my family to stay with Meemaw tonight."

Rude as it was to presume she had room for guests, I would use Dell as leverage mercilessly. I had brought her little girl home, and Meemaw would grant me this favor in kind. None of the wargs would want to see Graeson harmed on my account, and the good ones wouldn't want him to wake from his fugue with my blood on his teeth.

"Okay." She bobbed her head. "Are you sure you don't want to wait for Bessemer?"

"No." A snarl laced my voice and perked Graeson's ears. I'd had about all I could take of the alpha's interference. "I'm good."

That Bessemer hadn't put in an appearance all these hours later made it clear to me that his hopes aligned with Imogen's. He wanted me gone, and he wanted his beta cowed. Two birds, one stone.

I planted my boots and tested my weight on them. The wolf sat up to see what all the fuss was about, but seemed more curious than anything. Pushing to my feet in slow motion, I gave him plenty of time to protest. He sat there until I managed to stand, and when I wobbled, he darted next to me. I leaned on him with a grimace, afraid I'd draw back a bloody nub, but the madness that had seized him seemed to have abated now that he had a captive audience of one.

I waved at Imogen, hoping it wasn't a true farewell, and found her eyes as round as saucers.

Graeson hadn't killed or maimed me...much. Clearly that shocked her.

That made two of us.

Together the wolf and I picked our way back to the trailers. The homestead was as we'd left it. The driver's-side doors on Isaac's truck still stood open, and a basket of laundry had exploded over the ground. Aunt Dot must have dropped it when we peeled into the clearing.

I grabbed the plastic bag Mai had smuggled from Edelweiss, shut the doors and locked the truck. My leg wasn't up to gathering the clothes. Those would have to wait until tomorrow.

At my home, three tiny speckled eggs nestled inside a handful of grass on the highest step. A sweeping sense of déjà vu rocked me back on my heels. They were partridge eggs. I recognized them, because Lori and I had found a nest in the grass one summer while on vacation. Dad had given us a book to help us identify the species, which I did after Lori had given up on skimming. As a treat, he took two of the delicate eggs, thanked the nest for providing for us, and boiled them to go with our dinner.

This was the third item to show up on my steps that directly linked to me, to my family, to my past and my memories.

Cold rage ignited in my gut. There was only one reasonable explanation for it, and it made me sick. Bessemer had sifted through Graeson's memories. The alpha knew secrets I had only ever told Graeson. But what if a side effect of joining the bond was leaving mental residue behind? I had never told Graeson about the eggs or the scrunchie or the shampoo, but had Bessemer gleaned those from the bond some other way? And what about the rabbit? Had he known Lori and I kept one as a pet? Or had Aisha truly used it as a lure?

Half afraid that if I stopped now I might not get moving again, I stepped over the nest and into my home. No, I realized. That wasn't entirely true. I was just afraid I might spin on my heel and hunt down the alpha to bend his ear for a while, something neither Graeson nor I were fit to do at the moment. Grilling the alpha would have to wait, preferably for when I could stand with the beta at my back.

The wolf followed me without complaint, which I took as a good sign. I dropped the bag on the kitchenette table and limped into the bathroom, where my attempt to shut out the wolf for privacy was met with a rolling bass rumble of threat.

Heaving a sigh, I left the door open and handled business. While I was sitting, I untied my boots and kicked them into the corner. My pants were already halfway off, so I peeled those down my legs gingerly. This interested Graeson enough that he entered the bathroom with me, cramping the small room with his size while he inspected my leg. When he retreated, I tried to shut the door so I could strip for a shower. He was having none of it, hackles rising when I cut off his eye contact with me.

Defeated, I pulled my shirt over my head and started the shower. He allowed this and flopped down in the doorway, head on paws. A bra and panties were all that preserved my modesty as I stepped into the tiny glass enclosure. The bloodstained ensemble reminded me of Graeson's earlier bikini comment, and I blushed. I got the distinct feeling he wasn't home, but I wasn't taking any chances. Wargs were blasé about nudity, but I wasn't that kind of shifter.

The heat from the water relaxed my tense muscles and washed away the blood caking my leg. It lubricated my inhibitions too. Soggy and tired, I wanted to feel clean and safe again. Graeson's dozing posture made stepping out of my underwear that much easier. My bra landed in the basin with a *splat*, and my panties followed. While I was bent over, I braced myself and inspected my calf. The cocktail of warg blood had done me good. The raw edges were knitting together much faster than they would have otherwise.

Not until my teeth began chattering did I realize I had used up all the hot water. Packed into the tight stall, I dried off then made the short grab for gauze from my medicine cabinet. The one good thing about the size of my bathroom was pretty much everything was within reach of everything else.

After slathering my leg with antibiotic ointment and binding it in gauze, I wriggled into pajamas, skirted the wolf and hobbled into the kitchen in search of food. The uncertain temperament of my houseguest meant I couldn't afford not to eat. I had to replenish what the shifts had cost me in case I had to sprout claws in order to defend myself against the guilty-looking wolf drifting shadowlike in my wake.

"I have a frozen pizza, some of those microwave pocket things and an unmarked container, contents unknown," I told the wolf, wishing I could turn back time and ask Isaac for steaks or roasts or whole chickens instead of a few staples. "Let's try the fridge."

A carton of eggs, an unopened pack of bacon and a container holding biscuits I knew must be homemade because of their size and shape.

"You sneak." I glanced over the door at him. "You left groceries at my house."

The wolf flicked his ears.

"I can do breakfast. Nothing fancy," I amended before he got excited, "but it'll get the job done."

First I cracked open a bottle of ibuprofen and tossed back a handful. I washed them down with the half glass of remaining orange juice then set about hard scrambling eggs and microwaving bacon.

Graeson sat there watching the whole production. The man might have judged my dry eggs or slightly burnt bacon edges, but the wolf made whiney-growly sounds of encouragement.

A muffled ringing noise sent me dragging into the bathroom to dig out my cell. "Ellis."

"Where are you?" Aunt Dot snapped. "They won't let us leave. They said that Cord—"

"I'm at home, resting." I cut her off before she got too worked up. "Graeson is with me."

"He's with you?" she shrilled. "They said he was trying to kill you."

I flinched. "Um, about that..."

"Tell them to let us go," Isaac boomed in the background. "We can't just sit here while some crazy wolfman is stalking you."

Had I expected the captives to be happy? No. Had I expected them to try and break free the second Meemaw turned her back on them? Honestly...yes. But I hoped the fact I had requested they stay put, which proved I was indeed still alive to make such requests, might sway them.

Apparently I hadn't hoped hard enough.

Exhaustion plagued me. "Put Meemaw on the phone."

"Camille," she cackled. "I'd ask how you are, but if you're giving your family hell, then I imagine you're just fine. How's Cord? Did you kill him?"

"No." My heart thumped once, painfully. "He's right here. We're about to eat dinner."

She clicked her tongue. "Hasn't anyone ever warned you against feeding wild animals?"

"Dad did once." I hadn't meant to answer her rhetorical question, but my brain was mush and the words fell out of my mouth. "He wanted me to stop feeding wild rabbits lettuce from my taco bowls."

That's how I'd ended up taming Bunnicula, who Lori named after our favorite hand-me-down book at the time.

"You'll never get rid of Cord now." Another staticky burst of laughter. "You'll tame him right proper."

"Tame I can work with," I assured her. "Tame means I can swat his nose with a rolled-up newspaper if he tries to eat me again."

"If he was going to kill you, he would have by now." She sounded confident. "Crazed as he was, I thought for sure...but here you are. He must truly love you."

The word—the weight—of *love* made my skin simultaneously crawl and tingle. "Or he remembered that he'd stashed bacon in my fridge and needed me alive if he ever wanted it back." If she knew him at all, then she understood how seriously he took his breakfast meats.

"You've both made your choices," she chided. "There's no use in playing coy with me."

"Coy is one thing I'm not." I glanced at the wolf and found his head cocked in a way that made me question how good warg hearing was exactly. "It's just that he was much less furry when I decided to fight for him."

Even now the thought of losing him, through his wolf or the selection, squeezed my heart until it ached.

"The wolf is part of him," she said kindly. "The man will return. He must for them to remain in harmony. Loving you... It's a good thing. It will help him find his way back." Hostile murmurs erupted in the background, and she raised her voice. "So you're rescinding your order for your family to stay here tonight? Do you think that's wise?"

"It wasn't an order." I flushed. "It was a favor I didn't have time to ask."

Meemaw seemed tickled to be holding my feet to the flame. "As you say." A contented sigh. "I'll send them on then."

"Is it safe for them to travel alone?"

"Yes." She didn't hesitate. "You made it safe for them."

"Okay." I rubbed my forehead. "I appreciate this."

"Go eat, rest." A rustling noise came on the line. "I'll send Dell to you tomorrow if not the next day."

"I'd like that." Heat stung my nape. "I didn't think to ask—is she doing better?"

"Yes. She's a stout one." Meemaw's voice hummed with pride. "Here's your cousin."

A cold edge seeped into his tone. "We're on our way."

"Stay away from my house," I warned him. "Go home and lock up. Graeson seems settled, but I'm not willing to bet your life on it."

"I'll keep my phone on me." A pause. "If he sniffs you the wrong way and I'm there to see it, I'll put him down."

"That won't be necessary." I hoped. "Good night, Isaac."

The call ended, and as though it had encased me in a bubble, once it burst, the scents of burning food rushed to me.

"Oh crap." I popped open the microwave. The bacon was burnt down the middle. I checked the frying pan. The eggs were a harder scramble than I'd ever made, but they weren't black, so I plated them. "Sorry about this, big guy. I'm usually not this scatterbrained."

But usually I hadn't been chased through the woods by a warg out for blood either.

I set his plate on the floor, and he inhaled his portion. I carried mine to the table and shoveled food in with one hand. The other crinkled the plastic bag Mai had stolen while searching for clues.

Clothes. Belt. The hard ridge in the bottom corner told me her badge was in the mix too. Socks. A bag or purse. Papers. All that was missing were her shoes, assuming she had been wearing any.

My fork scraped the dish. Empty. A quick check showed me the wolf had cleaned his plate too. His forlorn stare at its pitiful state almost made me laugh. I cleared the spot in front of me and ripped the tab to open the mailer. The smell hit me first, and I gagged on my meal.

Escaping the booth, I retrieved a pair of latex cleaning gloves from under the cabinet and snapped them on before bringing the bag to the sink. I dumped the contents in the dry basin and recognition clicked. This outfit matched the one Ayer had worn in the surveillance video. No wonder they reeked. She hadn't changed clothes between the time the footage was recorded and when she showed up at Edelweiss two weeks later.

I patted down the grimy pants, liberating a handful of receipts from gas stations and fast food joints from the pockets. Those I put in a pile on the counter. Armpit stains and a few crusted drops of brownish-red fluid were all the shirt had to offer. The light jacket held more receipts, some cash and a brochure for a new indoor shooting range. I set those aside too. The belt surrendered no clues, and the socks had holes in them.

Before I got ahead of myself, I retrieved my phone and began snapping pictures. All this evidence had to be returned to Mai, and I wanted reference material before that happened. I spread the clothes out on the floor, shooing the wolf away before he contaminated the evidence, but he was not to be shooed.

The threatening vibrations rising up his throat gave me pause. Maybe letting him supervise wasn't the best idea I'd ever had. He pressed his nose hard against the shirt and blasted an exhale through his nose. He stared up at me, eyes dark with a message I was unable to decipher. Before I could stop him, he hiked his leg and hosed the garment.

Satisfied with his work, he plopped back down on the floor, belly on the laminate, head resting on his paws.

"What—?" I gaped at him. "Why—?"

The only piece of clothing not soaked in urine was a single sock.

"You are a bad, bad wolf," I scolded him.

Nose wrinkling at the smell, I cataloged each item front and back. I even turned the socks inside out and searched for clues in the nap. All that got re-bagged and sealed up to help the stench dissipate.

Mai was not going to thank me for this.

The receipts were thankfully higher than his leg height. At this point my calf hurt too much to keep standing, so I scooped them off the counter and deposited them on the table. Those proved much more interesting. I grabbed my laptop and started mapping them by date and location. The path led straight from Wink, Texas to Butler, Tennessee and back.

Butler. That sounded familiar. I made a note then carried on documenting the crinkled slips of paper through photos and an expense list I broke into columns by fuel, food or other.

Finished with that task, I stuffed them back into the damp pants and sealed the bag for good. Isaac could do the honors and drop it off at the post office for me tomorrow.

My gloves came off with a snap of latex, and I tossed those in the trash. Old habits die hard, so I uploaded the pictures to my laptop then emailed a copy of them to myself at a generic address and then forwarded a set to Thierry. I wanted backups in case the evidence—or Ayer—went missing a second time.

With that done, I sat at the table and tapped my pencil while debating sleeping arrangements. The door to my bedroom was shut, but I had no doubt where the wolf intended to bed down for the night. The thing was, with Graeson mentally MIA, I wasn't sure how much I trusted the wolf beside me.

Swallowing a yawn, I pushed to my feet and headed for the bedroom. As expected, the wolf shot past me and leapt for the middle of the bed. I stood there, considering folding out the kitchenette booths into their twin-bed configuration. My calf twinged at the thought, but I grabbed a pillow and comforter then returned to the kitchen.

Ears perked, Graeson barked.

"Forget it." I grimaced. "You're not the boss of me."

He bounced on the mattress and barked again.

"No."

Bark. Bark. Bark.

"Bad wolf."

Paws hit the floor with a powerful thump that shook the trailer, and claws skittered. He bumped into the bend of my knee, and I landed half on top of him. He took my pillow between his teeth and yanked it from under my butt. Once he deposited it near the foot of the bed, he came back for the comforter.

"Graeson," I groaned. "Stop that. I'm not playing tug-of-war with you."

Except I was. He threw all his strength into pulling it out from under me, but my weight was enough to keep it pinned. He growled playfully and tossed his head, tail wagging.

"You're warped."

He didn't disagree.

Shifting to the left, I slid far enough over that he could free his prize. Mouth full of fabric, he jumped on the bed, spat out the comforter and nested in it while shooting me a look that said clearly, *"What are you still doing down there? See how comfy this nice bed is? There's plenty of room for both of us."*

Aware I was taking orders from a lanky dog with big teeth, I crawled into bed and let him curl around me. All that fur soon made me sticky with sweat, but Graeson wouldn't budge. Once he started snoring, I caved to temptation and began stroking his velvety-soft inner ears.

"I know you're in there," I said, thinking of the man hiding deep beneath the wolf's skin. "You can't hide forever. You won't heal until you come out and face this." I shut my eyes. "I can't do this without you."

The wolf smacked his lips, and warm drool permeated my shirt.

"Good talk," I murmured, eyes closing. "I'm glad we had this conversation.

CHAPTER FOURTEEN

The next morning Dell arrived on my doorstep bearing gifts. Meemaw must have been up at the crack of dawn to have baked three types of muffins then packed them on a tray with homemade jam and fresh local honey.

The rich scents perked my stomach and wiped the siren song of returning to my comfy bed from mind. "How are you feeling?"

"Better." The way she said it made me think *better* was relative. "Meemaw was smothering me. I had to get out of there. She allowed me to walk this far, but I can only stay for an hour before she sends the cavalry."

The muscle in my calf still pulled, but I could tell without checking it was mostly healed. "I'd invite you in but..."

"It's fine. He's got what he wants. He's not going to hurt me." Her confidence made me nervous. "Here. Can you take this?"

"Sure." I accepted the tray, the better to smell all the homemade deliciousness, and couldn't help but wish Graeson was here, on two legs, to enjoy the meal with us. This was so much better than the burnt offerings I'd scraped together for dinner.

The wolf sat in the kitchen, ears perked, eavesdropping. Well, maybe not eavesdropping exactly. "How much of what he hears does he understand?"

"It depends." She busied herself with a packet of butcher's paper resting on the corner of the tray. "It's an individual thing for us all, and in his current condition I couldn't say for sure."

"Mmm-hmm." Knowing how Dell always had his back, I figured it was more likely she didn't want to rat him out.

Happy to avoid my gaze, Dell balled up the paper and stacked four meaty discs in her palm. Confident in their bond as always, she stuck her head through the door and whistled.

Graeson's ears perked, and he trotted over to investigate, leaning his weight against my leg until I was knocked against the doorframe.

"Lookie what I've got." Dell wiggled one thick slice. "Mmm. Slabs of country ham fresh from the smoker with your name written all over them." She twisted and hurled it Frisbee-style into the yard. "Fetch, boy."

The wolf pranced in place, toenails clicking.

"Oh no." Dell peeled off a second piece and hurled it in a different direction. "All that poor, delicious meat. So alone and uneaten. If only there was a hungry wolf nearby."

Whining as he peered up at me, Graeson all but begged me to go with him.

"You're a grown wolf," I told him. "You can go get your own ham."

The third piece flew, and he restrained himself with a whimper. The fourth slice, though, proved to be too much of a temptation. He was airborne in a blink, sailing over the steps in a single leap, snapping his jaws closed on the ham before it hit the ground.

While he walked the yard collecting his treats and then watering the grass, I ushered Dell inside. I settled her at the table then grabbed glasses and milk from the fridge. We ate in companionable silence, breakfast a quiet race to eat all I wanted before she devoured the rest.

"So, let's talk about Edelweiss." Plate cleaned, Dell leaned back. "The last thing I remember is pacing the road after you left. Did you see Ayer? Did she give you anything good?"

"Honestly?" I recalled her catatonic state. "I'm not sure."

I woke my laptop, which had made the trip into the kitchen with me first thing so I could check for email from Thierry—none yet—and showed her the pictures I'd taken.

"What's with that weird yellow staining?" She squinted. "It looks like when a guy tries to write his name in urine in the snow." Her eyes flicked over to me. "What? Guys out here are the reason people need warnings like *don't eat the yellow snow.*" She dipped her finger in a small pot of raspberry preserves and licked her finger. "I hope she wasn't wearing that shirt when it happened."

"Um, no." My cheeks heated. "That would be my assistant's fault."

"*Cord* did that?" Her mouth fell open. "Eww."

"My thoughts exactly." Eyeballing the squishy package, I couldn't wait to get it out of my house. "I'm glad someone else gets to explain that to Ayer when she checks out and they reissue her belongings."

Her head cocked to one side, Dell waited for me to explain what I meant, and I did. I filled in all the blanks from the time I left her on the roadside with Thierry until when Isaac, Aunt Dot and I delivered her to Meemaw. I glossed over the confrontation in the woods with Imogen, or tried to, but Dell coaxed each tidbit out of me in excruciating detail.

"Wow. You actually did it." She eyed me with newfound respect. "I heard you wiped the forest with Imogen, but it seemed so insane. A rabid wolf is chasing you, and you stop for a challenge? Really? Who does that?"

A tingle of apprehension coasted down my spine. "Who did you hear it from?"

She snorted. "Everyone."

"I didn't think anyone else saw." I had been willing to bet we were alone but for the wolf at the time. "They saw it all and didn't think to help?"

"No one can interfere with a challenge." Dell swirled the contents of her glass. "And no one in their right mind would step in front of a crazed wolf hunting for his mate. That's just asking to be murdered."

"What about Bessemer?" Imogen had sounded so sure he would help if we waited long enough.

"He made the rules." She shook her head. "He won't break them."

Eight words that validated my decision to walk home or die trying.

The telltale click-clack of claws announced Graeson's return. He took one look at us seated at the table and jumped onto the bench beside me, where he began sniffing our leftovers. Satisfied there were no ham discs hiding under the tray despite the scent from the crinkled butcher's paper, he gave a short bark at Dell.

The sound wasn't aggressive, exactly, but seemed to say *no ham, no Cam.*

"I think that's my cue." Her forehead creased, and she rubbed the space between her eyes. "I should be getting home."

I shoved the wolf out of the booth and walked Dell to the door. The nest from yesterday sat forgotten where I had left it, though Aunt Dot had cleaned up the rest of the yard. Half of a gray rock that had been split down its middle rested among the eggs.

Before I flipped it over with my toe, I knew what I would find. A geode. Its interior sparkled with purple crystals that reminded me of long, hot days with my family in the mountains. To this day I wasn't sure if they were only tourist bait or harvested locally. What did it matter? The two were indelibly linked in my mind, making this a fourth strike against whoever was leaving me these tokens.

"I'm going to smash it with a hammer." Lori eyed the *egg-sized rock in her palm. "I saw it on TV once."*

Cradling mine to my chest, I dared her with a scowl that would have sent Isaac and Theo running. "You're not smashing mine."

She bolted for the toolbox Dad kept in a low cabinet in our parents' bedroom.

Forbidden toolbox.

Forbidden room.

Her infractions piled higher and higher.

I had a bad feeling about this.

"I don't need your stupid rock." She stuck out her tongue. "Mine's bigger anyway."

Was it? I compared the two, and my heart sank. It was. Lori always got the best, the biggest, the shiniest. It wasn't fair. I hated being second best. We were sisters. She ought to share. She ought to be nice to me. But she was as mean to me as Theo was to Isaac.

Sometimes he and I wished we weren't Gemini, that we didn't have twins.

Ping. Ping. Ping.

Lori's rock split down the middle, and I gasped. Inside the rough and ugly stone was a treasure, a real live treasure. Purple crystals filled the inside and sparkled like a thousand whispered secrets.

She'd done it again. Lori broke the rules. Lori went where she shouldn't, did what she oughtn't, and still got rewarded. Instead of one rock she now had two, and both halves glittered with gems that a princess might wear on her fingers or her gown.

Envy burned cold in my heart. One day I would be the risk taker, and Lori would be the one left behind.

"—doing here?"

I blinked up at Dell, aware a question had been asked but unsure what it had been. "What?"

She frowned at the nest and the rock. "What's the deal with those?"

"I'm not sure." I scooped up the fistful of grass and its contents. "But I'm going to find out." A chill dappled my skin. "I wasn't sure the first time—the rabbit, remember?

Then the scrunchie." Which I had tossed in an empty plastic shoebox and left on the kitchen table. "I found the nest last night and the geode this morning. This isn't random. Someone is leaving them here."

"Do these mean anything to you?" She touched the geode's gleaming interior.

"They represent memories from my childhood." I turned the rock over with my finger. "My mother. My dad. My sister."

"It couldn't be bad, could it?" Her bare toes curled against the grass. "The wards protect you, right?"

That was the sticking point, wasn't it? "No one with ill intent could get close enough to reach the first step. Whatever this means, whoever is leaving the items, I don't think they want to hurt me." My brow puckered. "Which leaves the question of—what do they want? Why leave these items?" I checked the eggs, but there was nothing more to them. "I'll ask Isaac if he can set up surveillance." He kept his door locked during what he considered normal business hours except in case of emergency. Since I wasn't sure this qualified, I shot him a quick text with my concerns and my request. "I want to know what this is about, and if it's linked to the selection or something else."

The something else being Bessemer, but I needed hard evidence before calling out the alpha.

"I wish Cord was here." Her face scrunched. "I mean, really here. Not just wolf here."

"Me too," I admitted.

Dell's arms were around me, squishing me with her warg strength, before it registered she meant to hug me.

"I miss him." The admission left my throat tight. "I want him back."

I worried that his being furry was permanent. I'd never owned a pet, and I wouldn't own him, but he might as well be one if he never rose off four legs again.

"It will be all right." A big squeeze. "He'll come back to us. I know he will." She worried her bottom lip between her teeth. "I have to go before Meemaw comes after me with a switch in her hand." She darted toward the woods. "I'll be back later to train with you and Isaac. We'll talk more then."

Training. *Ugh.* The session with Isaac had helped. My attack on Imogen was proof of that. I'd recalled enough warg magic to rip out her throat. The adrenaline boost had been enough that I'd completed the most intricate change I'd ever made, notwithstanding my full transformation into Lori, of course.

"See you later," I called back, marveling that I was now the type of person who said such things and meant them, and returned my attention to the geode. It weighed heavy in my hand and on my mind.

A hard bump sent me bouncing off the doorframe as Graeson padded into the yard, and I dropped the nest and the eggs, which splattered. At first I thought he meant to follow Dell, and the tightness in my chest panicked me. I should want the wolf out of my house, shouldn't I? Being with his pack might help him heal in ways I couldn't.

I understand him better than they do.

It was a selfish thought, but I couldn't shake the rightness of the sentiment once it occurred to me.

The delicate tickle of the wards caressed me as I ventured out into the sun. Aunt Dot must have dialed up their strength in the wake of Graeson's rampage. Out here birds called. Bugs chirped. Leaves rustled. And the wolf made a slow pass, marking every major tree in the clearing before hesitating beside a clump of gnarled vines creating a jagged fence strung between two scrawny pines.

His snuffling noises drew me to him, curious what the wolf found so interesting. I slipped the geode into my pocket to add to my growing collection and followed. He glanced up and saw I had joined him, which he took as an invitation to enter the woods. I trailed after him as he wound around to the back of the brambles and entered through a narrow gap someone had hacked into the dried vines.

Graeson dipped his head to the ground then sneezed, scattering...wrappers? I shoved into the camouflaged hidey-hole and lifted one of the crinkly squares. Clear cellophane crimped on three sides with a ragged gap left in the bottom of the fourth.

"It's a sucker wrapper." I brought it to my nose and inhaled, the scent of artificial strawberries cloying.

Movement drew my attention toward a smudge of pink amid the shadowy greens.

A naked girl around the age of seven waved and started toward me. With a shrug to the wolf, I waved back. A few steps closer and her eyes shot wide as they bounced from me to Graeson. She squeaked and, in a burst of magic, her limbs flowed into the fluffiest, most darling puppy I had ever seen. Her pelt was the color of warm caramel, and one of her paws made it look as though she had stepped in a bucket of chocolate that dyed her front leg up to her elbow.

"Hey." The wild look in her eye had me scrambling toward her. "Wait."

The pup whirled and vanished in a burst of frenetic energy.

"I wonder what that was about" was my first thought. My second was that now I had an idea of where Isaac could point his security cameras. I shot him an update with a picture attached and the general direction.

Graeson kept his thoughts to himself but marked the area in case whoever was using it decided to come back. I knelt there, eyes stinging from the aroma, and peered through the crisscrossing vines into the clearing.

My trailer sat front and center.

Riffling through the wrappers at my knees, I shook off the creeping sensation that whoever had made this blind was hiding, watching as I tried to make sense their clues. As close as the shelter was to the edge of the woods, and my home, it made a perfect escape route after each delivery.

Questions pelted me like raindrops in a summer storm. Was this Bessemer's doing? Or Aisha's? Since they shared mental space, did it really matter? Did the wrappers indicate they had spent a significant amount of time here or simply that they had a sweet tooth?

More troubling was the possibility the girl was involved. She certainly seemed to be heading straight for the blind, and kids and candy went hand in hand. Would Bessemer stoop so low as to involve a child in his schemes? Or was she curious about the pack's newest member, wanted to get her first glimpse of a fae, and I was being paranoid?

I had no good answers to any of my conjecture.

Standing, I dodged the wet spots and returned to the safety of the wards and my home. No challengers had arrived to petition me today. Perhaps rumors of my death had been greatly exaggerated, and I would last another day or two in blissful quiet without having to rip or tear or shred my hosts.

I needed to touch base with Thierry. Leaving an email trail was damning enough even if those were more difficult to track. Tempting as it was to dial up the anonymous number I felt certain was Thierry's burner phone, I couldn't be sure it didn't belong to a friend of hers—or to Shaw—and adding phone logs into the mix would give someone looking in the right place a way to track her assistance to what some might consider a rogue agent. *Me.*

I imagined a cartoon light bulb flashing in the air over my head as I sat at the table, hands falling from my laptop's keyboard.

Butler, Tennessee.

A clarion moment of recollection vibrated in my skull, and I knew why the name seemed familiar.

The divinations.

The Garzas.

Butler, Tennessee was the site where the witchy Garza brothers had predicted Charybdis would surface had we not stopped the kelpie at Sardis Lake.

The kelpie was dead. Their prediction was nulled. The paper trail leading from Wink to Butler was months old. Whatever Ayer had done there, whatever was meant to lure Charybdis there, those plans had been cancelled out.

Hadn't they?

There was one way to find out. Time to invite myself over to the Garzas'. "This would be so much easier if you could talk," I told the wolf snoring on the floor, his fur tickling me where his chin rested on my feet. "Wake up." I lifted my toes, wiggled them. "We've got work to do."

The wolf wasn't impressed with my work nonsense and yawned to display sharp teeth.

"Save it." I pulled on my shoes and grabbed my phone. "If you were going to eat me, you would have done it by now."

He didn't disagree, just hefted himself upright and shook out his fur. He was waiting at the door by the time I had my boots laced. I debated texting Isaac to let him know where I was going, but decided against it. He would want details, and I didn't have time to give them to him.

This would go so much quicker if I could call Dell, but wargs didn't carry cells. Why bother when they could tap into the pack bond to relay messages? Telepathy was far more dependable than phone service out here in the boonies, which meant Graeson and I were going for a walk.

Wolf on my heels, I set out for Silverback Lane.

Today the shade-dappled path bustled with activity. How so many people had remained hidden from sight boggled the mind. There weren't enough houses here to accommodate them, so there must be other lanes yet unexplored.

A wisp of a girl gasped as we passed, and my stride hitched. I recognized her. It was the fuzzball from the woods. Eyes wide, she bolted. My muscles tensed to follow, even as my tender calf twinged, but a fae chasing a warg child was a fae asking for a lesson in disembowelment.

Dark blond hair streamed behind her. Pale blue eyes darted a glance over her shoulder. Round face. A gap in her front teeth perfect for holding the handle of a sucker.

Dell would know the girl. I could ask her who she was and if she had a history of mischief.

"I understand congratulations are in order," a husky voice rolled over my shoulder.

My shoulders snapped straight, and I fixed a neutral expression in place before turning. Graeson mirrored me, leaning his weight against my leg and a bit in front, as if holding me back from lunging. I hadn't realized my hands were fisted until I noticed the wolf was the one restraining me. Who was I becoming that a wolf called rabid yesterday was today the coolheaded one?

Every instinct tingled at Bessemer's nearness. His smugness rankled. I wanted to bare my teeth and growl at him. It wasn't a Gemini instinct. It was pure wolf. The sting of pelt beneath my skin shocked me out of my aggression. I hadn't tried to recall the warg shape. I hadn't drawn on magic at all. It had leapt to me, slid under my skin and stretched it taut.

I cleared the gravel from my throat and replied, "Are they?"

The antagonistic bent of the words made me cringe. Graeson shifted his paws, placing one on my boot and leaning all of his weight to that leg as if to say, *Zip it.*

"Yes, they are." Imogen joined her alpha in squaring off against me. "I told Bessemer about our fight."

Of course she did. *Tattletale.* It was barely a fight.

Gods have mercy, barely a fight and I had almost killed her. Graeson would have gutted her if I'd left her behind.

Was this my life now? This casual violence? This anticipation of teeth and the sting of claws emerging from my fingertips unwelcomed?

No immediate answer came to me, so I stood there and waited for one of them to elaborate.

"Imogen is the most dominate female in our pack, aside from my own lovely Aisha." Bessemer didn't spare a single sideways glance at Graeson. He only had eyes for Imogen. "She tells me you bested her." He paused, perhaps hoping I would contradict her story. I might have, if I had any idea what she'd told him. "None of the other females are willing to fight someone of your..." he rolled a few words around his mouth, "...caliber."

Lightness spread through my limbs, a weight lifted from my shoulders. "The selection is over?"

"Yes," he admitted with reluctance. "There's a formal ceremony, but it requires Cord's participation." A smile more at home on a snake than a wolf slithered across his mouth, and it reinforced how well he was matched to his viper of a mate. "There's also the small matter of the moon."

"Let me guess," I sighed, relief vanishing in a blink. "If he hasn't shifted back to a man by the next full moon, you'll have him mauled by rabid chipmunks or drop him in a pit of squirrels with his jaws wired shut and a nut pinned under his tongue."

The buttery rich sound of Bessemer's laughter disarmed me. "Nothing so barbaric."

Clearly he and I had very different ideas of barbarism. I glanced between them. "What then?"

"He's expelled from the pack," Imogen said, once it became apparent Bessemer was content to keep me in the dark. "The longer a warg stays in his wolf skin the more animal he becomes until there's no coming back. Some can last days, some weeks. A few of the more dominant wolves are capable of retaining their humanity for months. Past that..."

"Past that he's no longer a warg," Bessemer finished for her. "He's a wolf, and what use do I have for a pet?"

The sting of claws piercing my skin as they curved over my fingertips anchored me. Smelling the blood welling in my palms, Graeson shifted his gaze to me. This time it was more of an urgent *shut it* than his earlier and more polite *zip it*. Clearly Graeson-as-wolf comprehended more of the subtext than I gave him credit for, but I wasn't backing down from this.

"He's a dominant warg," I argued.

"He's a broken warg." Bessemer curled his lip. "He sits at *your* feet, looks to *you* for guidance, as if *you* are his master."

That was the problem in a nutshell, and it might or might not have had something to do with me. Graeson had told me himself he'd been *off* even before Marie's death. From my perspective, made stunningly clear by Bessemer's urgency to expel, kill and/or tame him, the issue wasn't who he looked to for guidance, but the simple fact that he no longer looked to Bessemer.

Graeson was an alpha in the making. When he returned from the place where his grief had spiraled him, and I had to believe he would, and soon, Bessemer expected retribution. He expected challenge. He expected Graeson to be out for blood. And he was wise to feel Graeson-as-wolf's breath on his nape, hot and moist and tangy with blood as yet unspilled.

"I am no one's master, and if Graeson is broken, it's because you crushed his sanity beneath your boot when you stamped out the pack bond."

"A mating should strengthen each partner. I had to act, the sooner the better, to wake him up before it was too late." Bessemer hissed between his teeth. "This choice the two of you made will destroy you both. I won't let it take my wolves with you."

The snarl curling my lip caused Graeson's ears to twitch forward, and Imogen to step back. I'd fought for him, bled for him, and he was *mine*. Instinct roared in my ears, and fur stung my arms as the needlelike hairs pressed through my skin.

That night, belly rounded with Graeson's cooking and happy to be in his company, I had weighed the value of his choice against pack expectation. Later, with Imogen, I had measured duty to his race against what he might contribute to his pack—full-blooded children—and wondered if I had any right to erase those future babes with hazel eyes and wolfen souls. But then it had been me or her. In a flash of consequence where choice had been ripped asunder, I'd saved us.

My life.

His soul.

I had protected him from waking with dried blood in the corners of his mouth and the burden of knowledge that he had brought me here, to his home, as his guest, and he and his people had killed me with his jaws and their prejudice.

And I had no regrets.

Bessemer and Imogen clammed up, and I had a second to wonder why before I saw the reason dart down the hill and slam into his leg. Naked as the day she was born and covered in mud, the child who had waved at me in the forest climbed onto his hip and planted a smacking kiss on his cheek.

"Look at this." She dangled a dead squirrel in front of his nose. "Now you don't have to go hunting tonight. *I* caught dinner for us."

"Emily, Emily, all teeth and claws. I'm impressed." He regarded the little mud ball, pride sparking from every pore. "Take it to Aisha and tell her to clean it. We can have stew for dinner."

"Okay, Daddy."

Daddy?

That same cartoon light bulb was back and brighter than ever. I didn't believe in coincidence, and this one was too good to be true. Finding the girl so near the blind wasn't concrete evidence she was involved in leaving the gifts on my steps, but her proximity added another layer of suspicion that her parents were somehow involved. Yet another nugget to relay to Isaac.

Done mopping up his praise, Emily turned her attention to the gathering of adults she had interrupted without hesitation. She noticed me standing there for the first time and froze halfway to the ground.

"It's all right." He patted her head. "This is Cord's...mate. She won't hurt you." The ice in his glare rivaled lesser icebergs. "Will you, fae?"

"I don't harm children." I tested a smile I hoped conveyed my nonthreateningness to her in case I lucked into an opportunity to question her later. "It's nice to meet you, Emily."

Bessemer's gaze scythed between us as though sensing there was more to my polite interest in his daughter. Guilty conscience speaking perhaps? His daughter thawed under his regard, wilting until her feet sank into soft grass. There would be no reaching her now, not while her dad was nearby.

"There you are." A bony hand closed over my elbow. "Did you get turned around again? Dell's been waiting on you half the day." Meemaw started as if the folds covering her eyes had prevented her from spotting her alpha until this moment. "Oh dear, I didn't interrupt?"

"Not at all," he assured her through tight lips.

Capitalizing on the stalled-out hostilities, Imogen rested her hand on Bessemer's forearm. "Do you have time to discuss the expansion project?" She patted Emily's head with yearning clear in her bright eyes. "That's what brought me to the Lane."

"Of course," he said, shooing his daughter ahead of him. "I'm hungry." His gaze burned hot over Imogen. "Let's have this conversation somewhere more private."

A squirming sensation left my gut tight, fear that Imogen was entertaining him to deflect his interest in me. What had changed there? Why was she championing me now? Had I proven my dominance and settled that score? Or had she humored me and let me claim the victory for other reasons? Reasons that involved an opportunity with a male one rung higher on the pack's social ladder.

The pair set out for the log cabin-style mansion on the rise, and I stared in the direction Emily had gone before a sharp tug at my elbow brought my attention back to Meemaw.

Wrinkles parted over dark eyes. "Do you want to give him another reason to kill you?"

"Does he need one?" Besides the fact I was fae and breathing.

Her gnarled hand gripped my jaw and hauled my face down to her level. "Imogen is in heat."

"Heat?" Dread ballooned in my chest. "Since when?"

"Going on forty-eight hours as best I recall." She fanned her nose, the air no doubt ripe with pheromones for those able to scent them. "She's got her sights set on Bessemer at the moment, and he's looking right back." The older woman turned me loose. "Aisha hasn't given him children, and anyone who's seen him with Emily can tell he craves more. This is an opportunity for both of them."

"Who is Emily's mother?"

"Her name was Agatha. Aggie," she amended. "She died due to complications when Emily was eight weeks old. Bessemer has been burning through females in our pack searching for a replacement ever since. This time he might have met his match in ambition."

That explained Imogen's change of heart, but I kept circling around to what Graeson had said about females in heat breaking up otherwise solid relationships. "How did Graeson resist?"

"Some men can think with the head on their shoulders."

Laughter burst out of me, and I covered my mouth.

"I know my way around men." Her eyes sparkled. "Dell would hardly be here if I didn't."

Nape on fire, I ducked my head and let her lead me to her home, where she hustled me and Graeson through the door. "Now." She poured herself a mug of coffee that was two-thirds whiskey. "What brings you to the Lane?"

"The Garzas."

After a long draw on her brew, she offered to pour some for me. I declined. I wasn't much for alcohol...or coffee. Meemaw didn't strike me as the type to sip chai, so I decided my thirst could keep until I got back home.

Sinking into a battered recliner, she peered at me over the steaming expanse of her mug. "What do you need with them?"

"I have a few questions about the incident at Sardis Lake." I touched my bracelet. "I'm also hoping they might be able to help me locate someone the way they tracked the movements of Marie's killer."

Her eyebrows drifted upward. "Can you afford them?"

Money wasn't the problem. This was worth splurging for. I was more hesitant to leave a paper trail with *me* at its head. "Will they charge for a consultation?"

Laughter sloshed coffee down the front of her shirt. *"Ha."* She wiped tears. "Witches practically bill you to answer the phone. They might as well set up hotlines that charge by the minute."

I stood, realized I didn't know where anything was to get her a towel, and she waved off the spill. I sank down and crossed my ankles. "Dell's been keeping an ear to the ground for me, but she hasn't heard anything yet, and I can't afford to keep waiting on them to grant me an audience."

"She's the only one outside of Bessemer or Graeson who deals with them. The young one, Enzo, is smitten with her." Still hooting softly under her breath, she wiped tears from her eyes. "Witches consulting for free. That's the best joke I've heard in weeks."

A loud thud rattled the floorboards, and I started to rise.

"I'm okay," Dell's muffled voice called from deeper in the house. "That body-butter crap is slicker than a greased pig."

"That'll be her getting out of the shower." Meemaw set her mug aside with a shake of her head. "She said something about shaving her legs for tonight." A nest of wrinkles gathered on her forehead. "What are you girls up to?" Her gaze dropped to Graeson. "And are there men involved?"

Interested for the first time since arriving at Meemaw's, the wolf slanted cool hazel eyes at me.

"No," I spluttered, defensive.

More quiet laughter overcame my embarrassment.

"Oh. *Oh.*" It hit me. "There will be a guy there. A man, I guess. Isaac."

Twinkles lit her eyes. "The same mighty fine specimen who delivered her to my doorstep?"

"Yes." I linked my fingers in my lap. "He's a good guy."

The spark in her dimmed. "But?"

"He doesn't stay in one place for long" seemed the least painful explanation.

"Neither do you." She made it both question and accusation. "Yet there you are with a wolf at your feet."

Sweat dampened my palms where they rubbed together. "We're an accident of circumstance."

An untethered wanderer who met a man with roots that anchored him to a past with the power to destroy him.

"That's generally how love works," she agreed.

Heavy and solid, Graeson rested his head on my lap, ears swiveled forward like my response might be the most interesting thing he'd ever heard.

"Uh, sure." I fidgeted. "I guess it does."

"I thought I heard voices." Dell bounded into the living room, wet hair French braided away from her face, wearing cutoff shorts and an oversized T-shirt knotted at her hip with a hairband, and smiled at me. "I wasn't expecting to see you until tonight. What's up?"

Hating to keep pressuring her, I forced myself to ask, "Do you know if the Garzas are home yet?"

"Sorry, I haven't gotten a response yet, and I can't go the usual route. Miguel's wife—Isabella—her cousin lives at their compound. Bessemer uses her like a two-way radio since mental contact with Isabella is strictly forbidden due to her health." Dell tapped her temple. "Normally I could ring up Janice and get Miguel's attention that way but..."

"No, Dell, it's fine." The weight of the favor I'd asked hit me, and I wilted. "I would never ask you to hurt yourself that way on my account. I was thinking of a more direct approach."

"I don't see the harm in it," Meemaw ventured. "They're familiar with the three of you, and Dell is one of the few who knows the way."

Dropping into a chair, Dell tied on sneakers. "Miguel isn't big on uninvited guests."

"He'll make an exception for Cord." Meemaw leaned over to pat the wolf's silver head. "If for no other reason than curiosity."

I bristled without knowing why. "What do you mean?"

"Isabella is...not well. She's frail, and changes only when the moon demands it." Her fingers went to her throat. "He's convinced that if not for the stress of the changes, she would recover from her illness. He's been searching for a cure for as long as I've known him."

"A cure?" Wargism was biology, not a curse. They were born, not made. "Bessemer allows it?"

"An alliance with the Garza coven is no small thing." Her chuckle was deep, sad. "Bessemer knows as well as you and I there is no cure, so he doesn't see the harm. It puts the most powerful coven of witches in the southeastern United States at his beck and call in exchange for a few tests run on the stronger pack members each month during the full moon."

"That's why he would do the favor for Graeson?" I pieced it together. "He's volunteered before and might again in exchange for the information?"

"Graeson was opposed to the deal, and he hasn't changed his mind." Her wrinkled lips pursed. "The testing is brutal, and we lost a wolf to a misfired spell last year."

My confusion must have been obvious, because Dell stepped in to clarify.

"Cord plays guinea pig every other month. He lets the Garzas cast spells on him, drinks their concoctions, gives blood, takes injections. He's had twice the magical exposure as the other wolves, but Miguel allows it because his wife has also been frequently exposed by his attempts to cure her, and he figures Graeson is a much safer bet for surviving his tests than Isabella."

"Of course he has." I glared at the wolf. "Do you have any sense of self-preservation?"

He swiveled an ear toward me.

"I'll take that as a *no*." I raked my hands through my hair. "Why didn't you stop him?"

"Cam." Dell laughed my name. "He's the *beta*. No one stops him. No one tells him no. No one tells him he can't do a thing he wants to do."

"Until you," Meemaw added.

"Until you," Dell agreed.

Unable to resist, I massaged one of his silky ears between my fingers. "Maybe that's the appeal."

"That's not it at all. What I should have said—" Meemaw rubbed her jaw, "—is that he never listened. There have been plenty of females who sought to tame him, and all of them failed. He didn't respect them, didn't acknowledge their opinions or heed their warnings."

"He listens to you." Dell shook her head. "You can't know how weird it is—was—to have him in my head day in and day out and feel his hesitation, his uncertainty where you're concerned. He's a good guy, but he acts like a big brother who thinks he knows best about everything. The pack is like a gaggle of younger siblings that he protects the best way he knows how, even if it means stomping on their opinions and rights as he goes."

I found myself nodding along. "The last part is him to a T."

The wolf snapped at me, sliding teeth over my skin without drawing blood.

"Don't take it out on me." I smoothed my smarting fingers together. "I can't help it if Dell's got your number."

Ears pinned back, he managed to look unamused. "He's a lot more aware in there than I gave him credit for at first."

"Graeson sees and hears everything, but it's far away, like a dream." Meemaw sipped her last then scratched the lip of her mug with her thumbnail. "The wolf is a simple creature. He hungers, he eats. He tires, he sleeps. He mourns, he heals. He accepts loss as natural. Even if he sings his grief in the nights, he walks in sunlight too."

That made sense. "That's why Graeson defaulted to wolf when the bond broke."

"Yes." Dell studied him. "What Bessemer did wasn't right. Cord held on to the end. He was the last link broken. That means all that rebounded emotion—his and ours—slammed into his psyche and KO'd him."

"Are the others recovering as well as you are?" It shamed me that I hadn't asked after them sooner.

"Mostly." She held out a hand and wobbled it. "It's better than it ought to be, and I think that pisses Bessemer off too."

"You were out of your mind for more than twenty-four hours," I protested.

"The depth and length of the bond Graeson sustained with the others would have driven them mad if he had surrendered the burden of connection first. Only by waiting until the last did he manage to preserve their sanity." Watery eyes met mine as Meemaw exhaled. "It was a foolish thing he did. I've never seen a warg come back from where he went, not even soul-mated ones."

A bitter taste rose up the back of my throat and with it the certainty that Bessemer didn't hate me as I first suspected. He probably *loved* me, fae nature and all. I was the perfect weapon, a scalpel for him to excise the troublesome wolves from his pack, starting with those who obeyed Graeson. I was the choice Graeson had made, even if I fought him at first, and the repercussions of that decision were ours to face.

Uppity beta mates a fae? Kick-start the selection and hope it kills her. Upstart beta shanghais six wargs? Snap the bond and hope their minds break too. Usurper stuck in warg form? Initiate vague ceremonial proceedings and hope he commits the faux pas of appearing wearing his fur suit instead, qualifying him for an automatic banishment.

All this back-patting was well and good, but it didn't change the facts. "But he's not back, is he? Not really."

"Not yet." Dell pushed from her chair and crossed to me. "He just needs some time."

Thanks to Bessemer's latest proclamation, time was the one thing he didn't have. That none of us had.

"Give the Garzas my best." Meemaw scowled into her empty mug before setting it aside. "Be careful. Both of you." She waggled a finger at me. "Never accept a first offer, understand? Witches will respect you more if you haggle."

"We won't bargain away our firstborns," Dell promised. "Seconds and thirds though…"

Her grandmother swatted her bottom, and I laughed, an easy sound that once would have been confined to my own living room and my own family's shenanigans.

Strange days when I had a serial killer to thank for bringing me back to life.

CHAPTER FIFTEEN

Fur brushed the back of my hand, a silent *hello* from the sterling wolf trotting at my side. I took the hint when his wet nose bumped my knuckles a second time and rubbed between his ears. Ahead of us, to the left, loped a golden-furred wolf who entertained herself by snapping at pesky mosquitos while guiding us to the Garza homestead.

As luck would have it, they lived within hiking distance of Silverback Lane. *Luck* and *hiking distance* being relative since each time Dell had ventured to the witches' lair, she had been sent to fetch Graeson and gone on wolf paws there and back. The only person who might have offered his opinion on her route was more concerned with me itching the base of his left ear, which I had discovered was his favorite spot for me to scratch with my nails.

Being on two legs made each fumble, every heavy breath from exertion, that much louder and the trek that much lonelier. I wasn't sure which I longed for more—for them to join me or for me to join them.

What would it be like to dissolve into a sleek wolf's form? To shake out my fur and chase the horizon as seen through the pines guarding my home? To catch my own dinners and bump cold noses with a comrade? To hear the night's song whispered in my blood?

Such wildness in their hearts. Such freedom under their paws. Such boundless joy they found in nature and in themselves.

As glorious as the wargs were in their wolves' skins, all I could manage was a pale echo of their majesty. The sting of energy racing up my arm didn't surprise me. Without meaning to, I had tapped into the mysterious reservoir of recalled magic brimming with lupine attributes that somehow had cobbled themselves together to create the fine black-tipped pelt of my warg aspect.

Sniffing me fingertips to palm, Graeson sighed happily at the change in me. He licked my wrist, leaving a cowlick set by drying wolf drool, and grinned wide, bearing lots of teeth.

Mate, he seemed to say, *join us in the hunt. Good eats roam these hills, and their scents are freshest near the earth.*

A shiver wracked my soul, and the prickling rose higher. My cheeks itched and forehead stung with emerging hairs. A panicked gasp caught in my throat that sounded eerily like the birth of a howl.

I swallowed hard and sank to my knees. "What's happening to me?"

Graeson gave no answer.

Breathe in. Breathe out. In. Out.

A cold nose edged under my jaw. Dell. I wrapped my arms around myself and rocked while the wolves shared a commiserating glance.

Time passed. The sun shifted lower in the sky. The sensation of being swept through the change abated, leaving me hairless and declawed. My skin passed smooth under my palms. I was me again, the wild rattle of something *other* locked behind my ribs.

A damp tongue swiped over my lips, and I spat Graeson's kiss off while rubbing my mouth with the back of my wrist.

"Are you okay?" Standing over me, Dell chewed her thumbnail. "I didn't know what to do."

"Something's wrong." I tested my face, my neck, my arms and hands. "I shouldn't be able to shift without blood. You've seen me. My recall isn't this good."

"Should we turn back?"

"How far is it?" Trees all looked the same after a while. "Is the trip back worse than the one forward?"

"Ten minutes. Maybe twenty." She hesitated. "I don't know if visiting the Garzas while you're vulnerable is a good idea."

As close as Bessemer watched me, I doubted I'd get a second chance to cozy up to his witches. There was nothing for it. We had to push ahead and hope for the best. "I'll be fine. Don't worry about me."

"Stay close." A firm note entered her voice. "Give me a heads-up if you start feeling puny, okay?"

I stood on wobbly legs and lurched into motion after her. "You're not changing?"

"I can't shift back for a while." Her bare feet made no sound in passing. "Besides, I can help you better in this form, and I know where we're going without my super sniffer, if that's got you worried."

The hike became even more surreal as I followed the curve of Dell's spine down the shadowy trail. "Is it kosher if you show up naked?"

"They're used to it," she assured me. "Miguel is married to one of us, remember?"

Based on Meemaw's cautionary tale, Miguel spent so much time attempting to suppress his wife's nature that I wondered if witches shared the same prejudices as fae toward wargs. Most shifters were healed by the change. What was wrong with his wife that she was deteriorated by it?

Exhaustion weighted my ankles by the time we crested a short rise and encountered the first *No Trespassing* sign. The trail turned to a dirt road leading toward a house. I set foot on the path, and Dell tackled me. My back slapped the ground. *"Oof."*

"When they say no trespassing, they mean *no* trespassing."

A scorched earth smell had me craning my neck to peer past her. Black smoke rose from the spot still marked by my boot print in the loose dirt. "They hexed the perimeter."

"Yes, they did." Dell poked me in the shoulder. "You've got to be more careful."

"They must really not want the pack on their property."

"They live near us out of necessity." She lifted her head, flared her nostrils. "They bought this parcel of land for the express purpose of being able to tell Bessemer where to stick it when he tries to lord over them. They aren't pack, they don't live on pack lands or partake of pack supplies. All they want from us is our blood in their vials and our bodies primed for spellwork."

A grimace twisted my face. "What happens if his wife dies before he finds a cure?"

"Then we've armed our pissed-off, grief-stricken witchy next-door neighbors with all the ammo they need to take us out with spells, hexes and charms." She shrugged. "Assuming they don't hire another coven to take us out for them."

"Well—" I shoved her back, "—as much as I enjoy having a naked woman sprawled on top of me, do you think you can let me up now?"

A sly expression flittered across her face. "What's the matter?" She walked her fingers over her hips, up her sides and over her rib cage until she cupped her breasts. "Scared of a little jiggle?"

On another woman it might have played out as seductive. On Dell, who must be picturing tassel-tipped pasties on her nipples, judging by the way she was swinging them in circles, I had to laugh.

My snorted chuckles drew Graeson's attention, who made a point of ignoring Dell's antics, which only made me suck in air harder.

"It's all right, girls." She gave them one last grope. "One day you'll find someone who appreciates you."

"You're insane." I bucked my hips. "Get off me."

"Don't stop on my account," an easy voice drawled.

I bolted upright, knocking Dell onto the ground. I rose on my knees and flung out my arms to cover her nudity from...an invisible man?

"It's nothing I haven't seen before," he assured us. "Wargs aren't big on keeping their clothes on." Seeming to realize how that sounded, he cleared his throat and backtracked. "I meant that as a statement of fact. Not as a slur."

"Show yourself," I ordered.

"You have no jurisdiction here, Agent Ellis. This is my family's property, and I'm free to do as I wish."

The fact he remembered my name was a good sign, right? There he held the advantage. The Garzas had erupted into frequent shouting matches while casting their divinations. His conversational voice—and no face to match it to—stumped me. I had no idea which witch stood before us. "Are you Miguel?"

"No, I'm Enzo." A huffed sigh, as if the mix-up happened often. "You should have remembered me as the younger, more handsome brother."

"Ah." I relaxed my posture. "Yes. Enzo." The one with a sweet spot for Dell.

"What brings you to our door?" The voice moved closer. "We weren't expecting Graeson for another week. Unless... Does he have another job for us?"

"No, but I do."

"Okay, I'll bite." The air shimmered in front of me. "What do you want?"

"Information on Charybdis's whereabouts."

"Hmm." The magic shielding him from view dropped altogether, revealing the dark-chocolate eyes and tousled black hair I remembered. He wore a pair of faded jeans well, and his vintage T-shirt defined his torso. "I thought the kelpie died."

"It did." My lips tingled as the blood oath let itself be known. "But we have reason to believe the kelpie was an avatar, that the real killer is still out there."

He rubbed his jaw. "Do you have a fresh sample?"

"No."

"Then I don't see how you expect us to help." He spread his hands wide. "Without fresh biological material or a personal item of his or his current avatar's, we can't pinpoint him."

"What about Harlow—the mermaid girl? Can you cast for her?" I lifted my wrist and exposed the shell bracelet. Hours of her life were sunk into those pearls. Sweat certainly. Blood, possibly. "She made this and gave it to me. Will it work as a focus?"

His arms dropped. "The mermaid is missing?"

Not trusting my voice, I nodded until my throat loosened. "She was taken from the scene of the last crime."

"Let me see it." He held his palm out flat. "I'll be careful."

For the first time since she gifted me the bracelet, I removed it and set it in his hand.

Fingers closed over the pearls, he moved his lips in a soft incantation. Threads of light bled through the cracks in his fist, and his eyes, when he lifted them, swirled milky white.

"Yes." Magic distorted his voice until it echoed in many layers. "This will do."

A shiver skipped down my arms, and Dell pressed closer. Graeson, whose absence at my side I hadn't yet noticed, appeared behind Enzo. The wolf's posture remained calm and nonthreatening, but his eyes were sharp and focused, his body taut with the promise of violence.

Blinking away the haze, Enzo swallowed a few times. It didn't help. He still sounded raw. "Call off your wolf."

"He's not my wolf" popped out of my mouth on reflex, but the truth was I had won Graeson. He really was mine. A wriggling tendril of panic wormed through my chest when it hit me. By that logic, I was his too. Having never belonged to another person, I battled my instinctive response to shove the thought—and the person attached to it—away. But my resistance didn't make it far. A tilt of the silvery wolf's head, as if he read my distress or understood my words and rebuked them, had me ready to call him to my side and stroke his silky ears while I whispered nonsense into them.

The sad fact was that Graeson-as-wolf was more of a danger to my heart than the man had been. Holding the man at arm's length was easy when I recalled his betrayal. The wolf, though, was honest. I couldn't hold my grudge when I peered into that wild face and glimpsed the simple animal happiness he experienced when I was near. A contentedness, if I were being honest, that mirrored in me.

If—*when*—I got the man back, I was in real danger of transferring that easy affection onto him.

"I see," Enzo said at last. "Well, call *the* wolf off then." He glanced over his shoulder. "Graeson, man, I thought we were tight."

The wolf chuffed.

Dell laughed, a pealing-bell sound that captivated the witch.

"When are you going to let me take you out?" His eyes softened when they lit on her and, through no small miracle, he didn't glance lower than her chin. "I'm not all bad."

I whipped my head toward Dell, who flushed ten shades of red. "It's nothing personal."

He rubbed the spot over his chest. "Tell that to my achy-breaky heart."

"Sorry," she murmured, eyes downcast.

"Never be sorry that you're being true to yourself." Enzo placed his palm over his heart, a pledge. "I'll be sorry enough for the both of us. Trust me."

The slight curl of Dell's lips in my periphery told me she wasn't immune to the witch's charms. Enzo wasn't the only one holding a torch for unrequited like, and I had to wonder if her answer might have been different had she not met Isaac.

To clear the air, I stood and brought his attention with me. "Are you willing to help?"

A negligent roll of his shoulder. "For a price."

"Name it."

"It's up to Miguel. I'm still an apprentice." He gestured toward the dirt road. "If you're willing to gamble, follow me."

The deck was stacked in his favor, but a chance to know where Harlow was urged my feet forward.

Finally I was making progress.

A stern-faced man with eyes a shade lighter than Enzo's awaited us on the porch of a pale-blue clapboard house. His crisp slacks defied humidity, and he wore a button-down shirt fastened at the wrists despite the heat. The house itself was the centerpiece of a bizarre garden divided into four distinct quadrants.

Decorative flowering plants adorned the area to my right, their zone tidy and pruned. Herbs grew wild on the left but managed to be at once inviting and forbidden. The rear of the house boasted a vegetable garden sprawling lush and plump. Its opposite was a massive square pond overflowing with water lilies, hyacinths and cabbage-like pistia plants.

"Adele," Miguel greeted her. "It's a pleasure to see you again so soon." He reached behind him where a rocker sat and lifted a pink cotton bathrobe as though expecting us. "I hope you don't mind."

"Not at all." She stepped up, let him help her into it and tied it on her way back to me. "Your house, your rules."

"Agent Ellis." His greeting for me rang cooler. "Come inside, won't you?"

The wolf gave me a nudge to get me moving. He was acting more coherent, more human, by the hour. I hoped that was a good sign.

Inside the house was as strange as the outside. Most of the living space was what you'd expect, but the books weren't light reading. The tomes gracing his shelves were thick, leather-bound. Crystals reflected rainbows in the windows. Bone sculptures took up table space, and elegant taxidermy brought a bleak air to the room.

"Have a seat." He took one of the two chairs positioned opposite a couch. "Tell me what brings you so far from home."

Enzo waited until Dell had plopped down on the couch before claiming the other chair. Left the only one standing, I sat beside Dell, and Graeson came to rest at my feet, his tail curled around my ankles. All this Miguel watched with detached interest.

"She wants to find the mermaid." Enzo dropped my bracelet into his brother's hand. "I told her we could help, assuming you two can settle on a price."

Miguel rolled the beads between his fingers. "What business do you have with the girl?"

"She was abducted from the scene in Abbeville."

"I see." He studied the etchings on each sphere through narrowed eyes. "Is this personal or professional?"

"Both." Hoping it might sway him, I added, "She's a friend."

"We can find her." He closed his fist and sat back. "The closer she is, the easier it is."

I scooted to the edge of my cushion. "Does that mean she's nearby?"

A ghost of a smile shadowed his features. "What are you willing to offer me in exchange for this information?"

"I assumed there was a set price." Graeson had told me their help was expensive, but not what it cost.

"For Graeson there is." He studied me with a clinical air that left me chilled. "For you...for this...I need something else, something different."

I sank my fingers into Graeson's lush pelt. "Why don't you spell it out for me."

Dell snorted. "You told a witch to *spell* it out."

I elbowed her in the side. "You're not helping."

Overhead the planks groaned, and all eyes rolled toward the ceiling. I jumped to my feet at the heavy thump that followed. Miguel blurred past before I could ask what the sound meant, but Enzo caught him by the shoulder.

"I've got this. I'll get Isabella back in bed. She was probably curious about the voices and went to look out the window." He jerked his chin toward us. "You finish up down here."

We reclaimed our seats, the quiet pervasive, until Miguel spoke. "My wife is unwell." His fingers tapped out a hasty rhythm on his knee. "I don't have long to entertain offers, and I don't have time for coyness." He snared my gaze. "I want your blood."

I recoiled, and Dell scooted closer. "My…blood."

"My wife is a warg. You're a shape-shifter of a different sort. You control your shifts. If I can isolate the strains of magic that make that possible, I can create a vaccine. She could do partial shifts when the moon calls to soothe her inner beast." His voice went distant. "It's not a cure, but it's a hope for a better patch than any I've created so far."

Blood was power. A lot of bad spells used it as both fuel and homing beacon. Whatever magic was twisted from my blood would rebound on me if the brothers misused even a drop.

"You're asking for a lot." Not just blood but trust too.

"You want the mermaid located while she's still sane, I assume." His tone was merciless. "There's not much time left for that."

I gritted my teeth. "Tell me about Butler, Tennessee first."

"Butler. That sounds familiar. Let me check my records." He held out a hand, and a ledger materialized there. When he set it in his lap, it flipped to a page near the center of its spine, and he marked a passage with his finger. "I'll give you my oath your blood won't be used for harm or against you. One vial is all I need. Promise me that, and I'll read you the transcription word for word."

Oaths were binding when sealed with magic. It was as safe an offer as he could make me. "I accept."

"The creature walks among mortals. As death wears many faces, so must he." Miguel's shoulders relaxed as he read from the journal. "He is hunger, his cravings unending. This world will perish at the edge of his teeth. Butler, Tennessee will bear the brunt of that first bite."

He closed the book and willed it back whence it came.

I waited. No, he wasn't being dramatic. He was done. "That's it?"

"Graeson was specific. He wanted a location, not motivation and not identification." He picked at a thread sprung from a seam in his pants. "You're fortunate Enzo keeps such meticulous records. Had I been entranced alone, all I would have remembered speaking would have been the answer to his question."

"Meemaw did say not to accept his first offer," Dell whispered.

I glowered at her. "Not helping."

"Sorry." She winced.

I rubbed the tense spot between my eyes with my pointer finger. "The apocalyptic nature of the divination didn't, I don't know, concern you?"

"Not particularly." Tired of the loose end, he snapped his finger, and the thread knotted. "All divinations have bleak aspects, and most possible futures bear grim tidings. I can't drop everything to run off to save the day every time a world-ending forecast is made."

"How is the world possibly ending not your problem?" I challenged.

"For some of us..." his gaze drifted toward the ceiling, "...it's not a possibility but a certainty."

How accurate were his divinations that he could afford to ignore such dire warnings? Was he truly content to let the world run out of time since his wife's was so limited? Or did he place his materialistic faith in people like me, who, to borrow from Mai, must have a savior complex?

"Now, the mermaid." The bracelet dangled from his fingers, an incentive. "What will you give me for her?"

A growl rose up the back of my throat that was echoed by Dell and the wolf at my feet. "I agreed to pay you a vial of blood for your help."

"The blood was for the divination." He worried the beads through his fingers like a rosary. "This is a separate price for a separate act."

I didn't bother making an offer. I didn't see the point in it. "What did you have in mind?"

"Be our guest. Three days should do it." A slight smile. "I might need more blood or—"

"—a fresh guinea pig," I finished for him, rising to my feet. "The answer is no. You're not the only one running out of time."

The witch would draw out each nugget of information at a cost that would climb higher and higher. I had wasted my time coming here. What scraps I'd learned through the divination shored up Ayer's rantings, but neither told me what had drawn Charybdis to Butler, Tennessee.

The only way to find those answers was to fly up there myself and take a look around.

"What about me?" Dell scrambled up behind me. "Is there anything I can do?"

Miguel was shaking his head before she finished. "Enzo bargained with me to spare you from my agreement with the pack."

Dell blanched at the mercy she had unknowingly been granted, and her gaze skittered toward the stairs where her knight errant had gone. Knees wobbling at the magnitude of this news, she sank back onto the couch. "Why would he do that? He doesn't even know me."

"Infatuation," Miguel said with casual cruelness. "The difficulties Isabella and I face haven't deterred him. Let his inherent magic infect you, let it warp your natural energies until each shift is a step closer to your death, and then he might begin to understand the idiocy of his bargain." Lips mashed into a white line of regret, perhaps for speaking his mind, he stood. "Once you leave, whether you got what you came for or not, you won't be permitted back onto our property." He crossed to the front door and rested his hand on the knob. "There are rules, and they must be upheld."

Anger sprouted fine platinum hairs up my arms, and an idea formed. "Your wife is a warg."

"I've said as much, yes," he answered, condescension ringing through his tone.

"Locate the mermaid, and I'll give you a second vial of blood."

His brow furrowed. "To echo your earlier sentiments, the answer is no."

"Are you sure?" I lifted my arm and pushed magic through my limbs to hasten the spread of the warg aspect. "The divination was worth the blood of my base form, which possesses non-specific magics. Think of it as a control sample. How much more would it be worth to you if I saved you some work? What if I gave you that Gemini baseline with a natural infusion of the warg magic instead of your clinical variety?" I spread my fingers and allowed him to admire the curled tips of my claws. Power swept up my throat and danced along my jaw until my gums ached. When I spoke again, it was to lisp through fangs. "Fine tha mermaid, an' you can ha' this too."

"Your offer intrigues me." Eyes bright, Miguel began pacing the entryway. "Magic is coded into warg DNA. Gemini capture a scrap of that wild energy, distill it from their blood, absorb it and use it to augment their own." He continued thinking out loud. "It would cut out several steps in the process and eliminate the threat of two opposing magics rejecting binding with one another. Blood from a Gemini robust with warg magic." He stopped, seeming to come to himself. "Your blood may prove to be a magical universal donor."

I held my breath. "Is that a yes?"

"Yes." He vibrated with energy. "Quickly, let's go to my lab."

"Not so fast." I planted my feet. "I want the information first."

"That won't be possible." He took a thin knife from his pocket and slashed open his palm. Dipping his fingers in the red liquid, he wrote a few symbols that ignited in his palm. "This is a binding oath, a vow that I will give you that which you seek, but to ensure the quality of the sample and your cooperation, I must ask that your end of the deal be met first."

Having little experience with witches, I wasn't sure what I had just witnessed. "Dell?"

"It's legit," she confirmed. "He's sealed deals with Cord this way. I recognize the symbols."

"Okay." A thrill of hope zinging through me, I followed Miguel. "Let's do this."

Still unsure which of us had made the better deal, I consoled myself with the simple truth that I had already promised him blood and exacted an oath as to the limits of how he could use it. What harm had I done by giving him more blood? Magic-imbued blood? I wasn't sure. But if it helped his wife and got me to Harlow, I wasn't sure I cared about the ramifications.

I had never been a *worry-about-tomorrow-when-it-comes* type person, but desperation makes fools of us all.

The three of us followed Miguel down into his basement lab, which resembled a cross between a five-star kitchen and a morgue. He offered me a stool, and I used it to climb onto the stainless-steel table. He urged me to lie down, but I politely declined with a growl in my voice.

The procedures themselves were clinical. I was given a half hour to shift back into my own skin before he drew his control sample. Then, although I didn't need it, I accepted a drop of blood from Dell to magic-up my veins before he drew his last vial.

The fact Enzo arrived with a glass of orange juice and a small plate with two chocolate chip cookies they forced down me made me wonder how often they did this very thing. Then I decided I probably didn't want to know.

"Do you need anything else?" I hopped to the floor and rubbed my arms, adrenaline giving me hot-and-cold flashes. "How long will it take you to cast?"

Busy securing his treasures, it took Miguel a minute to answer. "I already have."

I whirled on him. "What?"

"I did that upstairs." He tossed me the bracelet without a backward glance. "I had to be sure I could hold up my end of the deal before we finalized the transaction."

"You've known all this time?" I fumed. "Why didn't you say anything?"

After locking the vials in a metal case and tucking that inside a massive refrigeration unit he also locked, Miguel faced me. "I had to be certain you would honor your side of the bargain too."

"Are you implying I'm not trustworthy?" I bristled.

"No. Not at all." He crossed his arms over his chest. "But I knew once I told you, nothing I said or did would keep you here, and I wanted to take my time to ensure I took viable samples."

A shiver raised hairs down my arms. "Where is she?"

"In the sprite's den," he said, and Dell's eyes rounded.

"The pond." Her breath caught. "Harlow's in the cavern beneath the pond."

The mocking call of gulls echoed through my memory, their poignant cries threatening to nail my feet to the repurposed oak floors. I drifted onto the front porch in a daze and wrapped my arms around my middle to hold myself together.

Dell leaned her shoulder against mine. "This is good news, right?"

"I thought I had it figured out," I murmured. "The tokens being left on my steps. I thought it was Bessemer or Aisha. He's alpha, and when he broke the bond I wondered if he had somehow fished those moments I hadn't told Graeson about out of the residual energy."

"That's not how it works." A sad laugh rocked her. "Not usually." She exhaled. "Wargs active in the pack bond can only see and hear what is freely shared. We can't go digging around in each other's heads. Only the alpha has that power. He can yank whatever he wants out of our heads, but he has to be close, and the bond must be active. There's no residue. No footprints left behind." She squeezed my arm. "Bessemer only knows what you told Cord, and Cord would have fought him to the breaking point to protect your secrets."

Rubbing my arms, I acknowledged, "That's what I was afraid of."

"I don't get it." She cocked her head. "What am I missing?"

"Ayer," I said, working out the puzzle. "She said Charybdis was in her head, that he told her what to do, and she had to obey him. She lost control of herself, and he took her over." That fit with what we had suspected about him using the kelpie as an avatar, but the breadth of his power was that much more terrifying after seeing his effect on a more sentient fae. "She said he taunted her with things that no one knew." I leaned heavy against Dell. "He was pulling that information out of her head, like what Bessemer did to Graeson."

"So the Harlow we find won't be the Harlow we knew. She'll have to detox away from his influence, like Ayer." Dell frowned. "It still doesn't explain the nest and other things. Even if he got in her head, she wouldn't know about those things, would she?"

"No, she wouldn't." Fear tightened around my ribs, a metal band compressing my chest. I hadn't seen or spoken to my parents in years. That was about to change. "One crisis at the time," I muttered to myself. "Let's get Harlow corralled first." I glanced at Dell. "We can solve the other mystery later."

She dropped her robe into a chair and jogged down the steps onto the path leading back to the woods.

With a hitch in my step, I followed, Graeson at my side. His whine drew my attention, and I patted his head. "Any insight from the peanut gallery?" Palms slick, I dampened his fur with my touch, but his contribution to the discussion was a lick to my palm. "So we wing it."

As though my words were the blast of a starting pistol at the beginning of a race, Dell launched herself toward the shade of the trees. Dread pounding in my heart at what we might find, I jogged after her.

Miguel had been wrong to doubt my staying power. Had I known a few hours ago what I knew now, I would have asked for more cookies, another glass of juice, done anything to avoid facing the reality that Harlow was here and every bit as dangerous as Charybdis himself, because she was no more in control of her actions than the kelpie had been.

CHAPTER SIXTEEN

Night had fallen during our visit with the Garzas, and clouds hugged the moon, refusing to share even a single beam of her light. Yet I had no trouble tracking the gleam of Graeson's tail as he bounded ahead of us. I should have stumbled or hesitated, but I didn't. Magic thrummed in my veins, the swirl of Dell's blood freshening my recall when I summoned my warg aspect to aid me, and the darkness kept no secrets from me.

I saw as wolves see and glided through the forest as silent as my companions. The hammering of my pulse in my ears deafened me to all but the most persistent crickets. Their song pierced my heart, and I wanted to join them, but I had no song to sing. I was a child of the moon, a creature of twilight, and not myself at all and yet more myself than I had been since the night the ocean swallowed half my soul and left the other half to drown in grief.

"Have you and Isaac been practicing without me?" The warm current of Dell's voice flowed through my head without effort. *"You've almost caught up to Cord."*

Running with my wolf flushed my system of fears and doubts and left room only for exhilaration. *"Is this how it always feels to be a warg?"*

"Reckless? Wild? Free?" She tilted her head back as if she felt the caress of the moon despite it being overcast. *"Yes to all of the above."*

We ran until my chest heaved and my legs were noodles made limper with every step. The smell hit me first, sharper, more pungent than ever. Rotting debris. Decaying fish corpses. Moldy leaves. The scents were so pure I tasted them and gagged. The high of running evaporated between one breath and the next as reality set in.

Graeson slowed, glanced over his shoulder. Swollen with recalled magic, I didn't balk at the caress of a mind against mine. Expecting it would be Dell, I stumbled when a guttural voice rumbled, "Stay put," before the wolf trotted off to scout the area. It stunned me so much I came to a full stop and stared after him, wondering if I was losing my mind.

"Oh my God."

I spun toward Dell, heart thumping. "What is it?"

"Your face," she breathed. "Good Lord, Cam. Have you seen yourself?"

"Is it bad?" Careful of my claws, I rubbed my palms on my throat and sucked in sharp breath as I discovered the elongated curve of my jaw. My fangs weren't present. I hadn't realized the shift had altered me to this degree. Each time it came faster, smoother, easier. "Tell me the truth."

Fingers trembling, she traced the strange hollow of my cheek. "You're beautiful." She laughed. "It's just—wow. You're like a legend come to life. No one can hold a partial shift. Not even the alphas. We're wolves or we're people. There's no in between." Her fingers slid through my hair, and she presented a lock of hair out for me to see. Gleaming platinum strands clung to her hand, the ends black as if dipped in ink. "This is amazing."

"I don't know what's happening to me." I tried to find some part of me that was upset by the change. I discovered none. "I haven't shifted this easily since..." Not since Lori and I had practiced *becoming*. The change to her and back had been fluid, easy as breathing, painless.

Her aspect had been a comfortable pair of shoes I sometimes slipped on for a walk. "It's been a long time."

"*Please* show this to Meemaw," she pleaded. "She'll wet her pants."

I wrinkled my extended nose. "That's a good thing?"

"*Yes.*" She hopped from foot to foot. "Cord will lose his mind when he sees you like this."

The rush of embarrassment washed over me, and where my skin prickled the fur receded until I was left standing pink and plain and flushed. What would he think? A wolf might see the half-form as an improvement, but would the man? It shouldn't matter what Graeson thought of my appearance, but it did.

I wanted him to share the same tight-throated, dry-tongued appreciation of me as I had for him.

Realizing that made me want to curl into a ball. I had seen every inch of him nude. No one had seen me naked in, well, ever. I was a lights-off, clothes-on kind of girl. The exact opposite of the man who walked around bare-skinned and conversed with his pack, who were also in various states of undress, while I restrained myself from gawking.

It was the wrong thing to worry about now, but it gave my brain a direction to sprint in that didn't involve the wolf, the lake or the maybe-mermaid who might be closer than I ever imagined.

"The Garzas are never wrong." Dell rested a hand on my shoulder. "They're not always exactly right, but they're never wrong."

The wolf arrived before I got to ask what she meant. His paws were damp, and he shook out his fur with a snort.

I wiped mud flecks off my cheeks. "Did you find anything?"

He groan-whined a human-sounding answer that didn't make sense coming from a wolf's mouth.

"Nod for yes." Dell bobbed her head then turned it side to side. "Shake for no."

Apparently I wasn't the only one who'd noticed the shift in his cognitive awareness. "Did you find anything?"

Nod.

"Harlow?"

A low whine.

"Charybdis?"

Shake.

"So not Harlow but definitely not Charybdis?" Dell scratched her head. "I don't get it. Either she's there or she isn't."

As much as I wanted to agree with her, too many possibilities loomed. "Is it safe for us to look around?"

Nod.

Pilcher's Pond hadn't changed since our first introduction. The same sense of dread puckered my stomach and dampened my skin as I approached the dry bed where water ought to be. I'd arrived after Graeson had found Marie, after he and Harlow had removed her from the water. She had been curled on a tarp when we met, and I would never forget the look on Graeson's face that day.

He looked like a man ready to jump. All he needed was a push.

I hadn't understood then that his whole life was about serving others. Sure, he did it in his own pigheaded way, and the others in question might want to kick him in the shins for it, but he had a good heart. I saw that now. It wasn't just my stomach talking, even though the man was a fine cook. It was in the way he'd put his life on hold to raise Marie, how he valued and trusted Dell when everyone else overlooked her. It was the stoic acceptance of the six wargs I watched Graeson punish for their loyalty to him, each standing their ground, trusting him even then to take the maulings as far as they had to go but not a bite or scratch further.

And it was me. *I* had changed or been changed too.

Part of that was the crack in the doorway Harlow had opened with her bright smile and brighter hair. Some of it was the way Dell shouldered through the door and into my life like she had every right to call herself my friend before I even knew what to do with one. But most of it was the man who stood on the threshold with his foot wedging the door wide open, forcing me to let in more than the persistent few, but the rest of the world too.

Knowing all that, it was too easy for my own nightmares to superimpose themselves over memories of Marie. The pond had been brought low by summer drought, the water where she had been found cupped in the center of a cracked bed we had to crunch across to reach. The closer we came to the serene edge of the abyss, the thicker the mud squished.

This was where I'd met Harlow. She had been bobbing in that very puddle, holding a barrette rescued from the silt.

"Maybe this isn't such a great idea." Dell cupped my elbow. "You're as white as chalk."

Still a coward down to the bone, I nodded and gave myself permission to stand several feet from the moist nexus, where breathing was easier. "Do you smell anything?"

"No." Nostrils flaring, she expanded her chest several times as she sucked in oxygen. "Do you?"

My sense of smell was stunted compared to theirs, so I let the faintest brush of magic creep up my arm and into my nose. I inhaled through my mouth, over my tongue, braced for the brackish taste/smell of watery decay and got...nothing. A stringent tickle of magic-scoured woods, and that was all. "Someone cast an erasure spell at the water's edge."

Erasure spells had been developed by earthbound fae and were meant to restore balance to delicate natural areas that had been saturated in pervasive magic. The idea had been the spell would clean the air and ground all scents—including itself—so that in a few days the natural aromas would prevail and the local wildlife would reclaim the damaged location.

Of course, there were other uses for it too. All good magic could be twisted for evil. Such as the use we faced now. It was a signature of sorts that explained Graeson's confusion. Harlow couldn't cast magic. She used magical items, but she was human and was unable to create her own. He must have caught scent of her outside the spell's perimeter and identified her. Her and not Charybdis. But his spellwork was present so...

"I don't like this." Dell wrapped her arms around her middle. "He must have followed us back here after he grabbed Harlow, but why? We're hunting him. Shouldn't he be running in the opposite direction?"

"You would think so." I gazed across the quiet waters. "Hopefully we're about to get some answers."

She gave the murky pond her attention too. "How do we find out if she's down there?"

"I don't know." I slid my hands into my pants pockets to hide their trembling. "Without conclave resources, I can't just pick up a phone and call in a dive team. Everyone I know works for them, so even if I paid out of pocket, the conclave wouldn't have to dig deep to find out I was disobeying a direct order from a magistrate."

No matter how valuable my services were to the Earthen Conclave, I didn't kid myself that there wasn't someone else out there—not like me, because that was so unlikely as to be impossible—but an eager soul with similar talents looking for a place to belong.

"What would they do to you?"

The frail quality of her voice made me wonder what Bessemer did to those who disobeyed him. The six wargs who went to Graeson's aid hadn't disobeyed their alpha as much as vanished without his consent knowing he would never grant them permission. The savagery of their punishment lurked in my thoughts as a reminder of the violent nature of wargs, but it was easily banished with the truth that while they had two aspects, mine were infinite. There was no limit to the horrors of what I could become with the right drop of blood and a strong taste of magic.

What separated us—man from monster—was intent. Given these gifts, how would we use them? Bessemer abused his power, and worse was that he forced people like Graeson just as low in order to retain the status quo. Paint Graeson as a villain, and Bessemer appeared less sadistic by comparison.

"Fire me? Lock me up?" Or worse, assign me to Vause as her personal aid to endure unending remedial training. "I'm not sure."

"That sounds less dire than expected." Relief breezed through her expression. "Considering you're privy to sensitive information."

"The conclave won't maim or murder me if that's what you're worried about. Probably. I've made blood oaths to protect the deepest secrets I know, and spilling them would kill me." I permitted a smile to bend my lips. "They'd sooner sew my lips shut or wipe my mind and leave me an amnesiac. Though if I didn't remember how to use my powers and killed someone, then, yeah, they'd put me down."

She swallowed hard. "I think I'd rather get beaten to a pulp than lose my mind."

"Me too," I admitted.

Physical wounds healed. Mental ones...not so much. And never when inflicted by the most skilled fae.

Unconcerned with the muck, Graeson came to my side and gazed at the smooth surface of the water for so long I wondered what he was thinking. No, not thinking. Remembering. He had seen his sister's corpse, found her and hauled her from her watery grave. He had the images burned into his mind that I had fabricated through a career of solving drowning cases.

Which of us held the short end of that stick? The one who knew and didn't have to imagine, or the one who imagined because she didn't know? Neither of us would ever know peace on the subject. Each of us would be tormented in a different way. Perhaps that suffering made us equals.

"Bessemer drove all the fae from the pack lands." Dell worried her lip between her teeth. "You can't pay most fae to step foot on them after what he did to the sprite, and humans are out of the question."

Charybdis had brought the conclave here, and only Marie's death—tied as it was to the deaths of fae girls—had given the local marshals reason to trespass.

"That leaves us with one option." I massaged my temples. "I have her gear."

Her gear. I had it all. The tail. The gill goop. Everything.

I spun the pearl bracelet around my wrist, bile tickling the back of my throat, and wished there was someone—anyone—else.

"I don't trust that look, Cam."

Had I been standing closer to the pond's heart, I might have caught the faint reflection of my face arranging itself into grim but determined lines as the enormity of what I was about to attempt caught up with me.

"I'm going after her."

From here it seemed the water grinned with its concentric rings, each ripple of anticipation a shiver down my spine.

The knot of fear tangling my heartstrings kept me distracted on the way home, the press of fear so tight my lungs balked at expanding as if water would rush in to fill them before my head broke the surface of the murky water.

That's why I screamed when I tripped over the caramel-chocolate-dipped wolf pup who darted between me and the glowing lights of the caravan.

A blur of silver, and Graeson had her pinned lightly beneath his paw. The look he shot me was too self-aware for the wolf's features. It was a man's intellect that burned bright in his eyes, and his expression shared in my curiosity as to what the girl was doing so near our trailers, alone, so late at night.

"Camille," Isaac panted, jogging out of the woods to join us. "Get him off her. She's just a kid."

"He won't hurt her." That much I did know. "What are you doing out here?"

"I set up surveillance like you asked. I spotted a little girl dart out of the woods and set an item on your steps. It's late, and she was alone. I followed to make sure she got home safe. She spotted me, or maybe she smelled me, and panicked. She shifted, and here we all are."

"Emily, is what he said true?" I cocked my head and scanned the woods for hints of her father or Aisha. Gods knew if she had blasted a distress call through the pack bond, our lifespans had just been reduced to a matter of minutes. "Are you the one who's been leaving the gifts at my house?"

"That face says it all, doesn't it?" Dell knelt beside Emily and tapped her nose. "She knows she's in trouble."

A ripple of magic stung the air, and the pup's fur shed in clumps. As fluid as water poured from a glass into a bowl, Emily slid from one shape to another.

"Don't tell Daddy." Fat tears glistened on her thick eyelashes. *"Please."*

"Tell him what?" That she was out here? Alone? Or so near fae?

"He said fae are like rabid dogs." She hiccupped, holding in a sob. "They might look okay from a distance, but they'll bite you if you get too close."

Isaac snorted then sobered when he realized he was the only one laughing.

It sounded exactly like something Bessemer would say. "You came to get a look at me and my family?"

"Yes." Her bottom lip trembled. "I thought she was one of you. She was so nice, and so pretty, and pink is my favorite color."

Dumping a bucket of ice water over my head would have shocked me less. "You saw a girl with pink hair?"

Emily's head bobbed.

"Did you talk to her?" I grabbed her arm. "What did she say?"

"S-s-she asked me to do a favor for her. She said she was a friend of yours, and she wanted to surprise you." Emily scuttled closer to Dell. "She gave me weird gifts to put on your steps." She tugged against my arm. "She waited in the trees, and when I did good, she gave me a lollipop after."

A quiver started at the base of my tailbone and rolled up through my shoulders.

Isaac and Aunt Dot were safe, Theo was too, but Mom and Dad had all but severed ties with us. Who else would know the symbolism of those otherwise-random items? What had the newest token been? The possibility the scrunchie wasn't a plant but might be authentic chilled me to my marrow. I would get through this, and then I would suck it up and ask Aunt Dot how to contact my parents for my own peace of mind.

"A lollipop." Dell drew back with a frown. "Was there something special about them?"

Using treats as payment explained the sucker wrappers, but committing what her father would consider seditious for candy rang false.

Emily's chin hit her chest, and she sniffled. "They made it stop hurting. When I shift."

"Sweetie." Dell gathered the child in her arms and rocked her. "The pain is the price we pay for the wolf."

She curled around Dell. "Then I don't want to be a wolf."

"Yes, you do." A knowing smile skewed Dell's mouth. "I've seen you hunt. You're magic on four feet, the fastest pup in the pack."

Emily tipped a tear-stained face up at her. "I am pretty quick. I catch a lot of meat so Dad doesn't have to."

Dell smoothed the hairs from Emily's forehead. "Have you talked to your dad about this?"

"No." Horror rounded her eyes. "It would make his heart hurt, like when he says I remind him *so much* of Mom, and I don't like how sad he is when he remembers her."

The idea of Bessemer nursing an old wound might have delighted me hours earlier, but it seemed to signal the end of the world when seen through Emily's eyes. Graeson told me once there were dynamics within the pack I didn't understand. Bessemer's gentleness with Emily and her adoration of him sat like lead in my gut. What was he like when fae weren't on his lands? How were things when beta and alpha were in harmony? Would my leaving gentle the punishments? Would Graeson bowing down heal the wounds his presence inflicted or tear the pack wide open?

"What about Aisha?" Dell asked gently. "Have you talked to her?"

"She's *not* my mom," Emily growled. "I don't have to tell her anything I don't want to. Dad said so."

Another mystery solved. Aisha was the evil stepmother. How long had she held that position that Emily resented her? Would she feel differently if Imogen took her place? *I thought wargs mated for life* was on the tip of my tongue, but one glimpse of Emily's moist cheeks wired my jaw shut.

Now that the seed had been planted, it was all too easy to cast Bessemer in the role of the widower made bitter by grief. He was alpha, strong enough to survive the loss of a mate, especially when they had a child, but at what cost had he endured? And did he realize his attempts to mother Emily by surrogate were poisoning his pack by spawning avarice among the women to be the one who warmed his bed, who thawed his cold heart?

And I thought Graeson was complicated.

Blindly hating Bessemer was so much easier yesterday. Today...right now...I was being shown a different perspective, and I didn't like what I saw. That maybe—as helpful as Graeson tried to be—he was part of the problem. A big part.

"Cammie," Isaac began, an edge of temper sharpening the nickname.

Holding up my hand to silence him, I returned my focus to Emily. This was a one-shot deal. Once her father caught wind of her involvement, I would never see the girl again. Of that I was certain.

"Emily." I squatted to put us almost at eye level. "When do you meet the pink-haired lady again?"

"When the sun comes up." She blinked up at me. "Dad goes for a run every morning before anyone else is up to check in with the sentries, and I come down here."

Sentries would be guarding the borders, meaning she was safe to steal away without fear of him catching her. As hostile as her relationship with Aisha sounded, the alpha female must have no idea or else she would have turned the girl in to her father.

Night sounds filled the silence while I picked at why that felt wrong. "Why did you switch things up and come down here tonight?"

"I have a doctor's appointment in the morning." She dashed her hand beneath her nose. "I forgot about it, so I didn't tell the pink lady. I sneaked out of my room to come down here. I went to your house first, and I was going to leave her a note in our secret place, but then he—" she jerked her chin toward Isaac, "—started chasing me, and I got scared and ran."

"Where do you meet?" I nodded toward the blind Graeson and I had discovered. "There? Or somewhere else?"

"Cammie," Isaac threatened. "I don't trust that look on your face. It's the same expression you got when you were thinking of doing something that would get us both in trouble."

"There." Hushing Isaac with a flick of my fingers, I watched as Emily's gaze tagged the same spot. "I run the thing from the day before to your porch then go to her for the candy and a new item for the next day. Then I crunch the sucker on the way home so I don't have to lie to Dad when he asks who gave it to me." She wet her lips. "I don't want to get anyone else in trouble."

"She's a kid." Dell, still tuned in to Isaac's worry, clutched the girl tighter. "She's the *alpha's* kid."

Wondering where that righteous indignation had been while Graeson schemed to use me as bait, I snorted. "You act like I'm going to tie her up in the woods and sacrifice her to Charybdis."

Emily's forehead puckered. "Who's Charybdis?"

I shook my head. "No one."

"What the hell are you all talking about? Charybdis is part of that case you and Graeson were working together, right? That's how you two met." Tired of being ignored, Isaac grabbed me by the shoulders and spun me on my heels to face him. "What exactly followed you here? How long have you been hiding it from us?" He slapped a hand over my mouth and arched an eyebrow, only removing the gag when Graeson took exception to how Isaac was treating me. "So help me, Camille, if you tell me to shush one more time, I'm going to tell Mom the truth about what happened to your Precious Moments figurines collection."

Gods I hated those things, and she bought me a new one every year for my birthday. Their teardrop eyes, so full of sorrow, had kept watch over me all night while I slept when I was a kid. As an adult, I couldn't move into my own place and secure them in an out-of-state lockbox fast enough.

"I found out today, all right?" I shoved him off me. "When I visited the witches, they told me—"

"What witches?" His glare transferred to Dell as though she were to blame for my bad behavior. "When?"

"Earlier." Tired of his manhandling, I swung my arm outside his reach then sliced my hand through the air and struck his throat in the space below his jaw. He released me with a shocked gasp, and I leapt backward. "Look, I'm sorry I didn't keep you in the loop. It was stupid and dangerous, but I didn't know about this. Not until I saw the witches. I don't know how or why the killer followed me, but he did, and he selected a new avatar to help him."

"This Harlow girl," he wheezed. "Isn't that your friend?"

"Yes." I shook a hand through my hair. "She was abducted at the last crime scene, and we have reason to believe she's under his control now." I tugged on the strands. "We call her his avatar, but we don't know what it means, really." The kelpie was a killer before Charybdis. How much of what it did went against instinct? Not much I'd bet. For all we knew Charybdis had only encouraged its natural inclinations. "We don't know how he infected her, how she's being controlled, or why he chose her. We don't know anything." I amended the last to, "All I know is I have to save her."

"Tell me what you need." Simple. Straightforward. Typical Isaac.

I took his hand and squeezed it in thanks. "It's easier if I show you."

Arms loosening, Dell smiled at the girl to reassure her. "If you're not using Emily, then who...?"

I shut my eyes, exhaled and opened them. "Me."

Emily and Lori shared a similar height, build and hair color. The illusion would work at a distance.

"You," Dell groaned, hating the idea already. That made two of us.

Dell had never properly met Lori, or the shade of her that remained. That was about to change.

"Sunrise in the woods gives us shadows to play with. All we have to do is fool Harlow—Charybdis—for a few minutes." The more I spoke the more I convinced myself this had to work. It was this or the water, and I voted for this. "Between you, Graeson and Isaac, we can cover the area. That way if she runs, we'll have a head start catching her."

"Catching her could be dangerous." Dell worried her bottom lip. "We don't know what magic she has access to through him. We don't know how much control he has over her." She winced as she drew blood. "There's too damn much we don't know."

"This is getting confusing." Isaac rubbed his forehead, following along as best he could with his limited information. "Let's stick with calling Charybdis Harlow. That's the physical body we're looking for, right? We just assume the lights are on and no one's home."

"That works for me," Dell said with a slight flutter in her lashes.

"Confronting Harlow is a big risk, but I can't leave her out there. As long as she's under Charybdis's influence, she's dangerous." Another thought hit me, and it should have occurred to me sooner. I turned to Emily. "Did the girl tell you why she didn't deliver the gifts to me herself?"

"She said you liked to play tricks, but they only worked on fae." Emily eyed me as if expecting me to do something sneaky to prove her right. "She wanted to give you the presents herself, but one of your fairy spells made her feel like ants were stinging her."

"The wards," I murmured. "She couldn't get past the wards."

The wards blocked only malicious entities or those who wished me or mine harm. That Harlow couldn't cross them meant Charybdis's evil had tainted her psyche in a tangible way, proof positive she was his avatar. She had to find a loophole. To beat the wards, she enlisted the help of a child. A girl. There was symbolism there, the continuance of a twisted theme. Gods only knew what she planned for Emily when the last token had been delivered.

"That's why she enlisted Emily." Dell pieced it together. "Emily didn't wish you harm, so she could pass through.

Harlow…" Her lips mashed together before blurting out in front of the girl that her new fae friend wasn't one of the good guys. "That's bad."

I rubbed my tired eyes, but they kept settling on Emily. "You need to get her home before her dad misses her."

Dell stood and wisely kept a hand cuffed on the girl's arm. "What do you want me to tell him?"

As much as I dreaded the fallout and the anti-fae propaganda, Bessemer—and the pack—were entitled to know what prowled the woods alongside their children. "The truth." I massaged the base of my neck and scowled at the silver wolf. "Now would be a great time for you to ditch the fur suit. This is beta business. *You* should be the one marching Emily home, and *you* should be the one talking to Bessemer. Not Dell."

The wolf hung his head, and a low groan issued from his chest. Paws heavy, he loped into the trees and out of sight.

"Graeson," I called. "I didn't mean…"

"It's okay." Dell touched my shoulder. "He'll come around. Just give him some space."

"I'm going home before I cause any more collateral damage." Turning my back on the spot where Harlow had lurked, watching me and my family for days, raised gooseflesh down my arms. "Be careful, Dell. I mean it. If Bessemer wants his pound of flesh, send him to me." The threat of a shift rode the rise of those chill bumps. "If he puts a hand on you, I'm going to bite it off."

Behind her, Emily cocked her head at me. "Imogen says stuff like that."

Thoughts mired on Graeson, I managed a real smile at the hope Bessemer's latest bedmate might actually stick. "Sometimes it's up to us girls to tell guys when they're being silly."

She digested that nugget of wisdom with a bob of her head.

I had to give the kid credit. She didn't beg or cry or struggle as Dell marched her toward Silverback Lane.

She wiped her nose and eyes with the backs of her hands, straightened her shoulders and went to face the music.

Isaac stepped beside me, and we trudged for home, his gaze sweeping the night. "Where's the wolf?" He whistled. "Here, boy."

"He's not a pet," I snapped without heat. "He's a wild animal."

"With the heart of a man." He speared me with his gaze. "And the hots for my little cousin."

A flush baked my face stiff and itchy. "I'm not having this conversation with you."

"Not so fast." He caught me by the wrist when I tried to open my door and frowned at the small yard inside the circle of our trailers. "Looks like Mom has decided to inflict family night on us. We have to at least swing by and make our excuses." If he heard my groan, he ignored it and hauled me into the backyard. "It's your own fault her nesting instincts kicked in. You showed up with Dell, who was half-dead, then locked Mom up with the locals while your wolfman hunted you down. That's a lot for her to handle. You know she's pure momma bear when it comes to her kids." I warmed to be included in her brood, at least until Isaac added, "Huh. Now that I think about it, you got attacked by the wolfman and still somehow you ended up in bed together?" Any higher and his eyebrows would wing right off his forehead. "That's messed up, coz."

"You don't know the half of it," I muttered.

He turned me loose, plugged his ears, and said in a loud voice, "And I don't want to either."

Aunt Dot had arranged a snacker's paradise on the compact folding table near her home. Four chairs huddled around it, though only three people ever filled them. The normality of the scene, of her smile when she spotted me and her scent when she reeled me in for a hug, was exactly what I needed. Not the gloom of my trailer's blacked-out interior or another night spent in the company of a wolf, but this. Warm arms, genuine smiles. Simple. Easy. Uncomplicated.

"There's a meteor shower tonight." Aunt Dot shoved me down in my chair and slapped an icy can of soda in my hand then did the same for Isaac. "The person who counts the most wins. Winner gets breakfast in bed for a month."

"A month?" Isaac perked, winking at me. "It's on." Behind her back, he held up two fingers and mouthed, "Two minutes."

Sitting with Aunt Dot for a couple of minutes wouldn't kink our timeline. Giving him a thumbs-up, I popped the cap and took a long sip. "You two have upped the ante while I've been away."

Once assured she held our full attention, Aunt Dot launched into a recitation of how we, as Geminis, should have some interest in the skies because of our namesake constellation. Nodding along with the familiar lecture, I soaked up the normal before ruining Aunt Dot's family night with the ominous news I was, in all likelihood, being hunted by a serial killer and his new avatar.

Not five minutes later a bellow shook the trees and silenced the night birds, crickets and frogs.

"What on earth?" Aunt Dot's hand lifted to her throat. "What was that? Pumpkin?"

"That was the sound of an alpha warg realizing his daughter has been consorting with fae." I set my drink aside, stood and rolled my shoulders to loosen them. "Company's coming."

Isaac rose to his feet and positioned himself beside me. "How bad is this going to get?"

"This is Theo-discovering-you-swiped-the-keys-to-his-Camaro-and-wrecked-it-on-a-date-with-his-girlfriend bad."

"You said your brother wrecked that car—" she began.

"Not now, Mom." He shot me a *thanks so much* look that promised retribution via ceramic figurines. "You ought to go inside until we see how this shakes out."

"And leave my babies out here?" Her laughter rang cold in the night. "I don't think so."

We three stood, shoulder to shoulder, eyes on the forest beyond our wards.

We didn't have to wait long.

CHAPTER SEVENTEEN

The alpha burst from the forest's heart, all rippling muscle and simmering rage, with one hand locked around Emily's slender wrist and the other clamped on Dell's upper arm. The whites of his eyes shone with madness.

"You, fae. You did this." He shook Dell until she stumbled then hauled her back and lifted her until she was forced to stand on tiptoe or allow him to dislocate her shoulder. "You brought that evil back here."

Isaac tensed in my periphery, but Aunt Dot restrained him with a hand to his chest.

"I did." All the evidence pointed at that being true. I wasn't going to deny it. "I'm sorry. I didn't know."

"My daughter—*my only child*—met with that monster. She took spelled food from it. The same fae who killed our Marie." He flung Dell forward, and she landed in a heap. "Take that and get off my land." His face purpled, bones gliding beneath his skin as he fought the change and bellowed, *"Now."*

Trembling, Dell crawled on her hands and knees inside the safety of the wards. Isaac ran to her, cradled her in his arms and carried her inside his trailer before rejoining me in the yard.

Guilt drummed a painful tattoo in my chest.

My fault. I did this. I cost Dell everything. Please let Graeson be able to undo it.

Beneath that another primitive rhythm pounded. Dell was mine to protect, and I had failed her. The urge was visceral and flooded my mouth with saliva. My fingertips burned, the tips of claws pressing against the fragile pink barrier of my skin.

"I'm not on your land," I said, voice hoarse from my thwarted change. "I'll leave Villanow, but not until I've captured the fae." Harlow deserved better than to be torn apart by wolves. She was a victim too, but Bessemer's prejudice blinded him to that fact. "You have my word she'll be relinquished into conclave custody."

"Conclave," he scoffed. "They're your law, not mine. Fae who kill on my lands are mine to punish. The conclave had their chance. They won't get another."

"We don't have evidence the fae who killed Marie is here," I said calmly. "It appears he's chosen a new avatar, and as far as we know, she has committed no crime. She's his victim as much as Marie was."

"I'm done hearing your lies." He stabbed the air in my direction. "I gave your family sanctuary. I suffered your toxic presence among my kin for Cord's sake, because grief had carved him hollow and he seemed to think you'd fill him." His lip curled. "And this is how you repay our hospitality, how you repay Cord. The creature who killed his sister followed you here. It went after *my* daughter."

"I haven't lied to you, and I didn't scheme my way here. I came at Graeson's request." And oh how I wished he were here to back up that claim. "I've been hunting this creature for months. Until today I had no reason to believe it was in the vicinity, let alone on pack lands."

We might have made more progress too, if not for the pack drama Bessemer had instigated at every turn, but I was hardly going to throw that in his face now.

"Lies are the language of the fae." He cocked his head to one side, a predator scenting prey. "What hunting have you done if you didn't know it was here?"

I bit my lips before they had a chance to tingle. The last thing I needed was Bessemer figuring out I had been removed from the case or who had been helping me continue to work it off the clock. Armed with that

information, I had no doubt he would be thrilled to call
the conclave and tell them exactly what I had been up to
and how my actions had endangered the fragile accord
between fae and native supernaturals.

The fall was coming, but I didn't want Thierry and Mai
or any of the others helping to tumble after me.

"You had your chance to make this right." He glanced
around the clearing. Golden eyes winked in the trees.
"Now it's our turn." His voice rose to a stout cry. "We lost
one of ours to this unnatural creature. A child. As your
alpha and as a father, I give my word we won't lose
another. Tonight we hunt fae, and tomorrow we wake
with the knowledge our children are safe from their evil."

Summoned from the darkness, Aisha strolled to his
side. He didn't acknowledge her except to transfer Emily
from his grip to hers. Imogen emerged next, rolling her
hips with invitation, and his hungry smile welcomed her
to join him. She claimed the spot on his other side.

"Listen to me." Slowly, I approached them, leaving my
family in the backyard, near the pulsing heart of our
strongest wards. "Thanks to Emily, we know the fae's
routine. We know where and when to find her. Let's wait
for morning. Working together we have a better chance of
succeeding. We need her alive and unharmed to find out
where the killer's gone."

"We've heard enough." Bessemer bent to Aisha's ear.
Her mouth tightened and eyes shot daggers at Imogen,
but she took Emily and left. "The time for talking has
passed. Blood answers for blood." Shaking his fist at the
moon, he boomed, "Tonight we hunt!"

Bone-chilling howls lit up the night, the wolves' songs a
haunting melody that played while they dispersed.

"Hide behind your wards," Bessemer taunted. "I've a
taste for fae blood, and I'm not particular where it comes
from."

"I can't let you kill her." I could no more return to my
chair and watch the meteor shower with an ear cocked for

the sound of Harlow's screams than he could go home and wait for the dawn. "She's a good kid."

At least she had been before Charybdis sank his hooks into her.

She's human, I almost said in a bid for mercy. But Bessemer was past hearing, and he wouldn't believe me anyway. It might encourage him, in fact, the hope I was telling the truth and his prey was so much weaker than the rest of us.

Or...she had been. With Charybdis amplifying her powers, nothing was certain.

Not knowing was the worst part.

"Marie was a good kid too." Tight as a rope stretched thin, his voice strummed with determination. "There are a lot of children here, and I won't lose another one." His nostrils flared, and he hesitated when he might have turned. "Where is Cord?"

A pang rocked me. "I don't know."

"Convenient that he vanished before the call to hunt was issued," he noted. "Which side would he choose, do you think?"

"The side he felt was in the right." His personal sense of honor would permit him to do nothing less.

"The man, perhaps. The wolf? He will answer to me," he promised. "Make your peace with that."

Would he? Was that an alpha's power or an egotist's expectation? This was the first time the wolf had left my side in days. At this point Graeson was more man than wolf in temperament and, most times, in action. Did that mean he could resist the song of his kin? The lure to run alongside others of his kind? The promise of hot blood to rinse out his mouth? I wasn't sure. I hoped his will, his memory of Harlow, remained stronger than that.

Isaac crossed to me and slung his arm around my shoulder, grinning coldly at Bessemer. "Happy hunting."

The alpha paused, as though sifting the words for deeper meaning. Brow still tight, he turned and headed for the deepest shadows. Sooner than I expected, a new voice lifted the joyous chorus. That fast the alpha had shifted and picked up the scent.

Tracking the movement of the pack was simple. How Bessemer expected to catch a fae while making so much racket was beyond me. Once the stragglers had moved on, Isaac dropped his arm and rubbed his face vigorously.

The glimmer of hope that had risen in me when the possibility of confronting Harlow on land was a thing I could wake to and enact vanished in a cold rush of reality.

Back to Plan A.

"I need to grab something from my place." I would just have to hope it worked on humans *and* fae. "Then we have to get to the lake without being torn apart by wargs."

"Sounds doable." He backed toward his trailer. "Let me grab some gear, and I'll meet you back here."

"What about me?" Aunt Dot glanced between us. "What can I do?"

"Stay put," we said together.

"Someone has to take care of Dell." Isaac hugged his mom one-armed. "You have to keep her here. She's been cast out, and that means anyone in her pack can attack her without provocation or retribution."

"He's right." I squeezed her shoulder. "We need you to take care of her and keep our wards up. When we get Harlow back—" *please let us get her back,* "—we need things here at full power to keep out the wargs."

"You mentioned witches." Aunt Dot frowned. "If they're any good, they could dismantle the wards given enough time."

"They're good." Dell wobbled down the steps from Isaac's trailer wearing one of his dress shirts. "The best."

"Then we can't stay here." Aunt Dot shrugged off Isaac and went to steady Dell. She led her to the chairs and set her down gently. "Theo is in Orlando. We can always head there."

Normally, I would balk at the suggestion, but after tonight, Aunt Dot would want to mother hen all her chicks. "Okay." I tried not to grimace. "That sounds good."

"We can handle this." Dell's voice sounded pancake-flat. "You get the girl."

"You're coming with us to Florida." Isaac left no room for argument. "Put your things in my trailer."

This morning that would have jolted her awake. Now he might have been commenting on the weather instead of asking her to move in with him, even temporarily.

"Dell..." Unsure what to do, what to say to make this better, I rocked my weight from foot to foot. I had to go, but I couldn't leave her this way. "These people are your family."

"Not anymore." Tears overflowed her cheeks. "This hasn't felt like home in a long time anyway."

The cost of those words hurt me on her behalf, because I wasn't sure they were true. "What about Meemaw?"

"I can get word to her." She wiped her face and sucked in a breath. "It's not right to ask her to abandon her home...at her age...because I..."

Aunt Dot wrapped Dell in her arms, and Isaac gave me a nudge to get moving. "Mom will take care of her." He started backing toward his trailer. "Harlow will have heard all that racket. If she was on land, she won't be for long. The safest place for her is in the water where the wargs can't reach her."

A nod was all I could manage. I swallowed hard, turned and dashed into my house to grab the bag Harlow had abandoned in Abbeville. I didn't own a swimsuit, but I was a jogger in another life, so I pulled on a gray sports bra with matching spandex workout pants that cut off just below my knees and molded to my legs. I tugged a T-shirt on over it and shoved my feet into sneakers I could kick off before I...

Don't think about it.

A minute passed while I stood frozen in the bedroom with my hand on Harlow's bag and my heart lodged in my throat before someone pounded flat-palmed on the exterior. I jumped, and the spike of adrenaline thawed my fear. I slid the bag on and jogged out to meet Isaac.

Cutting short his lingering glance at Dell's back, he hefted a ratty duffle bag over his shoulder. "Let's go."

He stepped free of the wards and onto Chandler pack land ahead of me. I blinked, and he was flat on his back, buried under the weight of a snarling warg. At least one more set of golden eyes pierced the gloom.

Great. Bessemer had positioned sentries to keep us occupied.

Magic coasted over me, the change to half-warg complete in the time it took Isaac to throw off his attacker. His eyes widened when he spotted me. I didn't have time to let him gawk; I made a fist and knocked the second wolf out of the air. The first scrambled and leapt for Isaac, who had shifted so that his arms were as thick as tree trunks and shaggy as Spanish moss. Blunt fingers the color of swamp water dug into the warg's throat until it went limp in his grip.

"Don't kill them." The second wolf skirted me and pounced on Isaac, who was pushing himself off the ground. "Incapacitate them."

"Oh..." he panted through clenched teeth, "...I plan on it."

Dodging his beefy arms, I gripped the wolf's ruff and hauled him off Isaac, who clamped a fiber-thin silver collar around his throat with stubby yet nimble fingers. The warg howled and thrashed until I dropped him.

Isaac rolled to his feet, a silver loop glinting in his fist that he was quick to snap onto the other downed warg. "Why didn't they attack you?" He gestured toward my face. "Does it have something to do with your aspect?"

"I don't know." I wondered that myself. "Maybe they're loyal to Graeson."

It was the only reason I could fathom why they wouldn't harm his mate at Bessemer's say-so. For their sake, and Graeson's, I hoped their alpha never caught wind of their rebellion, or there would be bloodshed.

"We need to show this to Mom." He studied me a moment longer. "No offense, but you're not skilled enough to evolve or hold a shift to this degree unless..." He raked his fingers through his hair. "This level of imitation with a secondary shape is only seen in Gemini who are *becoming*."

"That's not possible." I smoothed my thumb over my spur. "I imitate Lori."

"Our resets are fluid," he said gently. "They must adapt as our twin ages, gets scars, puts on weight." He petted down the length of my forearm, a fierce curiosity blazing in his eyes. "You haven't taken Lori's blood in years, but you've been ingesting warg blood regularly for a prolonged amount of time. Paired with the mental bond and your attachment to these people..." He buzzed with excitement at the possibility. "Maybe your reset is, I don't know, resetting."

Dumbfounded, I stood there working my jaw like a fish out of water.

Isaac cinched his hands around my upper arms and gave me a light shake. "Later," he promised. "Mom and I will help you get to the bottom of this once your friend is safe, okay?"

Unable to use my words yet, I nodded at him.

Releasing me with a grin, he set off at a jog. I cast one final glance at the pitiful wolves and followed, shoving down the possibility I might be losing Lori all over again. This time for good.

"Hey." I caught up to him. "Since when are you packing silver?"

"Did you really think I was going to visit a pack of wargs unarmed? This one in particular?" He snorted. "A few calls were all it took for me to discover the Chandler pack alpha more than dislikes or distrusts fae, but hates them. I wasn't going to bring my family into a hostile situation unarmed."

"I didn't know it was this bad." Shame flash-burned up my nape. "I should have done the research."

"You trusted Graeson."

"I'm not sure that's true." Trust wasn't a byproduct of panic. "There's something you ought to know about Graeson and me, something I should have told you and Aunt Dot once I got here."

"That you're not really a couple?"

I stumbled over my own feet. "You knew?"

"Please." He scoffed. "You? In love? That fast? With the brother of a victim from a case you worked?"

My pace faltered as each point hammered home. "What about Aunt Dot?"

"Oh, she knows." He ducked his head to cover his laugh. "She let me listen in on his phone call. You know she's got a BS meter, and it shot off the charts when he started spinning his yarn."

"Why did she go along with it?"

"She didn't believe him." He cut his eyes toward me. "She figured he was a liar and that you'd tear him a new one, but...you didn't. You covered for him. You went along with his crackpot plan." He readjusted his bag. "She thought... She hoped you might..."

Pain slid between my ribs, sharp as a knife. "She hoped pretending might make it real."

And it had, hadn't it? Somewhere along the way I had fallen for Graeson. He was mine now, wolf and all.

The look Isaac shot me bounced my words back at me, like he thought maybe that hope hadn't been one-sided.

"Cammie, you lied to Mom. Me, well, it goes with the territory. But Mom?" His grin was downright wolfish. "You had your head so high in the clouds you didn't do your homework before a move. Usually you have binders filled with everything from maps to the grocery store to planned emergency escape routes. You always call the local marshal's office to get a heads-up on the local troublemakers."

"I didn't—" I spluttered. "That's not—"

"You could have told us to turn around, go back to Three Way. You could have said to head west, to Texas, where that new friend of yours is. You didn't. You let Cord lure you here, because you wanted to come."

"I put us all in danger."

He bumped my shoulder with his. "What is love if not a risk?"

I bumped back and sent him careening off to regain his balance. "No one said anything about love."

"I did. Just now." He mimed cleaning out his ears. "Weren't you listening?"

A mud-brown blur darted across our path, and I skidded to a hard stop, flinging my arm out to catch Isaac across the chest.

"Can you subdue him?" He jingled links in his hand. "Pin him, and I'll give him a new necklace."

"Will do."

Isaac sidestepped to the left, and the wolf took the bait. He sprung into the air, and I whirled on him, clamping my hands around his throat and jerking him back like he was a dog at the end of his leash. Jaw clenched, I hit the dirt. The weight of the struggling wolf yanked me to one side, and soon we were rolling in the dirt. "Anytime now," I ground out at Isaac.

A twist of Isaac's wrist and a snap of metal, and we had subdued a third warg.

The ease with which we had made it this far buoyed me with a false sense of hope. I should have known better. Bessemer was smart, and he was pissed. He didn't waste energy sweeping the woods to end up at the pond. Like us, he had gone straight there. Dozens of wolves mingled in the grass by the time we arrived, and golden lights I knew for eyes winked in the distance.

Fisting Isaac's shirt, I yanked him behind a pair of oaks grown together with a fat base and thick fingerlike branches arcing overhead. All those sensitive noses would sniff us out and quick. We had to act fast.

Isaac rustled his bag, wincing at the noise. "What's our next move?"

"I have to get to the water." I dipped my hand in Harlow's bag and found the tin with the gill goop. The tail would be a hindrance since I had no idea how to use one, so the shorts got tucked back in the bottom. "This should give me magic gills."

"Should?" He gripped my arm. "You haven't tested it?"

A warg passing by swiveled his ears.

"No time like the present." I twisted the cap, stuck my fingers in the icy slime that smelled of herbs and growing things, and smeared it down my throat. The burning started before I lowered my hand. Harlow once mentioned it took a few minutes to take effect. That's all I needed. "Here." I closed the tin and flung the bag into his arms. "Get home if you can, get safe if you can't."

"What if the magic doesn't work?" His eyes pleaded for me to reconsider. "It might be keyed to the girl."

Beyond our hiding spot, the warg's nostrils twitched, perhaps scenting the pungent salve, and his gaze swung our way. He flung his head back and howled.

We had been discovered.

"Go, go, go," I chanted at Isaac, giving him a shove.

Not waiting to see if he'd listened, I barreled into the wolf who'd tattled on us, and kept going. The leap to the basin sent dull shock waves through my knees. The slick mud nursed my sneakers, and I skated over its slimy surface. Cursing, I kicked off my shoes and grimaced as I sank in muck to the ankles.

Growls rose over my shoulder. They sounded...wrong. Distant. Fear for Isaac wobbled my ankle, but I steadied myself. A second's hesitation, and I would collapse in a heap and tremble at the water's edge as the wolves descended.

Don't look back. Keep moving. Isaac can take care of himself.

Thick brown sludge squished underfoot and slurped my toes. The divot in the dried bed loomed. The murky water sat mirror-smooth and waiting. I sucked in sharp gulps of humid air, counting down the seconds until I sank or swim.

My neck itched and stung, a rash of irritation spreading down to my collarbone, but I could breathe past it. Was that right? Harlow's tail required water to change. Was this magic the same?

There was only one way to find out. Muscles tensed, I leapt for the pond's heart.

"Ellis. *Wait*."

My head whipped toward the masculine voice, but it was an afterthought. I was airborne. Nothing, not even those fear-bright hazel eyes set in a face I had feared never seeing human again, could alter my trajectory now.

Impact.

My heart stuttered as the water closed over my head.

Muffled silence embraced me. Bubbles tickled my face as I expelled oxygen. The weightless, floating sensation should have brought me to the surface. It might have, had I not seen it, had not the moonlight pierced the abyss to show it to me.

A wisp of fabric. Ruffled hem. Fat moons. Grinning stars.

Lori.

But this was Marie's grave, not hers.

"Why are you here?" The scream flashed white before my eyes—more oxygen lost—but I kept screaming. "*Lori.* Wait."

The material flittered away, and I dove after it as though my life—and sanity—depended on it.

I kicked and clawed. I flung my arms and scissored my legs. The blackness became absolute. Darkness devoured me, cold and hungry. My heart pounded, frantic. My chest compressed. I raked at my throat, scoring flesh with my fingernails.

No gills. The water hadn't activated them but washed them away.

Either the magic was keyed to Harlow or to humans. I would never get the chance to tell Isaac he was right to worry.

The fist tightening around my throat gave a squeeze, and my vision went hazy.

"Wake up." Sticky fingers peeled open my eyelids. "Come on. Let's go."

I swatted Lori's hand. "What time is it?"

"Shh." She pressed a finger to her lips. "Or you'll wake up Mom and Dad."

I rubbed my eyes and yawned. "Where are we going?"

"To the beach." Her eyes sparkled. "The ghost crabs will be out. Don't you want to see them?"

"Mom said—"

"Mom said, Mom said," she parroted. "Fine. Be a baby. Stay here with your mommy. Maybe I'll go ask Theo if he wants to go."

"Stop calling me that. I'm not a baby." I swung my legs over the edge of the bed. "I'll go."

Sharp pressure constricted my middle, and a few paltry bubbles tickled my eyelids on their way to the surface.

Lori stood, arms outstretched. Ghost crabs scuttled over her feet, and she laughed and flexed her toes, daring them to pinch her. I buried mine to protect them.

"Isn't this great?" She flung an arm around my shoulders and jabbed her finger at the twinkling stars. "Look at all those. Gemini is out there somewhere. I bet it's up there looking down at us while we're looking up at it." She jumped and waved her arms. "Hey. We're down here."

Laughing, I yanked on her arm. "You're crazy."

"You followed me out here." She spun in a wild circle and kicked the surf. "What does that make you?"

The weightlessness of my body vanished. Had I hit the bottom? Was a plume of sediment rising around me, clogging my nostrils? Had I missed the entrance to the caves?

"Open your eyes, sweetheart." Warm hands cupped my face. "That's my girl."

I'm not your girl, I thought back at him on reflex, the taste of his blood in the back of my throat. Except now that I had won him, I suppose I was.

A figure carved from blinding light stepped into my field of vision, despite the fact I hadn't opened my eyes.

"Now you're just being stubborn." His mental laugh throbbed with relief. *"I thought I'd lost you."*

If he said more, I didn't hear it. Even the bright burn of him behind my eyes wasn't enough to anchor me anymore.

Alone in the dark, I drifted.

CHAPTER EIGHTEEN

"There you are."

Shifting onto my side, I groaned and coughed up the taste of pond water. My chest ached deep like the time I had contracted pneumonia, and I tasted blood from where I'd bitten my tongue. I opened my eyes and found Graeson, mostly dry, leaning over me.

The stark relief on his face transmuted to a radiant kind of joy that warmed me from the inside out.

"Thank God," he breathed. "I was getting worried."

"You weren't the only one." I rubbed my thumb over the leather bracelet on his wrist, which seemed to have survived his ordeal without so much as a single hair out of place. "I wasn't sure you were coming back."

"I'll never leave you, Ellis." He hooked a smile on his lips. "You're stuck with me now." He leaned down, cheek brushing mine. *"Mate."*

"Your wolf talks too much." The answer to "*how much does the man know of the wolf's dealings*" had been answered definitively for me. "He really needs to learn to keep his muzzle shut."

The mention of muzzle sent his gaze dipping to the calf he'd shredded, and regret filled his eyes.

"He and I have an understanding now." I sounded braver than I felt. He had decided there at the last minute not to eat me.

He grunted. "I noticed. He fought like hell to stay with you."

A filament of warmth whispered through me. "He did?"

The mystery of the wargs' nature was unraveling, and yet there were still so many layers to peel back I wondered if I would ever reach the heart of them. Of him.

"You're ours, Ellis." Heat flickered in his gaze. *"Mine."*

The single word, rumbled in his guttural and possessive voice, threatened to liquefy me where I lay. Forcing myself to remember he was no longer a wolf I could pet when the mood struck me, I shoved upright on wobbly arms and blinked at our surroundings. "Where are we?"

"The caves beneath the pond." He glanced around too, as if he hadn't dared peel his eyes away from me to examine the oddly civilized space where we found ourselves. This had been the sprite's home, and it still looked the part. There were sconces mounted to the walls, but no fire, and the walls glowed with bioluminescence. "We've been down here the better part of an hour, and I haven't heard a peep. I can smell her. It's Harlow, but it's Charybdis too. His scent is overlaying hers. His imprint is stronger, because the kelpie nested here too."

"So she might still be down here." With the pack in the forest, she hadn't had many places to run or much time to make her escape before we disturbed her. I pushed to my feet, and Graeson caught me before I stumbled. "How did you know to find me at the lake?"

"I went to the Garzas after you hatched your brilliant scheme." Sarcasm thickened his voice. "I wanted to quiz them about the magic you planned to use."

"Oh." I rubbed my throat. No gills. No goo. Just smooth skin and scabs from where I had clawed myself. "The magic didn't work for me. It washed off in the water."

"I had a little better luck." His gaze went serious. "We almost didn't make it."

"You don't have gills either." That I would have noticed. "What went wrong? Why didn't it work? What did the Garzas tell you?"

"Enzo said without a sample he couldn't be certain, that he'd bet the magic was keyed to humans. To have it keyed to Harlow specifically would require DNA samples, fresh ones, constantly, in order to keep up with minute changes in her biology." Graeson shrugged. "He figured there was a fifty-fifty shot it would work on me, but on you..." His eyes narrowed with admonition. "There was no chance of it working with fae biology, not when it was meant to allow a human to mimic a fae."

"I should have tested it beforehand." I suppressed the urge to fidget. "There wasn't time."

"You would have had plenty of time if you had died," he scolded. "All of eternity."

I dipped my head and let the words come. "Thank you for saving me."

His lips hitched as the weight of those first two words registered, but he didn't emphasize them, which helped ease my knotted gut. Thanks were favors owed, and I had just granted him a boon.

"You're welcome." An odd softening I had never heard in his voice lifted my head in time to capture his gaze as he added, "No thanks necessary."

Eager as I was to start exploring, right now a wall of bare man-chest blocked my line of sight.

The view didn't offend me as much as it might have once.

Graeson wrapped his wide palm around my neck and anchored me a scant inch from him. He didn't put his other arm around me, but he did dip his head and inhale the scent of my skin. I saw when chill bumps raised hairs down his arms and heard the low sound he made in the back of his throat.

For a second I had forgotten what this stolen moment forced me to remember. The rush of waking in a strange place had stunned me, but it was coming back to me how Graeson and I hadn't parted on good terms. The last I saw of him he was still a wolf, and I had snapped at him. This Graeson was all warm skin and...naked man.

"Are you okay?" I whispered, unsure why I was being quiet except it felt right.

"I am now." He pressed his lips against my temple, and my eyes closed. "I was…lost…there for a while."

I nodded, a jerky motion that tipped me forward. I dared to press my hands against his hard chest to steady myself. No. That was a lie. My palms itched with the need to smooth his contours and reassure myself he was here, whole. This place…it had been a home, but it had been the lair of a monster too, and it might have been the last place his sister was alive.

If I could have bound his head in bubble wrap to preserve his fragile mental state, I would have.

"We have to find Harlow." I stepped back, severing that timid physical connection. "I can go alone if…" If it was too much to risk what he might find.

"I'm not letting you out of my sight." He clasped my hand and speared his fingers between mine. "You tend to almost drown when I'm not around, and I'd prefer to be the only one giving you mouth-to-mouth."

A flush stole up my neck that sizzled in my cheeks. "Okay," I croaked, unsure what to do with my hand now that he held it. My elbow locked, my arm as foreign as a wooden plank sticking out of the sleeve of my shirt.

Comfortable with touch the way all wargs were, Graeson squeezed his fist and sent reassurance flooding through me until I seemed made of flesh and bone after all.

His keen nose led us to an arched doorway with ornaments cast from clay. "She's down there."

"You're sure?" The nervous, hopeful question popped out. "I— Sorry. I trust you. I just…"

The silence weighed on us. I wasn't sure what we'd find down there, but I sensed it would be nothing good.

Another comforting squeeze of his hand. "I know."

Together we walked the gently sloped path until it opened wide into a cavern that appeared to once serve as a sitting room. Couches and tables were organized in the same way you'd expect to find them in a house but...off...just a bit. The deeper we went into the room, the more odds and ends I spotted.

"This is all debris from the pond." Graeson voiced what had been itching the back of my mind.

"She used everything." Old Christmas ornaments hung from the ceiling on fishing line. Tires stacked two high made the tables I'd noticed. One wall's archway was framed by license plates. "This is amazing."

To think the sprite had lost all this—a home she had poured so much of her heart into creating.

We kept exploring, and I almost wished we hadn't. I was the one who found it, a time capsule sure to cast more fractures in Graeson's already shattered soul. I waffled on the threshold. In the end, I didn't have to speak a word. Drawn by my presence or by some faint scent, he arrived a heartbeat behind me.

The cramped room had been emptied of its furnishings. All that remained were a pair of couch cushions shoved together like a mattress with a thin sheet crumpled at one end and a bowl that might have once held water or food.

The wooden stiffness from my arm seemed to have infected Graeson's legs. He crossed the room, gait uneven, and squatted by the messy pallet. His hand hovered over the sheet for a full minute, maybe longer, before he fisted it and brought the fabric to his nose. His back muscles shifted as his lungs expanded. The wobble of his exhale, as though it snagged in his throat, fractured my heart.

Slowly, I crossed to him and rested my hand on his shoulder.

"He kept her here." His knuckles whitened on the pitiful sheet that had been Marie's only source of comfort in this cold place. "All that time she was right here." He punched the floor, and the scent of copper hit the air as his knuckles burst. "Right *here*."

"You couldn't have known." I toyed with the ends of his hair. "There's no way you could have guessed what we're dealing with now, then."

"What is...?" He shoved apart the cushions he'd disturbed and lifted a ring of some sort. "Her ring. She wore it every day. I thought it must have been lost when..." Raw and ruined, his voice scraped. "I bought this for her." He polished it with the sheet then held it up to me. "She spotted it in a rinky-dink shop in Atlanta when I took her to the aquarium."

The tiny gold band looked impossibly small balanced on the tip of his finger. A stylized wolf's head adorned the center, and diamond chips glinted in its eyes.

"It's beautiful." I kept my fingers tunneled in his hair. "I'm glad you have it."

"I don't have anywhere to put it." He reached for my hand. "My fingers are too thick to wear it."

Honored at the task he'd given me, I spread my fingers. "It might fit my pinky."

The ring slid on, chill and damp, as though the heat from Graeson's touch failed to permeate the metal.

Twisting the ring to situate the wolf, he shook out the cushions and sheet before rising. No other treasures were discovered, and we resumed our search for Harlow. Not until I found myself spinning the slight ring around my finger did it hit me that Graeson had put it on the same side as I wore Harlow's bracelet. I rolled my shoulder, the extra weight on that arm imagined, but I still felt tipped to that side.

I retreated to the doorway and turned my back on Graeson, keeping an eye on the hall. He deserved a moment alone in the room with the specter of his sister, so I guarded us from ambush while he grieved.

I whirled toward him when his palm landed on my shoulder and searched his carefully blank face for signs he was ready to go.

"This will be the last time we get the chance to explore this place," he said, voice grinding like crushed boulders. "We should clear the cavern as we go."

Nodding silent agreement, I followed him into the hall. The musty odors told my heightened senses the rooms we passed were empty and had been for a long time, but we stopped in every one to be certain we left no evidence behind. Erasure spells were Charybdis's trademark, after all.

I swept the last room on my side before Graeson finished his and waited in the passageway. A forked tunnel loomed ahead. I inhaled in each direction, frowning at the heavy scents overlaying the hallways. Knowing Harlow was so close made my heart pound. If we rescued her physical body from Charybdis, she could detox somewhere like Edelweiss, where the staff could apply what they'd learned treating Ayer to her.

Graeson joined me and gestured ahead, leaving the choice of direction up to me. Even his sensitive nose must have trouble parsing the fresher path due to the dankness and moldy smells. I chose right, and we walked straight into a dead end.

The wall curved, like a bubble, and inside of the circular alcove, a rusty nail protruded. Hanging from the nail a wad of fabric *drip, drip, dripped* a rivulet that diverged around me. The pattern... It wasn't possible.

Fat moons.

Grinning stars.

Lori.

A crack rang out when my knees buckled, and I crashed to the floor, a supplicant before my own version of a holy relic. I smelled blood, but I didn't feel the pain. I felt...nothing. Less than numb. Anesthetized.

"Ellis."

Hazel eyes flecked with gold filled my vision as Graeson squatted in front of me. His arms threaded under mine and held me upright until my head stopped spinning.

"What's wrong?" He raked his gaze over me, searching for wounds. "What happened?"

Trembling lips pressed together, I shook my head and pushed him back to give me breathing room. It took a few tries before I could stand, and a few tries more than that to get my legs to swing one in front of the other. Slowly, painfully, I approached the alcove. Reading my shock, Graeson flanked me, giving me a moment to absorb what I was seeing while watching our backs.

I gathered the tattered nightgown in my fist and searched for the tag. I flipped it up with my thumb, and there they were, initials written in the strong block letters of my mother's hand with a black permanent marker.

LGE

Lori Grace Ellis.

I crushed the gown to my chest. I was already soaked through. More water wasn't going to hurt me. Holding this—this hurt. It was impossible. Lori was *gone*. Taken by the sea. Her body was never recovered. That meant this gown, the one she wore that terrible night we explored the beach, should have been as lost as she was. Yet here it was, in my arms, as my sister never would be again.

The pattern was over a decade old. The fabric should have been out of print. The gown couldn't be an original. Was this meant to be yet another taunt? Another token that would have showed up on my steps one day? Where had Charybdis found it to give Harlow? A thrift store? Did killer fae shop on eBay? How had he known the significance? How had he copied Mom's handwriting? How had he known to?

"My sister—" my voice broke, "—wore this the night she..." A sob attempted to break through, almost snapping my sternum in the process. Arms folded around me, I held the gown plastered to me, a hug that would never reach the tiny body that had once worn it. "This... It can't be hers. It's not possible."

Understanding dawned, and his forehead wrinkled. "Are you sure it's the same one?"

That pattern haunted me. I knew it as well as I knew the blackness coating the backs of my eyelids.

"It's the same pattern. The initials—it's a match for my mother's handwriting." I kept flipping the tag back and forth. "How does he know these things about me? About her and my family?"

"I'm not sure." He reeled me into a tight hug and kissed my forehead. "None of this makes sense, but we're going to get you those answers. I promise."

Clutching the material in my fist, I gathered my nerves and pried myself out of his arms. "We should get moving."

"Are you sure you're okay?" He searched my face. "I can go on alone if you need a minute."

"I'm going with you." A fierce urge to protect him simmered in my middle. "I almost lost you too. I'm not risking it again."

Pleased warmth suffused his expression before the weight of our circumstances snuffed his masculine enjoyment. With a somber nod, he set out for the remaining hallway, and I covered the rear. He paused in the entryway of yet another bedroomlike chamber, and his nostrils flared wide. "She's in there."

Dread pressed down on my shoulders, all the rock and water overhead crushing me while I stood there warring with myself. I wanted to see Harlow, and I was terrified of seeing her. I wanted her back, wanted her safe, but I wasn't sure she could come back from what Charybdis might have done to her, and she would never feel safe again.

She was my friend, my responsibility, and I took point. I entered the room with Graeson at my back and pulled up short at what I saw.

Harlow perched on the edge of a rusted metal cot. Back straight, feet planted on the ground, she kept her hands linked in her lap. Her hair was a brighter shade than I remembered, more fuchsia than cotton candy. Her clothes were a flattering cut and trendy, her makeup flawless. She stared ahead at the wall opposite her, not acknowledging our arrival. I cut across the room until I stood in front of her, heeding Graeson's quiet warning not to get too close. She blinked glassy eyes but didn't move or speak.

Her vacant gaze reminded me so much of Ayer's drugged indifference it broke my heart. That couldn't be her future. She had to snap out of this.

"Harlow." So much hope smashed into one word. "It's me, Cam." Movement at my shoulder prompted me to add, "And Graeson."

The girl didn't respond.

"Look at this." Graeson tapped a row of boxes flush with the wall. "This is where she kept the suckers." He squatted and riffled through a second box then a third. "Clothes with tags still on. Makeup." The fourth box made his shoulders tense. "You should take a look at this." Reluctant to leave Harlow, I hesitated until he said, "I'll keep an eye on her."

We switched places, Graeson angling his body to keep our path out clear while keeping Harlow in his sights, and I knelt on the damp rock and dipped my hand into a box with three items remaining. A man's hiking boot, an old jar filled with brittle yet flawless leaves, and a piece of blue raspberry-flavored rock candy. I gripped the boot and yanked the tongue out as far as it would go. Written in the same neat hand that graced the nightgown's tag was a new name—Derik Ellis. My father.

"These must be the items Harlow had left to pass off through Emily." I replaced the boot and glanced up at him. "Seven items. Seven is a magical number."

Meaning the rabbit was a ploy of Aisha's or I was wrong about Charybdis sticking to magical theory.

Eyes on Harlow, he inclined his head toward me. "Do they have any significance to you?"

"This belongs to my father." I tapped the shoe. "The leaves remind me of a game Lori and I played one summer." I picked up the crinkly wrapper last. "This was our favorite flavor. Our parents bought these for us at general stores when we went up in the mountains."

Rising to my feet, I rejoined Graeson in staring at Harlow, who hadn't so much as fidgeted since our arrival.

"Can you hear us?" She gave no sign of listening to me, but it wasn't her I wanted to engage. "I don't know your true Name, but I know who you are." I took one step closer. "You aren't Harlow any more than you were the kelpie or Marshal Ayer."

"How dare you address me. You who are but a child." Harlow's lips moved, the too-deep voice coming from her mouth, but the cadence of her speech belonging to someone else—something else. "You cannot begin to fathom who or what I am." She turned her head toward us, and her eyes had gone black and gleaming, as empty and cruel as the kelpie's had been. "You have cost me much, Camille Ellis, and I will have what is owed repaid."

Graeson's hand closed over my upper arm, and he anchored me to the spot before roiling anger blocked out my rational thoughts. "I owe you nothing."

"You ruined an event I spent ten of your lifetimes planning. What would you call that, if not a debt?" Harlow fingered the hem of her shirt. "This girl is a start, but I will require much more compensation." Casual malice danced in the depths of her eyes. "How is your family, by the way? Have you seen your parents lately?"

"Leave my family out of this," I growled, magic flushing my skin.

"You are in no position to make demands. Bargain, perhaps. Think very hard and you might find something you possess of value to me." A shudder rippled through Harlow, and she wet her lips as though deriving pleasure from the fury wafting off my skin. "You have my attention now, Camille Ellis. I grant you permission to summon me when you have made your peace." A smile tilted her mouth. "Until we meet again."

Blind rage at him threatening those I loved propelled me several steps forward before Graeson caught me around the middle. "He's baiting you," he murmured. "Attack now, and the only one you'll be hurting is Harlow."

Slumping in his hold, I took a long moment to tamp down all the blazing animosity Harlow didn't deserve. Taking my outrage out on her would make me as pathetic as Bessemer, and I wasn't about to follow in his sadistic paw prints.

Gaze fixated on Harlow, I froze at the gradual change sweeping over her. Like a reset switch had been thrown, the light vanished from her eyes, and her head turned until she faced forward once again. Abandoning the fabric of her shirt, she slid her hands back into her lap, fingers linking. The pose was the same, as if she hadn't moved, hadn't addressed us at all.

"This is bad," I murmured. "She's like a radio transmitter and receiver all rolled into one."

Graeson's attention never wavered off her. "What should we—?"

"We'll talk about it later, once we get her someplace secure and warded for sound." I tapped my ear and broke from his arms, the temptation to stay in their shelter becoming harder to resist. "He's just proven he can drop in and listen whenever he wants. I don't want him overhearing any plans we make."

Crossing to Harlow, I murmured a Word I learned in marshal academy, one that bound her hands together at her lower back. I used another to muzzle her in case Charybdis turned out to be a biter. Graeson cupped her elbow and helped her stand then led her down the hall. With one final glance at the box of items meant for me, items I had no way to carry or capture since I'd left my phone behind so it wouldn't get waterlogged, I committed each one to memory then exited the bedroom for what I hoped was the last time.

After a shorter walk than I remembered on the way in, we reached the large antechamber, and I got my first good look at it. The entrance was as elegant as the rest of the place and its decorations as peculiar due to their scavenged nature. The sconces I'd noticed earlier were discarded citronella torches. The glimmering path leading into the first room, the main living space, was paved with bottle caps. From here, the exit resembled a giant pool. And on a rock sat a familiar tin I hadn't noticed in my haste to get inside the caves.

Harlow's unfocused eyes brightened at the sight of it, as though the power of the memories connected to the item had peeled aside the veil Charybdis had lowered over her mind.

"The gills don't stick." Graeson had noticed Harlow's fixation too. "Is it just me or are they supposed to do that?"

"That's how they work," she whispered on an indrawn breath. "They're meant to dissolve..." her focus wavered, "...once you don't need them."

Just as before, the flicker of awareness waned all too quickly, and she zoned out as her expression slipped back into blankness.

"I wish I could make this work for you too, Ellis." Graeson scooped up the tin and twisted it in his hand, but Harlow had checked out, and not even the lure of her gear roused her again. "I don't know the first thing about jury-rigging magic."

"Don't worry about me." I plastered on a brave smile, trembling inside at the idea of hitting the water a second time. "I'll manage."

"Getting out won't be too bad. It's not as far up as you think." His focus shifted toward the ceiling. "It's when we breach the surface that things will get sticky. Bessemer saw me go in. You too. He doesn't know about the caves, as far as I'm aware, but he'll figure it out or someone else will tell him. He'll be waiting." His gaze touched on Harlow. "They'll know it's her. They'll see we went in and came out with another fae—one with pink hair."

"We have to be ready for anything," I agreed.

"You and I are a match for any of them." Heat sparked in his gaze. "Your she-wolf is the most beautiful I've ever seen."

My gut pitched. "I don't have a she-wolf." There was no spirit animal inside me. "I don't have a wolf period. I just get hairier now than I used to."

"You haven't seen her, have you?"

"No." I didn't trust that knowing glint. "I haven't exactly had time to sit around admiring myself lately."

He raised his hands, an easy surrender, but I knew I hadn't heard the last on the topic.

The cool lap of water several feet away didn't spike the same dread in my heart as it had only hours earlier. My world was in chaos, and my fears were greater than sucking water in my lungs now. I rubbed the fabric of Lori's nightgown through my fingers. What did it mean that this had survived? I didn't kid myself that somehow she had too. That kind of hope destroyed people.

"I don't want to hurt anyone." The pack had, mostly, done me no harm. "Do you think they'll listen to reason?"

What I meant was him. Would they listen to their beta?

"You saw firsthand how it is when a warg gets its blood up. In a group it's impossible for all but an alpha to control the bloodlust." Regret flickered across his features. "They're scared of fae, Bessemer taught them that. They're still mourning Marie and reeling over my decision to bring a fae bride home. They don't trust me. They think grief has warped me."

Ignoring the fae bride comment, I focused on the bigger picture. "So we fight our way out."

His pause stretched several heartbeats. "Yes." He set his jaw. "Bessemer's left us no choice."

Ready as I would ever be, I threaded the nightgown down the inside leg of my pants in the hopes the tight fabric would hold it in place as I swam.

Graeson smeared goop down both sides of Harlow's throat then doctored himself up too. "How do you want to do this?"

"You take care of Harlow. She might be able to breathe underwater, but with her hands bound, she can't maneuver, and I don't trust Charybdis not to pop back into her body while you're both vulnerable." I swung my arms to limber up before the long swim. "I'll stick close enough I can catch you if I start struggling."

Stalking toward me with Harlow in tow, Graeson fisted the hair at my nape and claimed my mouth with a kiss that left me breathless. "Be careful."

"I will be," I promised, while my brain scrambled.

With an arm looped around Harlow's middle, Graeson hauled her into the rippling water with him, and they both vanished from sight. I stood alone in the cave of a long-gone sprite with a bitter taste rising up the back of my throat.

Gulping air, I flung myself after them before fear changed my mind. Submerged in effervescence, I squinted after Graeson and kicked toward the muted light rippling overhead, a golden halo cast by the fickle moon.

For once the familiar panic didn't swamp my senses and send me reeling. The ghost of Lori failed to put in an appearance, perhaps held at bay by the talisman at my hip. Panic fluttered through me as my lungs pulled tight, their oxygen depleted, but it was an honest burst of fear.

I was a long way from being cured of my aquaphobia, but when my head breached the surface and I gulped lungsful of pine-scented air, an ounce or two of the fear and hatred of water I'd carried with me all this time rolled liquescent from my hair to be left behind.

Snarls greeted my emergence, and I snapped to attention. Graeson stood, flesh warping, over Harlow. She lay sprawled on her back, staring skyward, as if aid ever came to those who asked those distant celestial bodies for help. Crawling from the water, I took my place beside Graeson as her vacant gaze settled on me. A flicker of consciousness darkened her eyes as she mouthed, *See you soon.*

Before I puzzled out her meaning, the night erupted. Wargs rushed in from all sides, paws scrabbling in the slick mud. Bessemer, in his silver-backed wolf form, stood on the lip of the pond and watched, Imogen at his side.

I called up all the magic swimming in my veins and thrust the shift on myself. Pain was my reward. Sharp, fast, hard. My jaw clenched and body stretched as my limbs elongated and muscles twisted. I came through the other side panting and breathless, and damn if Graeson hadn't held off his change to first watch mine. A reverent smile, and he became molten, his wolf a silver blur eager to join in the fray.

Fur in earthy browns, grays and blacks dotted the landscape as the pack descended.

Claws unsheathed, stance wide, I prepared to stand against the tide, only to have them shy away from me and flow over Graeson. There were too many for one wolf to handle. Too many for one wolf and—whatever I was now—to defeat. That didn't mean we were giving up the fight.

I waded in, knocking wargs aside and peeling them off the dog pile forming over Graeson. I had almost reached the bottom when the sterling wolf surged upward, a howl on his lips. We fought them off, back to back, keeping Harlow penned between us.

The onslaught thinned, and I risked a hopeful glance at Graeson.

I didn't see the slender black wolf bulleting toward me until she hit me in the chest and knocked me sailing backward. I slid in the muck until the back of my head went cold and wet. Aisha stood on my chest, planted one paw on my forehead and dunked me underwater. I came up spluttering and hooked my claws into her sides. All that did was haul her closer, and she clamped her jaws around my throat. Her teeth were sharp on my skin, her breath hot and smelling of copper. I expected the snap—of her jaws, of my neck—but she savored her victory.

Eyes rolling in my head, I spotted Graeson mid-shift. The tension left my body, a weightless sensation ebbing from my center. This wasn't the way I wanted things to end for us, but at least he would be the last thing I saw on my way out of this world. That mattered to me. A lot, I realized.

Roaring a battle cry, Graeson pivoted on his heel and lunged at Aisha. Jaws ratcheting tighter, she rumbled an eager sound in her chest. Sharp points pierced my skin, hot blood trickled down the sides of my neck, and I gasped a soundless cry as the former alpha female brought her jaws together with a powerful clacking of teeth. I gurgled a scream that died in the throat I no longer had and sank into darkness.

CHAPTER NINETEEN

Sunlight bathed my cheeks and teased my eyes open. Exposed beams slashed dark lines across a white ceiling. Thick log walls and rustic décor swam into focus, and recognition kicked in about the time a grizzled face leaned over me.

Graeson was here, and he had brought me to his home to recover.

"Hey," I managed, wincing at the searing burn in my throat.

"Hey." Graeson braced his hand on the pillow beside my head, his thumb smoothing over my cheek. "Are you staying with me this time?"

Eyes tender, I blinked him into focus. "Hmm?"

"You've been unconscious for three days." His thumb ventured lower and stroked my bottom lip. "You've woken up a few times, and I've fed you and forced you to take blood. Your eyes weren't so bright then. You look like you're all here now."

I rubbed my thumb over the nail concealing my spur and found it crusty with dried crimson flecks. "I'm not a vampire."

"My blood helped heal you once." He wisely moved his hand before the thought entered my head to bite him. "I figured it was worth a shot." He tucked the covers in around my hips. "Aisha did a number on you."

"Harlow?" My hand went to the bandage wrapping my throat. "Is she okay?"

"She's gone."

"The pack?" I jolted upright, tangling my legs in the sheet as I swung them over the edge of the mattress. "We have to get her back before—"

"No, sweetheart, I mean she's gone." He grimaced. "I turned my back on her when you were attacked, and she ran for it."

"We have to find her." Head swimming, I fisted my hands in the sheets to anchor me. "We can't leave her out there for Bessemer."

"The pack swept the forest." When I would have protested, he added, "I searched the caves myself. She didn't go back there. An erasure spell was used. There's no trace of her."

Gone again. Free in the world half-mad with Charybdis's influence and no one to protect her. "Is Isaac okay? Aunt Dot?"

"They're both fine. They're in town fueling up and gathering supplies for the trip. Isaac mentioned hitting the post office while he was there too. The rest of the pack made it out with mostly bumps and bruises." Gold rimmed his irises where the wolf pushed against his emotions. "You were the only near-fatality."

"What happened after...?" My fingertips brushed the edge of the bandage that crinkled when I spoke.

"I returned the favor." Simmering fury roiled in his eyes. "Aisha has been exiled from the pack, not for what she did to you, but for abandoning her station as Emily's guardian."

I doubted she would be missed. "Clearing the way for his new mate by getting rid of the old one."

"So it seems." He fussed with the fabric knotted around my feet. "With Harlow missing and Aisha wounded, Bessemer called off the hunt." He rubbed my toes with his palms. "While you were recovering, he and I had a long-overdue talk about the health of the pack."

I scooted to the edge of the mattress. "Does that mean you talked him into accepting Dell back?"

"No." A half-smile crooked his lips. "It means she won't be going into exile alone."

"Oh no." I gazed around his bedroom, through the door leading into the living room and stalled out on the row of neat shoes lined along the wall. "You didn't."

"It's been a long time coming." His warm palm covered my knee. "The only reason he didn't kick me out when I started making waves is my mother was a Chandler. I was the only warg in the pack who could have challenged him at any time on the grounds of the land and people being my birthright."

A sense of awe rolled over me. "Your parents were the alphas?"

"My great-grandparents founded this pack." His thumb made circles on the inside of my thigh. "Families loyal to the Chandlers haven't been making Bessemer's job any easier either."

"You can't leave." I clapped my hand over his. "Graeson, *think*."

"I can't stay here." He tilted back his head. "The memories... I can't."

Tears pricked the back of my eyes at the magnitude of his loss. Marie. His pack. His home. His birthright. "Are you sure?"

His nod was tight. "Any children I have will inherit the right to challenge for control of the Chandler pack, but I gave Bessemer my word I don't want it. I've promised him twenty years of peace, time enough for his daughter to grow into her role, for his pack to strengthen and...for me to form my own."

My head spun. "You're founding a new pack."

"I am." He laughed at my amazement. "There's a mountain of paperwork involved. I'll have to scout property and forge alliances with neighboring packs, but it's all doable. My parents were well liked and respected. I can make it work."

"Are you doing this for Dell?" His loyalty to her and hers to him was so absolute I could picture him making a sacrifice this size for her. She was family, and he wouldn't abandon her. "I just—I want you to be sure."

"Dell is a good friend, and I wouldn't let her face this alone, but no. I didn't do this for her." He squeezed my knee. "I didn't do this for you either, so wipe the guilt off your face. This is for me. For them. This was my call, and it was the right one." He straightened from his crouch and sat beside me. "It was my duty as beta to strengthen this pack, but I let resentment over Bessemer taking the reins when I was too young to hold them poison me against him. I rebelled, and I was dominant enough to drag others with me. I caused strife and turmoil, and he should have booted me out years ago. He would have if not for Marie and our bloodline."

His weight dragged down the mattress, and I slid against him but wasn't in any hurry to move away. Was this goodbye? Was that where this was headed? "Where will you go?"

"Wherever you go." He didn't miss a beat. "What did you think?" He folded me against his side. "That I would give you up just because we're no longer betas? No longer Chandlers?" A chuckle worked through his chest and vibrated through mine. "We're alphas now, mate. These stragglers following us out of Georgia? They're fifty percent your headache."

"No." I sat up and shoved him off me. "I'm not an alpha. I'm not a warg. They won't listen to me—to a fae."

He caught my wrists and held me captive. "Did you wonder why they didn't attack you at the pond?"

The pack *had* been acting odd around me, odder than usual. "I'm not going to like what you're about to say, am I?"

"Wargs have their own creation story, and I think it's time you heard it." He linked our fingers. "It goes something like this." He cleared his throat for effect. "The gods created wargs in their image. They were swift and fierce and loyal. One of the gods, Citlali, grew so enamored with their creation that he fell in love with a

HAILEY EDWARDS

warrioress. Her name was Zyanya, and she was the most beautiful of all the females. Her fur was silken and the color of silver ingots. Citlali was a fire god, and one day, unable to rein in the impulse, he stroked his hand down her spine and the tips of her fur blackened." He trailed his fingers down my arm. "Zyanya, who looked to Citlali as a father, was unable to return his affection and told him she had fallen in love with a member of her pack. In his rage, Citlali gripped her—an ear in each fist—and tore her in two. Out of control, he strode through the pack, tearing each member apart."

I recoiled. "That's a horrible story."

"That's not the best part." He shushed me. "The other gods were furious that he had destroyed their greatest creation. They tried to put the two halves back together again, but the wargs were indelibly altered." He lowered his voice. "They remained half wolf and half human. They no longer functioned as one creature but two. From that day on, wargs were either man or beast, but never both."

And I thought Gemini lore was brutal.

"Once Zyanya had recovered, she petitioned the gods for the right to challenge Citlali, because her chosen mate had been put back together wrong, and she had been forced to take his life to spare him the agony of his deformity." Graeson paused. "The gods granted her request, and the battle was fierce. Zyanya did a thing no one thought possible and killed Citlali. When he left his mark on her, she became god-touched, a goddess in her own right, and in her rage over losing her mate, she triumphed where they had expected her to fail."

"So the pack thinks I'm a reincarnation of Zyanya?" I squinted at him. "Why? They know I'm fae."

"They've never seen anything like you." His smirk told me he liked it that way. "You can tap into the pack bond, you can maintain a half-shift, and even your scent is warg. They're figuring out what I've known all along."

My eyebrows climbed. "What's that?"

Mischief sparkled in his eyes, and I knew not to trust what he said next.

Graeson leaned forward, lips brushing my ear, and whispered, *"You're a goddess."*

The burst of laughter that erupted from me caught him in its wake, and we sat there, shoulders bouncing, wheezing, until tears that had needed an excuse to fall pricked my eyes, and I collapsed against Graeson, happy to be in his arms.

There was no time for lounging around now that my eyes had opened. Cradling me in his arms, Graeson carried me through the woods to my trailer. He stole a kiss that left me dizzy, shooed me inside and ordered Dell to stand guard while he finished boxing up his belongings. Apparently my regaining consciousness had derailed the packing of his kitchenware, and he wasn't going anywhere without his whisks or his impressive collection of frying pans. We had plenty of mouths to feed, so I encouraged his mania. For all he was giving up, he deserved to bring his favorite part of his home with him.

Bessemer had withdrawn his wargs from the area to give the exiled wolves and my family time to pack their things and ready for the long drive to...we didn't know where yet.

Dell sat on the bottom step of my trailer, muscles tense, with eyes narrowed on the woods as though afraid Aisha lurked just outside her periphery. Graeson hadn't been the only warg terrified of losing me.

"Are you sure you don't want to come inside?" I called out to her. "I can brew some chai. I'll even let you put ice cubes in it."

The fine hairs lifted on my nape when she didn't immediately answer, and my wolf aspect rose as I approached the door.

"Do you need a hand with anything?" Graeson ducked his head inside, craning his neck to see me. "Dell's gone to finish packing." His forehead creased. "Is something wrong?"

"No. I just—I was talking to Dell and didn't realize she was gone." Relieved to be back in my own home, I patted the counter. "I'm good here. It won't take but another fifteen minutes or so for me to get everything secured and ready to roll."

Noticing the clear plastic box on the table, he raised his eyebrows in silent question.

I waved him inside and gestured toward my collection. "These are all the items Harlow left me, minus the bunny."

"Not all." He bent down and picked something off the ground before joining me in the kitchen. "I brought this too, just in case." He held out a plastic bag weighted with soggy items that dripped muddy water onto my floor in slow drops. "I brought everything that looked important."

Taking the bag from him, I set it in the sink until I had time to pick apart its contents. I tore off a paper towel, dropped it on the floor and scuffed my foot to clean up the mess while Graeson looked on with amusement.

"Every little bit helps." I tossed the used paper towel in the trash. "We need to figure this out. The things Charybdis said through Harlow…"

"Are you sure you want to pursue this solo?" His hand found my nape, and his heat radiated into me. "Things have changed."

Everything—and yet nothing—had changed.

Charybdis was still out there. Harlow was too. Except now it was personal. "I can't let this go. He threatened my family." I bit my lip. "I'll reach out to Vause if we find something concrete." It might cost me my future with the Earthen Conclave, but this wasn't the suicide mission it once might have been. "I won't be reckless, I promise."

"I understand." His thumb caressed my pulse. "I had to ask."

"You're starting a new pack." I tucked my hair behind my ears and dragged my gaze to his. "You have people you're directly responsible for now." I huffed out an exhale. "I can't ask you to come with me."

A hitch in his grip was the only sign I had stumped him. "I see."

"Don't say it that way." It sounded too much like goodbye.

"You might think mate is a title you can shed like any of your other aspects, but it goes more than skin deep." He ducked his head and teased his nose across my jaw, breathing me in like the first clean breath of air after the rain. "I can't say I wanted you from the moment I set eyes on you. We both know that would be a lie." His lips tickled across my skin as he spoke. "I can say I wanted you from the moment I saw who you are." He placed one wide palm over my heart, and the heat curled my abdomen tight. "In here."

"This is crazy," I rasped, heart frantic under his touch. "I'm not a warg."

"You're not a coward either." His mouth brushed my chin. "You're mine, Ellis, and I'm not letting you go. You fought for me, very well I might add." The hand over my heart slid behind my neck and threaded in my hair. "You won me." A nip on my chin. "And now you're stuck with me."

All the years of not belonging crumbled at my feet, and I felt more exposed standing there in front of him, accepting that I was his as he was mine, than if I had been naked.

"We'll do this your way. We'll find your parents, make sure they're okay and warn them." He hooked a finger in the belt loop of my jeans and hauled me forward. "It's time I met the in-laws anyway."

A thousand arguments leapt onto my tongue like it was a diving board.

"Hush now." Strong arms slid around me. "Don't ruin the moment."

Another stolen kiss, this one a fraction longer, hotter, but still too fast for me to react to except to widen my eyes, and then I was pulling back. "Do you hear that?" A buzzing noise interrupted my scrambled thoughts. Leaning around me, Graeson picked my phone off the table and put it in my hands. "Oh." The number on the screen coaxed a tremor of unease through me. "It's Isaac."

Isaac, who never spoke on the phone except on pain of death. Or when forced to shop, which amounted to the same thing.

"Who's this? On second thought, I don't care," the gruff voice challenged before I got out a *hello*. "You know when that pump-blocking asshole's coming back to move his rig?"

Foreboding slithered down my spine. "Why do you have my cousin's phone?"

"Look, lady, I run the Murphey's on Round Pond Road. One minute this guy is filling gas cans, and the next he's gone. I checked the john. He ain't in there." Aggravation threaded his voice. "I found his phone when I searched his truck and dialed this number since it showed up in the call history so often. I was trying to ID him so I'd have something to tell the cops when they got here."

More like he was hoping there was money or a gun in the glove box. I didn't call him on it. I needed his help more than Isaac needed his twenty-dollar emergency fund.

"There was an older woman with him, his mother." Eyes crushed shut, I massaged my temples. "She drives a mint blue vintage Ford F100 pickup."

"Never saw her." Sirens whirred in the background. "Hey, you going to come claim the truck or...?"

"I'll be right there." I ended the call, scrolled through my contacts and dialed Decker Comeaux, an elf I'd met while working on Marie's drowning. A beep prompted me to leave a message. "Hey, this is Agent Ellis. There's an incident at the Murphey's on Round Pond Road. Meet me there as quick as you can."

A black tide of panic rose until I had trouble sucking in a full breath.

Thanks to his sensitive warg hearing, I didn't have to waste time catching Graeson up to speed.

Knowing me as well as he did, he guessed the turn of my thoughts with ease. "This doesn't have to mean Charybdis is involved."

"I can't risk it." I massaged my chest as though that might keep my heart beating. "I have to call Vause."

A tickle of sensation prickled my mind, the pack bond at work was my guess.

"Your truck's already hitched to your trailer." He caught my arm before I could shove past him. "I asked Dell to bring me the keys to mine."

Exiting the trailer in a daze, I had to move, had to do something. I started walking the perimeter of the wards, aware Graeson's keen hearing meant he would catch every word exchanged. Speed dial trilled in my ear, and I paced as Vause's phone rang five times then rolled to voicemail. I hung up without leaving a message.

I had tapped my phone against my bottom lip once when it buzzed with an incoming call.

"Ellis."

"This is Magistrate Martindale." A haughty huff filled the line, and I had no trouble picturing him as puffed with self-importance as a toad. "Forgive me. I just missed your call."

What was he doing answering Vause's phone?

"I didn't mean to disturb you." Having gotten used to dealing directly with Vause, I scrambled for the proper reverent tone one should use when addressing a magistrate. "I was trying to reach Magistrate Vause."

"I'm afraid that won't be possible." A whiff of a chuckle tickled the line before he shared the cause of his delight. "Irene is missing."

"Missing," I echoed, as though I had misunderstood.

"Vanished from behind a locked door twenty-four hours ago." After the delicious morsel of gossip had been devoured by my ears, his savor ended. "It goes without saying that no one outside the Earthen Conclave is privy to this information. Some fool ran late for an audience. He thought she must have cancelled and forced his way in, making quite a spectacle of himself. We might have hoped to contain these most unfortunate circumstances if not for that. As it is, I'm sure the news will be making the rounds by morning."

My back hit a tree, and I leaned against it. "Were her guards...?"

"One dead." He clicked his tongue. "One missing. Seelie the both of them. Had she accepted my offer of Unseelie guardians, this tragedy might have been averted."

Noncommittal noises bubbled out of me. Seelie I might be, but a fool I was not.

He must have taken the mumbles as agreement, as he sighed in satisfaction. "Now then." A ripple of pops, similar to knuckles cracking, rang in my ear. "What business did you have with Irene?" He slathered on what I'm sure he thought was charm. "I will be governing the Northeastern Conclave in her absence, quite a burden by one's self, but a task I am equal to. Anything you have to tell her, you can share with me."

"I..." I fumbled for an excuse and settled on, "I wanted to check on the status of my leave of absence."

"Oh. You're *that* Ellis. The Gemini girl. The one who cavorts with a warg and compromised a multiple-homicide case." The disgust in his tone at having wasted perfectly good gossip on me was evident. "I'll have my assistant call you with that information."

Click.

Across the yard, Graeson rubbed his jaw. "What do you think it means?"

The rumble of an engine stopped me from answering. Dell swerved alongside us and threw the sleek pickup into park. Extending her arm out the window, she slapped the flat of her palm on the door. "All aboard who's coming aboard. I'm driving."

"No, you're not." He glowered. "We need to be ready to drive out once Ellis and I return. There's no reason for you to go, not when an extra set of hands could come in handy here."

Graeson reached for the door handle, but Dell hit the lock button with the flat of her hand. "I'm going, even if I have to hitchhike to get there."

"Don't you trust me to take care of Ellis?" He could have reached inside and hauled her out, he was within his rights to punish her insubordination, but he leaned on his elbow in the window instead. "Why is this so important to you?"

Stubborn gold winked in her eyes, and she barely restrained her growl. "Isaac."

"We don't have time for a pissing match right now." I circled the truck and let myself in, scooting next to Dell. "My cousin and aunt are missing, Vause has been taken, and I won't trust the rest of my family is safe until I set eyes on them." I leaned over her lap and met Graeson's unflinching stare, not the least cowed by his newly bestowed alpha magnetism. "Are you coming with us or not?"

"You're not facing this alone." With a snarl curling his lip, he prowled around the truck and slid onto the bench seat beside me, resting his arm across my shoulders. "You and I are a team. Where you go, I go."

Lacing my fingers with his, I held on tight as Dell churned gravel with her tires. With the smoke from the explosion clogging my nose and my heart banging against my ribs in fear for Isaac and Aunt Dot, I let the tears hazing my vision fall.

Where you go, I go.

I just prayed I wasn't leading him into a trap.

HAILEY'S BACKLIST

Araneae Nation

A Heart of Ice #.5
A Hint of Frost #1
A Feast of Souls #2
A Cast of Shadows #2.5
A Time of Dying #3
A Kiss of Venom #3.5
A Breath of Winter #4
A Veil of Secrets #5

Daughters of Askara

Everlong #1
Evermine #2
Eversworn #3

Black Dog

Dog with a Bone #1
Heir of the Dog #2
Lie Down with Dogs #3
Old Dog, New Tricks #4

Gemini

Dead in the Water #1
Head Above Water #2
Hell or High Water #3

Wicked Kin

Soul Weaver #1

ABOUT THE AUTHOR

A cupcake enthusiast and funky sock lover possessed of an overactive imagination, Hailey lives in Alabama with her handcuff-carrying hubby, her fluty-tooting daughter and their herd of dachshunds.

Chat with Hailey on Facebook or Twitter, or swing by her website.
www.facebook.com/authorhaileyedwards
@Hailey Edwards
www.HaileyEdwards.net

Sign up for her newsletter to receive updates on new releases, contests and other nifty happenings.

Made in the USA
Middletown, DE
24 January 2017